A Summer's Adventure

Books written by Sally M. Russell

    An Escape for Joanna
* Finding a Path to Happiness
* Dr. Wilder's Only True Love
* Josh and The Mysterious Princess
* A Summer's Adventure
    A Surprise Awaits Back Home
* The Haven of Rest Ranch Series

A Summer's Adventure

Sally M. Russell

A Summer's Adventure
Copyright © 2019 by Sally M. Russell. All rights reserved.

No part of this publication may be reproduced, stored in a retrieval system or transmitted in any way by any means, electronic, mechanical, photocopy, recording or otherwise without the prior permission of the author except as provided by USA copyright law.

This novel is a work of fiction. Names, descriptions, entities, and incidents included in the story are products of the author's imagination. Any resemblance to actual persons, events, and entities is entirely coincidental.

The opinions expressed by the author are not necessarily those of URLink Publishing.

1603 Capitol Ave., Suite 310 Cheyenne, Wyoming USA 82001
1-888-980-6523 | admin@urlinkpublishing.com

URLink Publishing is committed to excellence in the publishing industry.

Book design copyright © 2019 by URLink Publishing. All rights reserved.

Published in the United States of America
ISBN 978-1-64367-708-8 (Paperback)
ISBN 978-1-64367-709-5 (Digital)
Fiction
19.07.19

This Book is Dedicated to:

Julia Rude and Mary Thompson, my two older sisters who spent many hours doing research before being successful in locating our relatives still living in Sweden. I treasure all the information they recorded, a visit by one of the families they met, and the continuing correspondence that has been shared.

"What I'm slowly getting around to asking, Mark, is whether you would even consider spending a rather dull summer with your old grandpa to go hunting for a family that may no longer be there? I do know that there's a small town of Hayes located not too far from Pueblo, CO, and that was my mother's maiden name." Hesitating a moment, he then asked, "What do you say, Mark? Will you go hunting with me?"

"It really sounds exciting, and I'll definitely go, Grandpa. You know I couldn't turn down a trip to Colorado."

> *Now to him who is able to do immeasurably more than all we ask or imagine, according to his power that is at work within us, to him be glory forever and ever.*
> —Ephesians 3:20-21

CHAPTER ONE

Shivers of excitement are going through Mark Gillette's body as he's driving the big shiny new Lincoln Navigator along Interstate 90 in Ohio. The car actually belongs to his grandfather, Lucas Gillette, who is sleeping soundly in the passenger seat. Mark had to grin as he'd glanced over and saw his grandpa's head a little crooked on the pillow, his mouth open, a soft occasional snore, and a smile on his face.

The two of them are heading from New York to Colorado on an adventure to try to discover a somewhat forgotten, or unknown, part of their family. Mark had never been as thrilled as when Grandpa Lucas had called and asked if he would come see him about a rather special subject. He had always loved his grandfather and been very close to him, but that day was the one he most likely would never forget.

Mark hadn't had any idea what he was going to do all summer. He was to graduate from High School in two weeks and then enter college in the fall, but the long hot summer loomed before him like a vast empty space which he had to fill in order to survive. While growing up, his life had always seemed to be lacking something, but he could never quite put his finger on what it was. The teen years had been filled with all the normal boyhood activities such as baseball, swimming, hiking, and camping during the summer months, and he'd had a lot of basketball, bowling, downhill and cross-country skiing in the winters. His interests at church had filled a lot of hours, too, being counselor to a group of younger boys and the activities with his peers, but there had always been a hunger to explore beyond the areas that were the usual for his very conservative family.

When he'd reached his grandfather's house, he had been a little concerned that the church may have asked his grandfather to try to change his mind about being a counselor at camp this summer. He'd done that the last two years, but had decided to decline this year because he wanted to do something entirely different before starting college, even though he still hadn't known what that was going to be. He'd just hoped that camping wasn't the reason he'd been asked to come today.

Grandfather Lucas had met him at the door and immediately asked him to join him in his study. His grandmother hadn't been there to welcome him, as was the usual custom, so if it hadn't been for the big smile that he knew so well, Mark would have thought he was in big trouble. When they'd reached the beautiful big room where he had played, read, and talked to his grandfather since he was a little tyke, he'd remained standing until he was told to please sit down. He'd then waited for his grandfather to speak.

"Mark, you and I have talked about many things and have also done quite a few things together over the years while you were growing up, but I have now made a decision to do something that I've been wanting to do for the last two decades, at least. My problem is that it might take this whole summer, and I desperately need someone I can tolerate, and also trust, to go with me to help with the driving and keep me company. It'd be impossible for me to do this alone.

I imagine you remember the few stories I've told you about my mother's family who supposedly settled in Colorado. She'd never wanted to talk much about the time she'd lived there, and there were always tears in her eyes when she did. It seemed as if she was trying so very hard to convince herself it couldn't be true, but she softly whispered once, when we were talking, that they hadn't acknowledged her as their daughter after she'd decided to come and stay with her grandma and grandpa for awhile. I tried to get her to tell me more, but she wouldn't elaborate, so consequently, I have very little information about them.

She did mention that there was a big ranch, but a very small town named after her father, Jeremiah Hayes, who had studied to be an attorney and also learned the duties of a mayor while living with the Whites after his mother and father died. She'd related that she didn't like the town or want to stay there after she'd lost her older sister during WWI. She'd also admitted that it was mostly because of all the letters her Grandma White had written to her about the grand things that went on in New York and the pictures she had sent of the big stores and lovely homes.

Of course, as a teenager, she had been intrigued and had finally asked her parents for permission to go and live with the grandparents and finish school in New York. After she'd arrived here, however, she said she never saw any of those things but had continued to believe her grandma that she would someday. She said she'd written lots of letters back to her parents, which Grandma had always offered to mail for her, but she'd never gotten any replies. One day she'd been told that her parents had probably disowned her because she'd wanted to come to New York.

After a few years, she'd met my dad, your great grandfather, and was married, but apparently had never mentioned that she might have some family in another State until Dad suffered a stroke and was on his death bed in 1972.

For some unknown reason, Great Grandma White never mentioned anything about Mom's family either, although it would have been her daughter. My Great Grandpa died shortly after I was born so I've come to believe she may have been afraid she would lose my Mom, too, if she'd informed anyone about this possible family out in the western part of the country. Her only child, Rebecca, had apparently married this Jeremiah Hayes and then gone off to Colorado with him in 1895. I guess I was about twenty years old when Great Grandma died at 103 years old, but I still had never been told about my grandparents who might be living in Colorado.

Dad called me to his bedside and told me what Mom had confessed to him about the possibility of some family out in Colorado. So now, before I get too old to travel, I have to discover if there is any truth to the few stories I finally persuaded my mom to tell me several years after Dad had passed away. Although she was still younger than I am now, she either didn't want to go, or was afraid to go, but her excuse was that she was way too old to travel that far, especially alone.

I didn't feel I could get away right then because I was the only one in the law office, after Dad had had his stroke, then it was James starting college and on to Law School, and Katherine in the process of planning her wedding after she'd finished college. Sadly, going to Colorado never got discussed again before Mom's sudden death in 1986, the year when I could've finally gotten away. Now, I feel very strongly that it is up to me to find out how the rest of that family has grown over the years and if they'll even want anything to do with us New Yorkers.

I understand there was an older brother, Nathaniel, so maybe his descendants are still around that area. My sister, Rebekah, apparently named for her grandmother, is very interested in the findings, but her husband's health keeps her from doing any of the actual searching. I'm hoping that what I find could possibly give our family and the next Hayes and Gillette generations a whole lot of happiness in knowing there are quite a few more of us than we could've ever expected. Your dad and Aunt Kate haven't been too excited so far about the information I've given them, but maybe, if we find some real people, they'll get enthused, too, about the family heritage. Your two siblings, Steve and Deborah, being in college and law school, have too many other things on their minds right now. I don't know about Kate's two Army career boys, but I feel you have always seemed interested in family ties.

What I'm slowly getting around to asking, Mark, after talking all this time, is whether you would even want to consider spending a rather dull summer with your old grandpa who wants to go hunting for family that may no longer be there. I do know that there is a small town of Hayes located not too far from Pueblo. I also know that there was a well-known attorney in Lakewood, NY, by the name of Hayes, who died from pneumonia along with his wife, in 1890. And, just recently after I thought to search, I actually found in the county records that a Jeremiah Hayes and a Rebecca White were married in 1894. So, what do you say, Mark? Will you go hunting with me?"

"It sounds really exciting, and I'd love to go, Grandpa. You know I couldn't turn down a trip to Colorado. I remember when I was still pretty young, you would tell me stories about a possible ranch in Colorado, and I had so many wonderful dreams of horses, cowboys, and even Indians becoming good friends just because my great, great grandfather was a man who everyone looked up to. The only thing I couldn't understand, and it made me so sad, was why Great Grandma never returned to Colorado, even for a short visit, to see her parents and the other relatives who might have been born after she left. I really can't believe it about her family disowning her, so to speak, so I just hope and pray that there are still some members of the family living there. We can hear their side of the story, and hopefully have a great big family reunion. When were you planning or wanting to get on our way?"

"Do you think you can be ready about a week after graduation? I don't want to pull you away from your family too fast, but I'm so anxious to get started now that I've done all the research that I can think of. I'm just looking forward to a very exciting adventure."

"Don't worry about my family. They'll probably be glad I finally have something to do to keep me out of their hair all summer," he laughed. "I'll be ready to go whenever you say the word, Grandpa, so just let me know when.

CHAPTER TWO

Exactly three weeks later, Lucas Gillette started the drive from Jamestown, NY, to Hayes, CO, with his grandson, Mark Gillette, as his passenger and companion. He could easily see the excitement and anticipation in his grandson's eyes and actions, but he also couldn't help but wonder how long it would last as the days of driving, sitting, and looking at highway stripes started taking their toll.

"I think we'll pick out some interesting places to stop along the way, Mark, and maybe we'll spend two or three days in some places if we're enjoying the area. That way, we won't get so tired of seeing only highways and industrial areas which are usually found along the outskirts of the cities and alongside the Interstate Highways. As we get farther west, I understand it turns into acres and acres of flat farmland, grazing cattle, and miles of very little to look at. Did you get a chance to read or see on the map any places of particular interest that you'd like to stop and investigate?"

"Don't plan to stop because of me, Grandpa, because I'm really anxious to get to Colorado and find our missing family. I also want to find out if there are possibly any horses on this ranch. I've wanted to ride a horse for years."

Lucas had chuckled. "I hadn't known about this horse craze of yours, but I hope the dream of riding will come true. I also know you're anxious to please me, Mark, but you don't yet realize how far we're going to be driving and just how hard it can become on your mind and your body, not to mention your disposition. We don't want to be two old grouchy guys when we meet this family we'll want to make an impression on, now do we?"

"I see what you mean. I did look at the maps of the different states we're going to be driving across, and it did appear to be a long, long way. I'll look at that map of Ohio again and see if there is anything that I think would be worthwhile stopping for."

When they'd reached Interstate 90 in Pennsylvania, the traffic was noticeably a bit heavier, but it was moving along smoothly and it didn't seem very long until they'd entered Ohio. "I know you've seen the Conneaut Historical Railroad Museum, Mark, but in less than an hour, we should come to a road that will take us to the Fairport Marine Museum. I've been there once before, but I'd like for you to see it. I think you'll enjoy it very much."

The museum was interesting, but Mark kept thinking it was too soon to do a lot of stopping and sightseeing. He and his family had seen most of the places in Ohio anyway, and he was much more enthused about being on the way to Colorado. When they'd gotten back to the car, Grandpa remarked, "We'll stop for some lunch somewhere on the west side of Cleveland and then I'll let you do the driving. It'll be time for my little nap that I like to take after I've eaten lunch, but we'll look over the route so you'll know where to turn off to get to Detroit as long as we're so close. I'd like to visit the Automotive Hall of Fame so I've decided we'll spend the night there. If we still have time this afternoon, we'll do it after we find a place to stay. Otherwise, we'll see it before we continue on in the morning. Does that meet with your approval?"

"Anything you say, Grandpa. That really should be interesting because I love cars."

When Mark got behind the wheel, his grandfather gave one final word of driving instructions as he got settled in the passenger seat. "Remember now, you wake me if you get confused or need anything."

Mark hadn't expected him to be asleep in less than five minutes, but it certainly warmed his heart to realize his grandfather trusted him that much with this new car that he had bought especially for the trip. Mark had always been considered a pretty careful driver and he'd had an old truck of his own for two years, but to get permission to drive this new Lincoln Navigator, while his grandfather was sleeping, no less, had to boost a guy's confidence just a little. They had checked the map and figured it was around 120 miles to the Detroit turn-off. As if an alarm had gone off, Grandpa woke up just as Mark was approaching the exit and had started slowing down to ramp speed.

"You made good time, Mark, and I had a wonderful nap. This trip would've been so exhausting if I'd had to drive it alone, but I'm really going to enjoy it with you along to share the monotony of driving. We probably could've flown, but I wouldn't have felt quite right imposing on absolute strangers, even if we'd really found a family, to get us where we wanted to go, and I hate rental cars. I haven't gotten one yet that I felt comfortable in. I know I can relax now with you behind the wheel, and it's been a while since I've taken a nice scenic vacation trip by car. Your grandma and I used to jump in the car without even a destination in mind. We'd find an interesting looking country road and just drive and enjoy the scenery until we'd get tired and hungry. My only regret now is that your grandma decided she'd rather not make the trip this time, but it sounded like she was pretty confident that there would be a next time, didn't it?" he chuckled.

"I sure hope we discover a lot of relatives and then all the uncles, aunts, and cousins can be united to become a big happy family. I wonder if Aunt Kate, Uncle Bill, William and Paul will be willing to join us. They always seem to be so involved with their careers and not too interested in the rest of the family."

"It is disappointing that we can't get together more often, and it will be wonderful if we can find more relatives to get acquainted with. We'll just have to wait and see, though. At the moment, I see it's only about 60 miles up to Detroit, but we'll want to change routes up here a little ways so we'll be nearer the Museum when we stop for the night."

They discovered that the University of Michigan-Dearborn wasn't a great distance from the Museum, so after they'd found a motel and eaten a nice dinner, they drove over so they could walk around the campus for awhile just to stretch their legs. Lucas noticed that Mark was quite interested in all the different buildings and the landscaping of the school, so it wasn't a surprise when he remarked, "I've read where the University of Michigan is one of the top universities in the country. Everything is really nice here, but I'm pretty sure The Law School is in Ann Arbor. Maybe we could stop there and see what that campus looks like, too. When I was researching colleges, I learned a lot about Michigan and had even considered applying there for my regular college classes.

Of course, Dad was constantly hinting and hoping that I'd decide on Amherst since practically all of our family has gone there. To be honest, I really wanted to stay a little closer to home my first year, too. Law School, however, seems to have been individual choices and I think several different ones have been attended."

"That's true, Mark, and you certainly couldn't find a better one than Michigan. We can definitely stop and see the campus at Ann Arbor, if you'd like. It might help make your decision a little easier when the time comes."

"I've really gotten interested in the architecture that the different colleges select, especially after we visited several campuses while I was making up my mind which one I actually wanted to go to. One had an assortment of buildings, both old and new, which I didn't really like too well. Another was totally Colonial. It was beautiful and I just stood and stared at the landscaping--it was so outstanding, I loved the overall appearance of the campus, but the college itself didn't quite fit all our needs, especially the financial since it was out of state," he chuckled. "Then there was the one that had these modern red brick buildings, squares or rectangles only. I thought the monotony of seeing almost identical buildings day after day would get to me pretty quick although the landscaping was really nice at that one, too."

"There are probably a few more colleges or universities that we can arrange to see before we get to our destination. I hadn't realized that you'd gotten so interested in the architectural field. Maybe you'll want to work toward a double major," he chuckled.

Grandpa had stopped and bought a newspaper on the way back to their room so he started reading the front page and handed the sports pages to Mark. After scanning them for a few minutes, he turned on the TV. It wasn't long, however, until he went to take a shower and then crawled into one of the queen-sized beds. It had apparently been a much more tiring or exciting day than he'd imagined because he drifted off to sleep rather quickly.

After touring the Automobile Museum the next morning, Grandpa was driving as he'd decided to follow Rt. 94 across Michigan so they could stop at Ann Arbor. It was a nice drive, and they took time not only to see the university at Ann Arbor, but also a little bit of Jackson, Battle Creek, and Kalamazoo that they would've missed if they'd gone back down to I-80/90 on their way to Chicago. After they'd stopped for lunch, Mark took over driving so Grandpa could nap. He'd turned south at Benton Harbor/St. Joseph and drove along Lake Michigan on the way down to Michigan City, Indiana. They'd learned that a Boat Show on the Lake was there, and both of them had always loved to go to various boat shows to look at all the different makes and models.

It hadn't been easy, but they'd finally found a place to stay so they could take time to look at all the boats they wanted to see in the morning. They would then drive on into Chicago to watch a Cubs game tomorrow night. Grandpa had called to make reservations for tickets and also a room while in Detroit the night before.

"I've heard so much about this Wrigley Field that I'm not going to miss seeing it in person since I'm this close," he'd remarked. "We really lucked out because they're going to be playing their old rival, the St. Louis Cardinals, so it should be a great game to watch. By the way, Mark, when I was checking the map last night, I realized that we can change our route plan slightly, or maybe a little more than slightly," he chuckled, "and get to see a couple more sights that I've heard about and think you'd probably enjoy."

"What are they, Grandpa?"

"Well, they are both on I-90 in South Dakota, and it looks easy enough to access the highway from where we're staying tomorrow night. We just stay on I- 90 all the way until we reach Mitchell, SD, where there is a place called the Corn Palace. It is supposed to be an awesome sight. It'll take us at least two days to get there unless we find something else we'd like to see along the way.

The other is Mt. Rushmore, which I'm sure you have read about and seen pictures of, but seeing it in person should be exciting."

A Summer's Adventure

"I have read a lot about Mt. Rushmore, and also about another museum containing Indian lore, not far from there, called Crazy Horse. Do you suppose we could see it, too?"

"I don't know of any reason why we can't. From there we'll go into Wyoming and get on Rt. 25 which will take us almost directly south to our destination. There are a few places of interest to see along that road, too, but we'll be on the last leg of our journey to discover if we have any family ties to get acquainted with."

"That is so exciting and my heart is beating so hard, Grandpa. I can hardly wait to find out if I have some long lost cousins, aunts and uncles, and maybe even great aunts and uncles if the genealogy has run about the same."

"I've wondered about that too, Mark, and I would think that it would be fairly close. My mom was the youngest, as far as she knew, so the older brother she mentioned could make their Family Tree a few years older than ours, but I wouldn't think by much. You may even have some second cousins, if each generation turns out to be a little older and the ones of your age group have married and have a child or two."

"Maybe I'll get to play with some little ones, or feed a baby," Mark laughed. "Who knows, but I'm sure wondering about this ranch. Do you think they might really have some horses and I could possibly go riding? That's one thing I've wanted to do ever since I heard those stories you told me. They caused me to have dreams about cowboys and Indians, but I have never had the chance to even get close to a horse. It must have gotten in my blood, though, because I've wanted to ride a horse for years now."

"I guess we'll just have to wait a few more days to discover the answers to all our questions, Mark. Right now, though, I think it's time to get some sleep. Goodnight, and I hope you can sleep tight because it's another long day tomorrow," he sighed.

"Goodnight, Grandpa, and thanks again for asking me to come along with you."

They got to see some fabulous boats the next morning, from 19' Runabouts up to a Yacht that was over 100' long. The one Mark really liked, though, was a brand new 40' Bluewater, and Grandpa finally had to take his arm and lead him away. "We've got to be on our way to Chicago pretty soon, Mark, or we'll miss the game tonight."

"That is such a beautiful boat, Grandpa. I hope I'm rich enough to own one of those someday."

Grandpa couldn't help but chuckle. "If you can always keep your mind on the good things in life, Mark, and keep God by your side, then you can accomplish all you need in life. Young people can be led astray too easily these days, with all the enticements that are out there, but you have the opportunity and the genes, from both sides of your family, to be in law, politics, or even finance, and any one of those are great assets to fulfilling a dream or two."

"I guess Great Grandpa Gillette was a good attorney. I do know that you and Dad haven't done too badly. And now that we know more about this Jeremiah Hayes, it'll be fun to find out what the other descendants, in the extended part of the family, have had as their vocations."

Mark continued to speculate on what they might find when they reach this town of Hayes, Colorado. Grandpa was listening and laughing heartily as they drove along Lake Michigan toward Wrigley Field and their reservation for the night. They decided to eat a late lunch before checking into their room, and then Grandpa was ready for a short nap.

Mark went down to the lobby and checked on transportation out to Wrigley Field, and then he wandered around to some of the nearby shops. An official looking sports store caught his attention so he went in to look around. He found Cubs baseball caps for them to wear to the game. He'd never seen his grandpa in a baseball cap, but he hoped he would at least wear it to the game tonight. By the time he returned to the hotel, he was thirsty, so he got two cans of soda from the vending machine near their room. He expected Grandpa to be a little thirsty, too, when he woke from his nap, and he was right.

They'd decided to eat at the game, of course, so they went out there early to take in some pre-game activities. They weren't the only ones with the same idea, and they found themselves in fairly long lines wherever they went. Grandpa must have paid well because they did have good seats so settled in with their hot dogs and fries, Tortillas with cheese, and a drink to watch all the pre-game goings on and to get a good look at the stadium. The over-all view was breathtaking, but the famous ivy-covered walls, the unique scoreboard with the clock at the top, all the team flags blowing to give the players the wind direction, and that viewing area across the street were a few things they had heard about or seen on TV, but were now seeing with their own eyes.

Grandpa, and the man who was seated next to him, were carrying on a pretty good conversation, and Mark heard Grandpa ask a few questions about Indians and powwows. He wondered if what was being discussed might give them another place to visit as they made their way to Colorado. He excused himself and walked around for a while, taking in more of the concession area, but the time seemed to go by rather quickly. He bought both of them another drink and got back to his seat just as they were standing for the singing of the National Anthem. It was an exciting game with a lot of hits, amazing double-plays, but not too many runs until the

6th inning when the Cubs got 5 runs from a couple singles and a home run, and then a double and 2 more singles.

During the 3rd inning, they'd gotten to see the most beautiful sunset, the unusual blue sky in the east, and the sailboats out on Lake Michigan with the red sky in the west reflecting on the sails. Mark didn't forget to take some pictures although he felt his eyes were actually glued to the extraordinary phenomenon.

The home-town fans were happy at the 7th inning stretch because the Cubs were still leading by 4 runs, and you could certainly tell it by the enthusiasm during the singing of 'Take Me Out to the Ballgame.' The Cards started a rally in the 8th, however, tied it in the 9th, and it had to go into extra innings. Both teams added two more runs in the 10th, but the Cubs won it with a home run in the bottom of the 11th. The fans were then singing a catchy tune, "Go Cubs Go," but Mark wasn't familiar with that one. The attendance had been announced as being 40,837, and he could believe that from all the noise.

It was after 12 o'clock when they got back to the hotel, so both of them were ready for a good night's sleep.

CHAPTER THREE

Over their breakfast the following morning at the hotel, Grandpa was telling Mark about the talk he'd had with the man at the ballpark. "He told me we'd be going right by the Wisconsin Dells and it would be a shame not to stop and see it. He said we really should plan to stay overnight and take the scenic boat ride on the river at night. He'd also thought that our hotel here might be holding a reservation or two in the area of the Dells that they could confirm for us. Would you like to do that, Mark?"

"I've heard that Wisconsin Dells is one of the most visited vacation spots in this area, and I'd really like to see it if we don't have to sleep in the car," he chuckled. "Let's check real quick about that reservation before someone else does."

It was a little slow moving on the Interstate in Chicago and the suburbs, but they got to Wisconsin Dells a little after 2 o'clock. They'd had their lunch at a drive-thru about noon and Grandpa had then had his nap, so they were now ready to sight-see. As they'd walked along the Dells River District and bought a few souvenirs, they'd spotted the Lower Dells Boat Tour sign. It had been pure luck that they were the last two allowed to get aboard, but they'd really enjoyed hearing the stories and viewing all the historic sights including the famous sandstone bluffs that so many people have been coming to see for over 150 years.

When they'd returned from that excursion, they made their reservations for the later Paddle wheeler scenic tour which was to be after dinner. They found a nice restaurant and had an excellent meal, but then they were truly fascinated with the Paddle wheeler tour up the Wisconsin River. Upon the return, they'd decided to stop at the Casino for just a little fun to end their day. They were really amazed when both of them won a small amount.

They still had to drive another six miles or so to reach the motel that had been held for them, but they were going in the right direction to continue on their way to the west in the morning.

Only about 80 miles remained in Wisconsin when they'd started out the next day, but before crossing the Mississippi River into Minnesota they'd stopped at a restaurant near the Municipal Airport for a drink and a snack where they could watch the river flowing by. They hadn't found anything else of particular interest on the map, since all those fabulous lakes, that the State is known for, were quite a ways farther north of the highway they were on. They decided to drive up to Rochester, because Lucas wanted to see the well known Mayo Clinic. It wasn't too far off the highway, and it turned out to be quite an impressive establishment. They drove back past the International Airport, stopped for lunch at Austin, and after that, it was time for Grandpa's usual little nap.

When he'd awaken, he was thirsty and it was also time to get gas in the car, so they stopped at a Kwik Stop, got the gas, two bottled iced teas and also purchased a six-pack of soda to put in their cooler. With his throat soothed, Grandpa started talking about finding a place tonight that would have a church with an early service the next morning. "Tomorrow is Sunday, Mark, and we can't forget to thank God for this opportunity and our safe travels so far."

"I've been trying to read my devotional book every day that I'd put in my backpack, but it's been a little hard to find enough time to really concentrate on the messages, so I'd like to go to church tomorrow if it works out."

They had been on the road almost nine hours so far today, just enjoying the scenery and all the small towns they were passing by. It had certainly been a nice change from the monotony of the constant driving and watching highway signs on some of the highways in Ohio. Even though it was Saturday, there had been very few cars on the road to draw their attention away from the afternoon sun constantly hitting the windshield. Thank goodness for sunglasses, but now it was time to keep their eyes open for a place to stop for the night. It was almost 6 o'clock when Grandpa suddenly spied a lake on the left and Worthington coming up on the right. "Why don't we try this one, Mark? We'll see if we can find a church to go to in the morning, locate a pillow to lay our heads, and then maybe we can drive down by that lake to look around. Perhaps we can even stick our feet in the water."

"Before or after we eat?" Mark laughed as he turned onto the exit ramp.

Everything had worked out fine. They'd really enjoyed the church service and then had reached Mitchell, S. Dakota, shortly after lunch. They then found the Corn Palace and were so glad they'd come to see it. The outside of the building was just spectacular, so their camera was really busy taking shots of it and also the amazing pictures inside which were made entirely from corn products. Large pictures along the halls inside the building showed how the outside had been changed every year since it was established, except for one or two, with the use of corn stalks, shucks, silks, and whatever else is associated with corn. It was unbelievable to learn that the inside pictures are changed almost every year, too, so even visiting yearly certainly would not become boring.

They'd also gone to an interesting Indian museum, but then had decided to drive on for a little while longer because it had been a beautiful day and it wouldn't be dark until much later. Grandpa finally got to take his nap while Mark drove toward Chamberlain where they'd decided to stop. It was located right close to the Missouri River, and they did take a little tour over to see Fort Kiowa, dating back to 1822, before they found a restaurant to enjoy a good meal. They then caught up on the news in their room before getting a good much needed night's rest. The rather hot days, even in the car with a good air- conditioner, seemed to be tiring and they welcomed the comfortable beds at night.

They only had to drive a little over three hours the next day to get them close to Mt. Rushmore, but there had been extensive road work so it had been a little slow getting to the little town of Keystone. They visited The National Presidential Wax Museum, which was really great as it had 41 of the American presidents represented. Individually partitioned rooms depicted some presidents in splendid likeness and in a scene that was familiar to his presidency, but there were also a few of the 41 with just an encased bust sculpture or a nice picture on the wall. It had been an interesting tour---getting to view some of the history of most of our presidents.

They'd had lunch at a busy corner buffet, and then had driven on up the mountain to see the impressive faces of the four presidents -- Washington, Jefferson, Teddy Roosevelt, and Abe Lincoln at Mt. Rushmore. That tour had taken longer than they'd expected so they went back down to Keystone and luckily had gotten a room for the night. A late leisurely walk along the main street of the small resort town, which was cooler due to the altitude, had been rather

A Summer's Adventure

invigorating as it had the typical souvenir shops with all types of trinkets to buy. Mark had seen a few other happenings that got his attention in a tourist town, but they'd finally found a nice restaurant where they enjoyed dinner.

When they'd gotten back to their room, they caught up on the national news of the day by watching the 10 o'clock news on TV. Grandpa had missed his first afternoon nap.

The Crazy Horse Museum displayed many artifacts and information about the early Indian heritage, but the sculpture in rock of Crazy Horse was far from being completed. It was started in the 1940's, they'd learned, but there had been several delays due to shortage of funds along the way. Not much was being done at this time, either, but Mark felt it had been worth their time to stop and see it because of the unique museum.

Instead of driving back north to follow the Interstate into Wyoming, they decided to take Route 16 over to Newcastle and then drive south along Route 85 down to Lusk. They would then cut over to Interstate 25 which would take them down to Cheyenne and all the way south to Pueblo, Colorado. The chance to get off the Interstate for awhile really did appeal to them, and they would also save quite a few miles by not going back up north and out of the way to the west. The unusual formations of rock along this area did cause a detour or two so they could get a closer view and take some pictures to show their family back home.

Their plan had been to stay at Fort Collins, where they'd stop to see the Colorado State University campus, but then Mark had noticed that Estes Park was on the road that goes through the Rocky Mountain National Park. He was ecstatic when he realized that they could drive clear to the top of the mountain, so they tried to get a room there first. They soon discovered, however, that June is an exceptionally busy month for tourists in this area and there were no vacancies. They tried Loveland, and some other small motels along the way, but finally had to drive over to Greeley to find lodging.

The next day, of course, Mark had loved the drive up the steep, narrow and winding road to the 10,758 ft. peak in the national park. Grandpa, unfortunately, had been holding on for dear life as he kept looking at the cliff right outside the passenger window that he feared he would be tumbling down any second. He was elated when they were finally able to stop and see the panoramic view from the Visitor's Center parking area before starting down the other side. They stopped for lunch at a restaurant and Visitor's Center on Grand Lake that had a spectacular view of the lake and all the surrounding woods.

They sat out on the big inviting deck or porch for quite awhile after they finished eating because it was so relaxing for Grandpa after his harrowing experience during the drive to the top of the mountain earlier.

When they reached the outskirts of Denver, they decided to get farther away from the huge metropolitan area by driving on south to the town of Castle Rock. They would be in Pueblo the following night, and then on Friday they would finally know whether their trip was going to be a rewarding one by discovering some family who would accept them, or only a big disappointment after their interesting, but long, eleven days on the road.

That night, as well as the following evening in Pueblo, they'd spent time laughing and having fun as they reminisced about the trip so far, but they really tried to relax and sleep well so they'd be ready for the big reunion they were hoping for in Hayes, Colorado.

CHAPTER FOUR

As much as they'd tried, Grandpa Lucas and Mark had a hard time getting to sleep Thursday night because of their excitement of now being so close. They didn't want to get to Hayes too early, though, and find everything not yet opened, but they were still up early and eager to get on their way. They ate a leisurely breakfast Friday morning and then even drove around a bit to see Pueblo. They walked for a half hour or more on the campus of the University of Southern Colorado before starting the last leg of their journey.

When they finally did reach the small town of Hayes about 10 o'clock, Lucas and Mark saw what they thought might be the business district. They could see a grocery store and a bank so they turned right and followed Cleveland Road, which they soon discovered was not the main street of the town. They kept going, however, and did find Main Street and the small business district which was now to their left. They saw that the street name changed from Main Street to Ranch Road at that corner so it must've been the starting of the outskirts of town at one time. A fairly new Animal Hospital and Kennel are on the northwest corner now and a Farm Supply Store is just a little farther down the road. A car wash and even a Kwik Shop has been added across the street.

As their eyes returned to the business district and they started to drive down the Main Street to see what their relative had left behind, they realized there had most likely been many changes over the years. One stark reminder was the movie theater situated on the south side of the street and a big shady parking lot next to it. The theater, however, had been nicely designed to fit the early American wooden fronts of the other buildings. A large historic hotel definitely drew their attention with its immaculate maintenance and beautiful landscaping, and the biggest store on the street still had the sign Mercantile across the front. Some of the other store fronts looked as if they'd been there for quite some time, too, but it did appear as if most had at least updated their signs or were different stores and owners all together.

It was a clean, very welcoming town, and Mark had just about turned onto a side street because he thought he'd seen a school with a large sports area behind it. Lucas, however, motioned for him to continue on down Main Street because he wanted to see all of it first. "Look, Mark, Jeremiah Park," he'd uttered softly when they came alongside the nice landscaped area, "and look at that statue. Your great, great grandfather must've been very well liked to have not only the town, but a park named for him, with a statue, no less."

"The Hayes Law Firm is right there next to the park, Grandpa, but it looks like a fairly recent addition to the town compared to some of the other buildings. Since we know Jeremiah studied to practice law like his father, are you ready to find out if this could be a part of our family? We'll either be welcomed or told to continue on our way," he laughed.

"It looks like some parking spaces over there at the side of that fancy law building, Mark, so let's pull right up there and storm the place," Lucas pointed and chuckled. "I've waited too long to put it off another minute."

They entered the office and glanced around. Both of them were drawn to a very cute petite blonde with a welcoming smile and the most expressive blue eyes. When it suddenly registered who might have come through the door,

A Summer's Adventure

however, those eyes became as big as saucers. She immediately reminded Lucas of his sister Rebekah, when she was just out of college, and also his daughter Kate about twenty-five years ago. This one stared at them for only a few seconds before she went running down the hall calling "Grandpa, Grandpa."

Lucas chuckled, "Well, Mark, I think the first question we had about this family has been answered. I'd guess that we most likely have some recognizable relatives around here and possibly even close by."

They glanced around the office area, while they were waiting, and smiled at the two other girls who had also been staring at them. Mark couldn't keep from chuckling when he saw how quickly they'd returned to their work after they realized they'd been caught.

"What in the world is wrong, Christy, that has you raising your voice like that in the office?" they heard a man's voice quietly ask as he'd apparently entered a connecting hallway from where they assumed his office must be located. "We're lucky there were no clients here at the moment."

Another door opened in the main hallway and a younger voice asked, "Christy, what in the world has happened that has you so excited? Do we have a celebrity visiting in the building, or is there something terribly wrong?"

With light from windows apparently causing shadows in the hallway, Lucas and Mark could just barely see the young lady pointing toward the front of the building as the three seemed to be congregating in an area toward the back of the building. Then they saw two men come into view and heard the young girl exclaim, "He...he looks..looks just like.. your, your...twin, Grandpa." She'd had to gulp as she was trying to finish the thought.

"What are you talking about, Child?" the older one questioned as he headed toward the area where Lucas and Mark were waiting. Upon reaching it, however, he took one look and could only gape and then mutter, "Well, I'll be. Although I never knew her, you have to be my Aunt Ruth's son. I'm Noah Hayes," he said as he extended his hand but then just threw his arms around this stranger to embrace him as he would a member of his beloved family.

"Yes, I'm Ruth's son, Lucas Gillette," he whispered into Noah's ear as he was also slightly overcome with emotions, but he returned the hug with as much enthusiasm as had Noah. They were almost the identical height, 6' or 6'1", similar build, and both had a little gray in their blonde hair. After the embrace was broken, he continued with tears welling up in his eyes, "and this is my favorite grandson, Mark Gillette."

"Hello, Mark, and welcome," Noah smiled as he put his arm around the shoulders of the young man. "This is my granddaughter, as you probably guessed from her calling out Grandpa all the way down the hall," he chuckled. "She is Christy Hayes Holcomb, and this is her husband, Jon. Come along, all of you. Let's go back to the conference room where we can sit down and really talk." Turning to the girls in the office, he smiled and said, "Amy and Beth, please hold all the unnecessary calls because I think an unbelievable reunion is taking place here. You've probably guessed the most obvious, since you know the family history as well as we do, but we'll fill you in later."

Noah was immediately on the phone to his wife, Eleanor. "Sweetheart, we're going to have a few extra for dinner tonight. Do you think you could get Marge and the staff to help you plan an extra special feast?"

"What in the world are you up to now, Noah? Your voice sounds like you'd just won a grand prize and you want a 4th of July celebration."

"Not quite that big," he chuckled, "since you have the wedding coming up so soon, but we have two very special people here in the office who just arrived from the State of New York, and they want to meet their family."

"Noah, you can't possibly mean that some of Ruth's family is right here in Hayes, can you? Oh, what an unexpected, but fabulous surprise. Can you tell me who and how they're related? I can hardly believe this is happening." Noah could clearly sense the elated sniffles, so common with his very sentimental wife. "I'd rather wait and introduce them in person, Eleanor, but I'll say that one has to be fairly close to my age, and I'd guess the other is about the age of Liz but the size of Brent--a grandfather and grandson. We've just come back to the conference room so I don't have too many details yet. I'll call you later, but I just had to let you know about dinner so you can try to get everybody there.

Goodbye, for now, Sweetheart."

"You shouldn't put that extra load on your wife, Noah, especially since I heard you mention a wedding coming up. We could all meet at one of the restaurants here in town after we get a room," Lucas remarked when Noah had cradled the phone.

"Nonsense. We keep a kitchen staff for spur of the moment dinners, but none have been as exciting as this one will certainly prove to be, and you'll definitely stay at the ranch."

"Well, this is the eleventh day we've been on the road, all the time wondering if we'd find anyone belonging to my mother's family when we got here. Mark has been so excited just thinking he might have some more cousins, as well as other family. He has two siblings back home, but only two cousins who are career West Pointers, so there's not a lot of family togetherness there. Can you fill us in on what relatives we have here in Colorado?"

"Let's see. In direct descendants, Mark would have five cousins, an uncle and an aunt, and a great uncle. A few spouses can be added to that number, of course. Christy and her brother, Brent, are both married. Christy works here as a paralegal, and Brent manages the ranch. Liz Becker, the youngest of the cousins, just graduated from high school earlier this month here in Hayes and is going to be married July 5th at the ranch. She and her fiance', Josh Holcomb, who incidentally is Jon's brother, have been waiting patiently, or most likely impatiently, for over two years for the day to arrive. She was just sixteen when they met three years ago, and only with their lives placed in God's hands have they survived. The two older siblings in that family are still in college, Mary in Pre-Med and Brad in Law.

The uncle is Joseph Hayes, my son, and his wife is Marge. They are the parents of Brent and Christy. They live in the main house at the ranch and over the years a fine breed of horses has been raised for riding, performing, and entering competitions. Actually, it all started with Jeremiah, and then my father,

Nathaniel, who dearly loved the ranch, took over the operation. He was joined by my son, Joseph, and then Joseph's son, Brent. Joseph had a heart attack two years ago so Brent persuaded Josh to become Assistant Manager and they now work the ranch together. That leaves Joseph to do as he pleases, and he and Marge have taken a few trips and cruises. The aunt is my daughter, Rachel, and she's the mother of the three cousins, Brad, Mary and Liz. Her husband is Dr. David Becker, a pediatrician in Colorado Springs. The great uncle, of course, is me. I was an only child, but I had the most wonderful parents and grandparents. I spent long hours with Jeremiah learning about the law, and that is really why I'm a lawyer now. I also have the most wonderful wife, Eleanor, who I met at college. I had to hire a future son-in-law to keep the firm in the family, however, since my son and my grandson both turned me down because they loved the ranch more. I guess I wasn't as good at persuasion as Jeremiah.

I loved my grandparents, Jeremiah and Rebecca Hayes, and I will never forget the times I found Grandfather holding Grandmother and trying to console her while she softly cried. He'd explain later, when we'd be talking, that it was Ruth's birthday, or the first day she'd started to school, or she'd lost her first tooth, her confirmation Sunday, her straight A report card was brought home, or the day she'd decided to go live with her grandparents because of the most flattering letters about New York from Grandma White. Jeremiah and Rebecca both had tried to tell her about the small town of Lakewood that they had come from and that it was only if you went way into New York City that you would see all that glamour. Being a typical teenager, she wouldn't listen and insisted she had to leave this undeveloped territory, especially after her older sister, Sarah, had died. I think Jeremiah told me she was only thirteen or fourteen when she left, and they never saw her again.

Since they didn't hear from her after the first six months, they never knew what kind of life she was able to have. Grandmother had sent letter, after letter, after letter, with money to make a trip home for a special event or during summer vacation. There were also birthday and Christmas presents for many years, but never was there a thank you or a letter from Ruth. Grandmother even made two or three trips back to New York, trying to find some clue to what had happened or where she might be, but she'd only found the house, where she had grown up, with new occupants. She was only able to learn that the Whites had moved to Jamestown the year after Ruth had come to live with them, but it was impossible for her to find them. It was as if they'd changed their name or just dropped out of sight. It was even more confusing since an occasional short note from Grandma

White, saying they were fine and Ruth was doing well in school, was always postmarked Lakewood but with no return address. I'm sorry, but I need to let you talk now. Let's hear about the family that has been hiding in New York for all these years," he chuckled as he leaned back to relax and listen.

"Well, Noah, you've confirmed some of my worst thoughts about why my mother didn't want to talk about her family in Colorado or come back to visit. I can understand now how she was led to believe by the Whites that her parents had disowned her when she came back East to finish school. She lived her entire life feeling as if she had no family except for the two grandparents until she married and had children of her own.

My dad, Adam Gillette, told me that he was in his last year of Law School when he'd seen her and wanted to date her, but she always seemed to disappear each day as soon as her classes were over. He'd finally met her one night when she'd actually been allowed to be out with another girl that he happened to know. He asked her for a date and I understand that she finally consented if they could meet at a church that was having special services so she could tell her grandparents where she was going. She told him they could, however, leave from the church for their date without attending the service. Dad said that she was actually very shy but also starving for affection because the Whites had been so controlling. During the rest of that school year, they'd met at the library where she was supposed to be doing some research for her junior year classes, but they'd actually gone on a date. He'd even taken her home to meet his parents one weekend when she'd told Grandma White she was going to an overnight seminar with a classmate, and that girl had actually picked her up and brought her to him.

Dad had started working at his father's law firm when he asked her to marry him. She apparently jumped at the chance, but asked if they could get married secretly by a Judge so she wouldn't have to tell her grandparents until they were legally married. They planned it so she would sneak out of the house on a certain night with just a few belongings, and he'd be at the corner waiting. They'd stay at his parents that night and be married the next day, but Dad and his parents had made arrangements for them to be married at home by the Pastor of their church. They took a short trip and then he rented a home that they furnished with the help of his parents and then a little at a time. Mom finally told me that it was at least two or three years before she and Grandma White actually reconciled their differences not only about the marriage but because she hadn't gone for her senior year of college. She wasn't even sure if her grandma had ever really accepted my dad.

Mom and Dad had two children. My sister was the older and was named Rebecca, but spelled R-e-b-e-k-a-h. It may have been the White's influence again that caused her to spell it differently, but I feel Mom wanted her daughter named after her mother, Rebecca Hayes. Rebekah married Reuben Ward, who was an architect, and they moved around a lot, in this country as well as overseas. They had two boys. One is still a bachelor, who owns and operates a Ski Lodge in New York, and the other one did get married but I'm not sure where he is at the moment. His job as an Archeologist has him traveling all over the world. His wife travels with him and they elected not to have children. Rebekah and Reuben returned to Jamestown, when his health started failing, so I do keep in touch with her. She is very much interested in the outcome of this trip.

My wife's name is Esther and we had two children, Katherine and James. Right after she finished college, Katherine married William Fowley, a West Point graduate and career officer. They have two sons, William, Jr. and Paul, both of whom are or will be West Point grads and also plan to make a career of the service.

James has been in the law firm with me since 1985, married to his wonderful wife of 25 years, Ann Louise, and they have three children. Stephen will enter his second year of Law School, and Deborah will be a junior this fall in college. Mark will start as a freshman, and right now is also planning to study law. That about covers it.

Mark, do you want to ask anything? I heard something mentioned a while ago and I've wondered how you've stayed quiet so long, except that Noah and I haven't given any of you a chance to talk," he chuckled.

"I don't think it's the time or place to ask about that, Grandpa. I'll wait until we go to the ranch for dinner. My stomach is telling me it's about lunch time, though. Do you think we could go to one of the restaurants we saw on our way down Main Street?"

Everyone laughed as they quickly glanced at their watches and realized it might only be a little after 11:00 A.M. here in Colorado, but it is after 1:00 P.M. for the New Yorkers.

"Let's definitely go to lunch, Young Man," Noah agreed as he stood. "You're at the age when they say most have a bottomless pit for a stomach. Christy, why don't you and Jon take Mark and see which one of the restaurants looks good to him, and Lucas and I will pick ours and have some more informative conversation. We have a lot of catching up to do for all these missed years. Does that sound OK?"

"Sure, Grandpa. I slipped out and called Liz a few minutes ago, and she was going to see if Josh and Brent could get away for a lunch break. Susan is visiting her mother today so she won't be back before dinner, but Liz should be calling back real soon. We'll see you back here about 1 o'clock."

"Sounds fine with me. Do you two want to freshen up a bit before we go?" "I would like to do that, please. Mark, would you like to wash your hands?"

"That would probably be a good idea," he chuckled as he followed the two men out of the conference room and down the one hall that went past Noah's office.

After showing them the location of the Men's Room, Noah returned and couldn't hold back a smile as he gave his granddaughter a hug. "Can you imagine this, Christy? It's such an unbelievable dream come true. I just wish it could have happened 20 or 30 years ago."

"I think it's wonderful, Grandpa, and Mark is so handsome and seems like such a well mannered young man. He must love, respect, and enjoy being with his grandfather a lot to agree to this long trip with him."

"Of course, Christy, he's got a lot of Hayes blood in him. He's tall, blonde and blue eyed, and haven't we all loved spending time with our grandfathers?" Noah grinned as he raised an eyebrow and looked at her with a sparkle in his eye.

Christy was grinning, too, and patted his cheek just before her phone began to ring. It was Liz calling to tell them that she was so sorry but Brent and Josh were not even close to the house right now, and Grandma really needed her to help with the dinner tonight.

"O.K., Liz," Christy answered, "that's perfectly understandable, and I want to thank you for helping Grandma. We'll see you all later."

"What are they like, Christy? Do they have that New England or Eastern accent that I hear on TV so much? Is one actually close to my age like Grandpa told Grandma? Are we going to be able to be compatible? Oh, I have so many questions."

"I can't answer all those right now, Liz, because Mark is hungry and we're going to take him to lunch right quick.

His poor stomach is two hours ahead of ours so we've got to get some food for the poor guy. I'll just say that I think you'll be pleasantly surprised when you meet both of them because they are really special. Talk to you soon. Bye, now."

A Summer's Adventure

```
                        Jeremiah Hayes 1869-1958
                                   m.
                         Rebecca White 1872-1952
```

```
Sarah 1898-1918   Nathanial 1902-1994              Ruth 1906-1986
                            m.                            m.
                  Annabelle Rogers '04-'98        Adam Gillette '01-'72
                            │                             │
                  ┌─────────┴─────────┐         ┌─────────┼─────────┐
                  Noah 1930-                    Lucas 1933-      Rebekah 1931-
                       m.                            m.                m.
                  Eleanor Dilworth 1931-        Esther Hall 1934-  Reuben Ward 1928-
                       │                             │                  │
        ┌──────────────┼──────────┐         ┌───────┴───────┐      ┌────┴────┐
   Joseph 1955    Rachel 1959              Katherine 1957   James 1960    Dean 1956   Ray 1958
        m.            m.                         m.              m.
 Margaret Brown '56  David Becker '55      William Fowley   Ann Louise Fey
        │             │
   ┌────┴────┐   ┌────┴────┐
Brent '80  Christy '82  Brad '85   Mary '87   William, Jr. '82   Stephen '84    0           0
   m.        m..           Liz '89              Paul '85          Deborah '87
Susan     Jon                                                     Mark '89
Ferris '81 Holcomb '79    Josh Holcomb '84
```

35

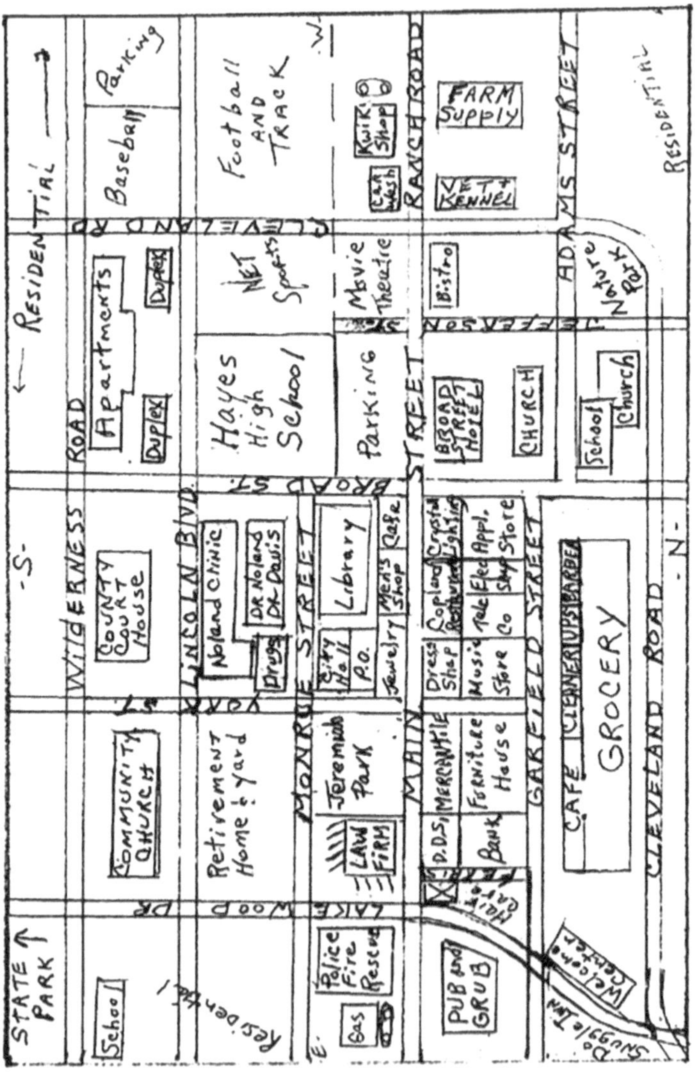
STATE PARK
School
Residential
Police Fire Rescue
Gas
PUB and GRUB
Welcome Center
LAKEWOOD DR
COMMUNITY CHURCH
Retirement Home & Yard
LAW FIRM
Jeremiah Park
D.D.S.
MERCANTILE
Bank
Furniture House
CAFE
CLEANERS
UPS
BARBER
GROCERY
CLEVELAND ROAD
GARFIELD STREET
MAIN STREET
MONROE STREET
YORK ST
WILDERNESS ROAD
LINCOLN BLVD
COUNTY COURT HOUSE
Noland Clinic
Dr Noland Dr Davis
Drugs
City Hall
P.O.
Jewelry
Library
Men's Shop
Dress Shop
Music Store
Copland Restaurant
Tele Co
Crystal Lighting
Elec Appl. Shop
Store
BROAD ST
-S-
-N-
E.
W.
Apartments
Duplex
Hayes High School
Parking
BROAD STREET HOTEL
CHURCH
School
Church
JEFFERSON
Bistro
Movie Theatre
NET Sports
Nature Park
ADAMS STREET
CLEVELAND RD
RESIDENTIAL
Baseball
Parking
Football AND TRACK
Car Wash
Kwik Shop
RANCH ROAD
VET + KENNEL
FARM SUPPLY

CHAPTER FIVE

Christy and Jon took Mark to the cafe when his request was a typical teenager's meal of a hamburger, an order of fries, and something to drink. When they'd been served, Christy started the conversation with a question. She'd remembered something that Lucas had asked Mark earlier.

"Mark, your grandfather said that he'd heard Noah mention something concerning the ranch that you'd wondered about for awhile. Would you like to ask Jon and me and maybe we can satisfy your curiosity? If it's about the ranch, either one of us can give you pretty accurate information. I've lived there all my life, and Jon was raised on a farm just over the line in Oklahoma and has been around here for three years, so we both know a lot about the ranch."

"When I was still pretty young, Grandpa used to tell me some things that his mother had finally told him about the family that might be living in Colorado. In my mind, at that age, the mention of Colorado meant cowboys and Indians and, of course, horses. I did a lot of dreaming about the possibility that Great, Great Grandfather Jeremiah made friends with the Indians, and it was always on horses. I have, since then, had a longing to ride, but there was never an opportunity to do it because none of my family seemed interested in that sort of activity. I guess, while I was talking to Grandpa on the trip, I asked if he thought the ranch might have horses. I got the shivers when Uncle Noah mentioned them, but I was just going to wait until we got to the ranch before I asked about the possibility of getting to go for a ride."

"Well, Mark, the ranch does have some marvelous riding horses, and we'll see that you get a chance to ride a lot while you're here. You won't confront any Indians, but there is so much to see as you ride the trails, and there are quite a few of us to go with and keep you company as you ride. Of course, there is a special wedding being planned for two weeks from tomorrow, and we hope you'll be able to stay for that. Was there any set time that you had to return home?"

"I don't think so. When Grandpa asked me if I would consider spending a rather dull summer traveling with him, he said it might take all summer because he had no idea what we would find. I'm enrolled to start college about the 20th of August, but I have no idea what Grandpa's plans are, especially since we've found some family to get acquainted with. I had absolutely no plans for the summer so was thrilled when he said he was going to Colorado to try and find a family that might not be there or even exist. But, who would refuse a trip to Colorado?" he chuckled.

"We're so glad you came, Mark," Jon smiled as he affectionately ran his finger down Christy's cheek, "and you couldn't have found a nicer family to become a part of. I'm living proof of that. The whole family is as sweet and loving as the two members you've already met, and it's quite an experience to get to know them."

"Could you give me some of the names again, Christy, so I'll be able to put the faces with the names when I'm introduced tonight? I'd really love to be able to pick out some of them before they're even introduced. It has actually been one of my hobbies."

"Sure," Christy replied. "The ones who live at the ranch are Grandma Eleanor, who is Noah's wife. There's no mistaking her, as she is the oldest and has the most beautiful smile, a wonderful personality, but eyes like a hawk. She doesn't miss much of what goes on around the ranch. She and Noah live in a house that Nathaniel built not far from the original one that had been built by Jeremiah. There's a story about that, of course, that you'll get to hear later, I'm sure. Then there's our youngest, Liz Becker, a cute little blonde with extraordinary brown eyes, who's been living with the grandparents for about two years while finishing high school here in Hayes. She is the soon-to-be bride; and Josh Holcomb, her fiance`, is tall, dark and very handsome, since he looks like a twin to this one," she grins as she pats Jon's cheek.

"Josh lives at the original homestead, which we call the Main House, along with my mom and dad, who are Joseph and Marge Hayes. Dad is a tall blonde, much like Noah, with a few gray hairs showing, too. He has the blue eyes, while Mom's are hazel, her hair is more ash blonde, and she is about my height although a little heavier. My brother, Brent, cannot be confused with Jon and Josh. Although he is tall, he's definitely a Hayes with blonde hair and bright blue eyes. He and his wife, Susan, who will be easy to recognize since she is our only brunette, live in a big wing off the Main house which they remodeled to their own liking. He manages the ranch and watches Dad like a hawk so he doesn't overdo and have another heart attack.

Mom and Dad have a large master bedroom suite in the wing on the opposite side of the house from Brent and Susan, and Josh has two adjoining rooms on second floor that Noah and Eleanor used for privacy when they were living there. I'm sure Brent and I were the reasons they were driven to where they are now although that's another story, of course," she giggled and then continued.

"Jon and I had been planning and building our home for over two years and we finally moved in April 25th, which we felt was the actual date we met in 2005. I'm sorry, Mark, I've gotten off the subject. However, the other house you'll see is the one Josh and Liz had built so they'll live there when they return from their honeymoon.

I'm not sure if all the Becker family will be able to come down tonight, but there are four of them besides Liz. Rachel is my dad's sister, a short one who is blonde most of the time but she loves to play around with hair color. She has the bright blue eyes, always a smile on her face, and she is lots and lots of fun to be around. Dr. David Becker is a pediatrician, loves all us kids, and has even mentioned he might bring his practice here to Hayes so he can be the doctor for his grandchildren, great nieces and nephews, etc.," she chuckled. "He will be the shortest of the men, but about 5'10", with medium brown hair and the most beautiful brown eyes. You and Liz are apparently about the same age, so Brad and Mary are slightly older than you. Mary will enter her final year of pre-med, and Brad will be starting his final year of Law School this fall. Mary has the blonde hair and blue eyes of a Hayes; Brad is taller than his dad but has the medium brown hair and sparkling brown eyes like him. I think that covers the whole family."

"Thanks, Christy, I'm sure I'll be able to tell, from your descriptions, who most of them are. I've always been pretty good at remembering names and faces, so I hope my luck holds as I'm getting acquainted with my extended family. This has to be the most exciting time of my life."

"From my un-businesslike display of excitement this morning, you have to know how surprised I was to see you two standing there with those smiles on your faces. I realized, of course, that you had to be some of our family because Lucas looked so much like Noah, and that only meant one thing--you were some of Aunt Ruth's family even though I couldn't make the connection immediately. I am so happy to discover that I have more family than I could ever have dreamed possible. Do you suppose we'll get to meet all of them one day?"

"I certainly hope so, but I'm especially happy that Grandpa got to make this trip while he's still healthy and able to travel."

They continued to talk about the family until Jon quietly broke into their almost non-stop conversation. "I hate to break this up, Sweetheart, but I need to get back to the office. A client is coming in that will be a little upset if I'm not there when he arrives, but I'm sure glad it was an afternoon appointment. You two can stay and talk, though, if you'd like."

"No, I think we need to get back, too. I'm almost positive I have a few things on my desk to get done, and we don't know what our grandfathers have up their sleeves, do we?" she chuckled.

As they walked back to the office, Mark remarked, "If your grandfather is anything like mine, he loves to be in the middle of everything."

"Oh, yes, that's my grandpa all right, but I must admit that he has more good advice and ideas than anyone I've ever known. He has actually been a wonderful friend throughout all my growing up years."

"Noah played a big part in getting Christy to accept our relationship right from the beginning." Jon added. "She wasn't the easiest person to convince that I was serious about loving her, so from the day I came for my interview right through the planning of our fabulous honeymoon, he was giving advice and running interference for us. He is one super guy, but maybe we've just discovered another one. I'd wager right now that they're having a great time together."

CHAPTER SIX

Upon reaching the office, Jon excused himself after assuring the two that he'd join them again as soon as possible.

Christy checked her desk and grimaced as she noticed a couple of things she needed to get finished today. "I'm sorry, Mark, but it looks like I'm going to have to desert you for a little while, too. Shall we find our grandfathers?"

"You go ahead with your work, Christy. I'll find our grandfathers and see if they'll let me wander around the town by myself. I don't think it's big enough for me to get lost in, is it?" he chuckled.

Mark was soon on his way down Main Street past Jeremiah Park, across York Street, and then looking in the windows of the Jewelry Store and the Men's Clothing Store. He then walked past the Cafe at the corner of Main and Broad Streets, where they had just had lunch, and then turned south on Broad Street to take a look at the High School. He glanced across at the nice tree-lined city parking lot but then noticed a fairly large library which was located on Monroe Street behind the Cafe and also part of the Men's Clothing Store. It had entrances on both S. Broad Street and Monroe Street that only went east from in front of the school.

A Summer's Adventure

The high school building, just south of the city parking lot, was very impressive, he thought, for a small town. There was a big sports complex behind it, and from what he could see from that distance, it appeared to have several tennis courts before a road divided the area. On the other side of the road was a football field with a running track around it plus a nice baseball diamond to the south of that with another parking area. He soon realized that the road was the continuation of Cleveland Road that he and Grandpa had driven on to find Main Street. Several sports had been very cleverly included in the one fairly good-sized area, and, of course, parking had been made very convenient for those attending the games.

Across the street from the school building, there was a doctor's office and the west end of a clinic that actually faced the tree-lined Lincoln Boulevard. While standing at the corner, he could see the large historic County Court House on the south side of Lincoln Boulevard to his left. The three-story building and its nicely landscaped grounds covered the entire block back over to York Street. An impressive big clock was ticking away the seconds and minutes in a steeple at one corner of the building not far from the entrance. To his right, in the block along the south of the High School, there were a couple of large duplex buildings, also facing Lincoln Boulevard. A large apartment building had been built behind them although it faced the next street which he thought was Wilderness Road if he'd seen the sign correctly. The founders must've thought it would be the end of the town, but he could see quite a few private homes had been built south of there, and the north and south streets continued way beyond Wilderness Road now.

He crossed the boulevard to walk past the court house, and he could see a charming old church in the next block. Looking back across the boulevard, he saw the entrance to the clinic which he had only seen a portion of from Broad

Street, and he was amazed at the great job of landscaping that surrounded that building. Proceeding on, he reached the Community Church, which was definitely a one-of-a-kind antique marvel. It had a quaint old-fashioned appearance in architecture and beautiful stained glass windows. With its shaded parking spaces and the outstanding grounds, it also takes up an entire block from York Street over to Lakewood Drive. With the church and the court house, along with the boulevard plantings and the clinic's great landscaping, he was really impressed. He actually hadn't seen it all yet as he was crossing the Boulevard and heading north. A fairly new Retirement Home had been built directly across from the church and east of the Clinic, and it had an entrance and a yard also manicured to perfection. He soon found that its beautiful back yard bordered Monroe Street which was just south of Jeremiah Park and the Law Office, which were also beautifully landscaped. *They must have some really talented 'green thumbs' living around this town,* he thought to himself.

As he'd continued his walk north on Lakewood Drive admiring the Retirement Home's colorful flowers and shrubs, plus its backyard seating areas in the shade of the tall trees, he could see a Drug Store, over on York Street just north of the east part of the Clinic and behind the doctor's office. The Post Office and City Hall were there, north of Monroe Street and if his calculations were right, they'd be behind the library that he'd seen on S. Broad Street.

Crossing Main Street at the Law Office, he noticed a Hair Care Salon in the little space between Lakewood Drive and Ferris Street, which looked like a short street that connected Main Street to a large parking area, but he couldn't actually see what was back there except it might be where they'd seen the Grocery Store. Going on down Main Street, there was a nice looking Dentist Office although the building was old and connected to the Mercantile. This one truly intrigued him, since he'd never seen a Mercantile before, so he went in to look around. He was a little stunned when the wooden floors squeaked or creaked with every step he took, and the ceiling had big wooden beams which actually showed the boards of the roof above. He was surprised at the wide variety of items they had for sale, though, and couldn't resist buying his very first cowboy hat. He chuckled, as he left the store, wearing the hat of course, because he suddenly felt like he was really in the old Wild West that he had read about, and he could soon be a ranch hand. "The Magic of a hat," he grinned as he fingered the brim like he'd seen so many cowboys do in the movies.

He then passed a Dress Shop, a nice looking Copland's restaurant, and a big Crystal Lighting Store on the corner which had entrances on both Main Street and N. Broad Street. The outstanding chandeliers were shimmering in the afternoon sun, and he could also hear some wind chimes making their melodious sounds. North of it was an Appliance Store, but across the street was the large Broad Street Hotel, which he and Grandpa had seen earlier. It was another old antique marvel which had to have been there for many, many years, but it still looked in good shape from meticulous care and upkeep. A lot of landscaping had been done which gave distinction to the hotel and also a parking area between the hotel and a big church on the next corner which was Adams Street that only went west from Broad Street.

Turning back to the east on Garfield Street, which began at Broad Street and continued as far as he could see, there was an Electronics Shop, the Telephone Company, and a Music Store behind the stores on Main Street. In the second block, after crossing York Street which ended at Garfield, there was a large Furniture Store, and then a Bank. Looking north, across from all of those, he saw another Cafe, a UPS Store, a

Dry Cleaners, and a Barber Shop which all backed up against a large Grocery Store.

He decided to venture into the Grocery when he remembered that he needed some tooth paste, aftershave, and also a new comb to replace the one he couldn't find this morning. He'd had to borrow Grandpa's. The store turned out to be an enormous building, and he was having trouble finding the items he wanted. He'd been glancing down every aisle as he strolled along a wide front aisle until he began to feel more like he was lost in there than in the whole town he'd just been touring.

He finally noticed a young girl stacking boxes of cereal on a shelf, so he decided to approach her. He was only going to ask directions to the tooth paste aisle, but when he said

"Pardon me" and she turned toward him, he couldn't remember a word that he wanted to say.

He was in a trance, or spellbound, or completely captivated, but he could only mutter, "Oh, you are so-o-o beautiful, what's your name?"

"May I help ya'll find something, Sir, or do ya'll make it a habit of going around trying to get the attention of working girls with ya'lls un-welcomed remarks?"

"Oh, no, I'm sorry. You just made me lose my concentration for a minute," he said as he tried to smile. "I'm trying to find the tooth paste aisle. I'm new in town and this is my first time in the store. I'm visiting the Hayes family, but the ones at the law offices were busy this afternoon so I thought I'd check out the town."

"That's an unlikely story, but I'll show ya'll the tooth paste aisle. Follow me," she said in a rather disgusted manner.

"Could I walk beside you instead of following you? I don't want to appear as if I'm stalking you. I'm really sorry if I offended you."

"Most people let us lead, but suit yourself. It's not far to the item ya'll said you were looking for."

"Would the aftershave and combs be in the same area? My grandfather and I have been on the road for over a week, and I'm out of several things."

"I'll bet, but ya'll do have a slight accent that isn't from around here, so where did ya'll come from?"

"New York."

"Oh, yeah," she laughed. "What other big lies are ya'll going to try to sell me? Next, I suppose, ya'll will try to tell me that ya'll are related to the Hayes family and even know all of their names. Ya'll are not fooling anyone by picking the Hayes family to claim being related to. We all know the Hayes family AND the story about the town's beginning."

"Well, actually, I *am* related and I do know their names, but you really don't have to believe me. I would really like to get to know you, but I guess I made a lousy start to be able to accomplish that."

"Sir, here is the aisle ya'll asked about, and I hope ya'll find what ya'll are looking for, as long as it's not me. I don't want to get to know ya'll because I don't associate with liars. I'd rather ya'll just left our town as soon as possible." She then turned and walked away.

"Whew," he muttered. *I guess everyone is this town isn't as friendly as my new found family, but I'd still like to see if I could get a smile from this cute Miss Un- congeniality. She can't be very old, and so gorgeous, but I sure made a fool of myself by getting so tongue-tied. Maybe Christy will know who she is and can help me, because I'd like to at least prove to her that I'm not a liar.*

After paying for his purchases, he stepped into the cafe, which turned out to be part of the grocery store with an inside and outside entrance. He ordered a soda to go. He then went outside and glanced around to see if he could determine what the other buildings were that he'd seen over on this Lakewood Drive. He knows now that it is the road that takes you north to the highway because it's the one that he and Grandpa had come in on. Of course, they had seen the grocery store and the bank and had thought they were the start of the business district, so they'd turned onto Cleveland Road and followed it around to Main Street. The road had gone on from where they'd turned onto Main Street, but he hadn't been sure how far it went until he'd seen it behind the school. It then appeared to go on into a residential area.

Of course, he realized now that they would've found the Hayes Law Firm a lot sooner if they'd just stayed on Lakewood Drive. He saw a fairly new Do Snuggle Inn and a Pub & Grub restaurant on the other side of that road and the back of a nice building that appeared to be some sort of a Civic Center on this side.

He cut across the large parking lot that he'd seen from Main Street and where Ferris Street also ends as it enters the parking area. He went past the bank which had an entrance facing Ferris Street as well as the one he'd seen on Garfield. He continued along the side of the Dentist office to reach Main Street, and he was, once again, across the street from where he'd started his little tour.

He'd actually seen several residential areas peeking through the trees and foliage, as he'd walked around, and he thought he'd seen a school building about two blocks east of the Community Church, which he assumed was an Elementary one. Another school, which would also be an Elementary one, since it had playground equipment, appeared to be attached to the church located on Cleveland Road and wasn't far from the church he'd seen north of the Hotel.

Looking to his left now, he saw a rather large building on Main Street, just east of the Law Firm and Lakewood Drive that apparently is shared by the Police, Fire, and the

Rescue Squad. He could see that Main Street continued on to the east for quite a ways as had Garfield, Monroe, Lincoln Boulevard, and Wilderness Road. To the west, he knew Main Street became Ranch Road and went way out of town, but Adams, Lincoln Boulevard, and Wilderness Road had continued into residential areas going west also.

It's a rather compact little town, but it seems to have everything that is needed to provide its citizens with a good life, he thought as he crossed Main Street and entered the Law Firm to see if his new found cousin had finished her work. He glanced at his watch and was a bit surprised that he'd been gone for almost three hours.

"We were beginning to wonder if we'd have to send a search team out to find you," Christy laughed as she watched him come in the door. "I see you found yourself a cowboy hat, which looks very good on you, by the way---a true, red-blooded cowboy. Did you practically see the entire town?"

"I think I saw most of the business district and was very impressed, but I didn't get to the residential areas. I only saw some roof tops through the trees over by the high school, a few houses up a little higher over to the west and quite a few houses south of the Wilderness Road. I didn't really look very far north of the Grocery Store, but I could see some scattered homes, or maybe small farms, behind the nice looking Do Snuggle Inn and the Pub and Grub restaurant over that way," he related as he pointed toward the northeast. "There also appeared to be some homes over to the east of that beautiful antique church where I saw a building I assumed would be an Elementary School as he pointed to the southeast."

"You really did take a tour, Mark, but we'll drive around so you can see the homes and farms before you leave. We actually have three Elementary Schools, but the Westside School can't be seen unless you get into the residential area to the west. The Do Snuggle Inn and the Pub and Grub

Restaurant are rather new and are owned by the same family who thought the names were very clever. They both do a great business, so I guess it worked. We'll be ready to leave in a few minutes. Jon is just finishing up a little paperwork. Our grandfathers already took off for the ranch, so you can ride out with us."

"Thanks, Christy. I have something, or someone, to ask you about later, but I'll go wash up a bit before we leave for the ranch. Can I drop this paper cup in a waste basket in the rest room, or would you rather have it put somewhere else? I got myself a drink in the grocery store cafe."

"In the rest room will be fine, Mark. We have a person who comes in and cleans a little each evening after we leave."

"I'll be back shortly then."

Christy is really curious now. *I wonder who he could've seen or met that he wants to know about. I hope he doesn't keep me waiting too long.*

Jon was just coming out of his office when Mark was returning to the reception area. "Well, Mark, how was your tour of our little town?" he asked as he put his arm across the young man's shoulders. "You must've seen quite a bit of it in the time you were gone. Your grandfather and Noah thought they would drive around a little, before heading to the ranch, and maybe pick you up so you could go with them. They called to let us know they didn't find you so we wouldn't leave without you."

"I was probably in the grocery store, unless they left a little earlier, because the only other place I went inside was the Mercantile where I bought my new hat. Do you think I'll pass as a cowboy on the ranch?" he laughed.

"It's really a nice hat and you look like a member of the family already. Be sure to take it off, though, when the family members come at you with their arms outstretched. It might be a bit awkward with the wide brim, but a gentleman always removes his hat when he's meeting new people, so that shouldn't be a problem," he chuckled.

"Thanks for reminding me, Jon. I haven't worn too many hats, especially this kind, except when it's really cold outside, and I don't remember meeting any strangers while I was wearing one. Maybe I should leave it in the car so I don't cause any problem."

"That would probably work, but don't think you have to hide it. Brent and Josh always wear their hats while they're working, and we all wear hats when we go riding to keep the sun out of our eyes and the wind from blowing our hair all over, but we aren't big on wearing them like into town or when we're at the house. You'll definitely want to wear it when you go with the guys to the barn and whenever we go riding."

"I really appreciate your advice, Jon. I'm just so excited about seeing the ranch and maybe getting to ride. It definitely seems like a dream come true."

CHAPTER SEVEN

They joined Christy and were soon on their way to the ranch. Mark wasn't sure how or when to ask Christy about the girl he'd seen at the grocery store, but he finally decided it might be easier in the car than at the ranch with all the others around and listening in.

"Christy, I went into two stores while I was out touring this afternoon. Of course, you know by my hat that I stopped at the Mercantile, but I also went into the grocery store to get a few items I was out of. I had to glance down every aisle because I didn't know which one would have what I wanted. Finally, I saw a young girl stocking cereal boxes on the shelves, so I decided to ask if she could give me directions. When she turned around, I made a fool of myself because I couldn't think of a thing to say or even what I'd wanted to ask her. Oh, I was so stupid, Christy. She was gorgeous and I just blurted out "Oh, you are so beautiful, what is your name?

Well, you can imagine what kind of a reply I got. She was as cold as ice and finally told me she hoped I left this town very soon, plus a few other choice words. I'm wondering if you'd know who she is and help me prove to her that I wasn't lying when I mentioned that I was visiting the Hayes family."

"I know several of the girls who work there, Mark, so what did this one look like and about how old do you think she'd be?" It was hard to keep a straight face, but Christy was remembering some of her own embarrassing moments when she'd started college so it made it easier to understand how Mark must've felt.

"She can't be very old, probably 16 or 17, with the prettiest shiny brunette hair that falls down to her shoulder blades, at least. She has perfect olive skin and dark eyes that, of course, wanted to kill me at that moment. She has a small build, maybe 5'4" tall, and looks like she could be French or Spanish, I would guess."

He noticed that Jon and Christy were both smiling as they glanced at each other, so he assumed they apparently had some idea who he was describing. "If you two know this girl, please tell me if you think I would have any chance of meeting her under a little different set of circumstances. Don't keep me in the dark. She can't be engaged or maybe married, can she? I didn't see a ring on her finger."

With a chuckle in her voice, Christy replied, "Mark, there can only be one young girl in this town that would fit that description, and she just recently went to work at the grocery store for the summer. And, yes, we know her very well since we brought her and her family up from New Orleans about two and a half years ago. Hurricane Katrina had destroyed their home and the business her father worked for. There are five in the family and they have all become great additions to the town. They do have a French heritage, and in this town, the only other person you could've seen, fitting that description, would've been her mother, Carole. They could pass as twins, except for some age difference, but of course, the mother doesn't work there. We'll definitely see that you meet her and assure her that you're not a liar," she giggled.

"It must be great to live in such a small town that you can know almost everyone. Did you really bring her family here from New Orleans? That would explain the slight

Southern accent I detected. There must be a wonderful story that goes along with that, and I'd love to hear it."

"We don't have time for the story right now, Mark, because we're almost at the ranch. I will tell you that she has lost a lot of her accent, but it probably did show up if she was upset. If you get acquainted with Jaclyn Lambre, which is her name by the way, you might be able to hear their story from her. It was a horrible ordeal for so many."

"I hope I get a chance to talk to her, Christy, and smooth over my stupid remarks. But, now, I guess that this is the ranch that my great, great grandfather homesteaded. It certainly doesn't look anything like what I envisioned in my dreams, thank goodness. I had it looking more like the dusty barren land in the movie, 'Giant,' he laughed. "This is really beautiful with all the lush green trees, the flowers and shrubs, and I can see at least four homes scattered out and around."

Jon slowed down so Christy could tell him about the houses. "The large one we'll come to first is the one that Jeremiah built for himself and Rebecca, which we call the Main House. I understand he wanted a big family, since he had been an only child and so had Rebecca. They did have three children; but Sarah, the oldest, went overseas as a nurse during World War I and then died from the wounds she received while close to the front lines. Of course, you already know that your great grandmother Ruth went back East so it left only Nathaniel and his young wife, Annabelle, to try to produce descendants. After several years with no children, Annabelle got very discouraged and wanted a home of her own, so Nathaniel built the one you see on the right of the parking area. They had only the one son, Noah, who lives there now with his wife, Eleanor.

The first one on down there, on the left of the Main House and past the beautiful yard with the trellis where Josh and Liz will be married, just got completed this spring for

Josh and Liz after they return from their honeymoon. They are still getting it furnished but have plenty to get started with. There is plenty of room for Brent and Susan to build their home some day between the Main House and Josh and Liz's. Our house is the last one you see way over yonder as we decided to leave some room closer to the Main House in case someone else connected with the running of the ranch wanted to build later on. We love the view we have of the mountains and also the trail leading to the grove of trees which surrounds one of the small ponds on the ranch. You'll get to see all of it before you leave, but it looks like some of the Becker family has made it already from their home in Colorado Springs. You have a lot more family to be introduced to so we'd best get moving. You aren't nervous, are you?"

"Not really. I love meeting people, but it is really a thrill to realize that these are going to be real newly-found relatives. I just hope I don't get tongue-tied like I did at the grocery store," he chuckled.

"You may get squeezed a little with all the hugs you're going to receive, but there'll be no wishing you'd leave this town like Jaclyn wanted you to do. I can't understand her being so insulting because she's really a very friendly and helpful person after going through the horrors of the hurricane, although at times she does appear to be apprehensive about being left alone if there are young guys around. Of course, she'll change her mind about you when she finds out who you belong to," Christy giggled.

As soon as the car stopped, three smiling faces were waiting at the door. "I hear we've acquired another cousin to get acquainted with," Brad remarked as he opened the back door and was the first to speak. "Hi, Mark, we've been waiting for almost two hours, or maybe I should say two decades, for something like this to happen. Come out and meet some of your long-time unknown relatives. We can't let Christy have you all to herself."

Mark left his hat on the seat as he got out and shook hands with the young man who he noticed had the medium brown hair, brown eyes, and approximately 6' tall. "Well, let's see, from all of Christy's excellent descriptions, and with two lovely ladies standing beside you, I must assume that you are Brad. Do I get a hug from a male cousin or is that reserved just for the female ones?" he laughed. Brad's arms were immediately open and the two embraced like two very old friends who hadn't seen each other for a long time.

As he stepped back, Brad said, "I'd better introduce you to these two before they have my scalp in their hands."

"Please, Brad, let me see if I can remember what Christy told me about these two very lovely cousins and see if I can call them by name. I think I have to look into their eyes to be sure which is which." Taking the arms of the closest one in his hands, he smiled as he looked at her face and eyes. "This is Mary, and I'm so glad to meet you. I understand you are a pre-med student and will someday be a wonderful doctor. I hope all your dreams come true." He gave her a quick hug and a kiss on the cheek.

He then looked at the other one who had already captivated him, when he'd first seen her from the car, as had the one in the grocery store. She had the sweetest smile on her face, and he had to chuckle as he moved toward her. He held her shoulders with his hands as he stooped down to look into her eyes. He was so entranced he could only whisper, "You have to be Liz, with those beautiful brown eyes sparkling like a soon-to-be bride, and the one who's about my age. I wish we weren't related because I might've tried to steal you away from this Josh fellow." Without hesitation, he put one arm around her waist, pulled her quite close to him, tilted her chin with his free hand and gave her a kiss on the lips that was much more than a new cousin kiss. He then whispered, "I just had to have my first real kiss be from the cousin who stole my heart at first glance." Looking at her blushing face, he grinned as he turned to the others who were speechless, and asked, "So, how did I do?"

Liz could only gasp but then accuse him of not playing fair as she tried to downplay her very surprised reaction to the kiss. Finally she managed enough control to say, "No one can do a better job at describing people than Christy, so you were apparently well schooled on what we all looked like and our future plans. Brent and this Josh fellow, as you called him, should be coming from the barn shortly, but there are some adults who are also very anxious to meet their overly friendly visitor. Did our helpful Christy describe *them* to you, too?"

"She sure did. Shall we see how well I can do with my newly discovered aunts, uncles, and great aunt?" Apparently recovered from the unexpected greeting, Liz grabbed his hand and pulled him with her toward the group of adults waiting on the large deck.

"Hey, everybody, this is Mark, our unpredictable, but handsome new found cousin, and he said he'd like the challenge, from Christy's descriptions, of trying to call you all by name. So give him your best smile and undivided attention." She then turned toward the newcomer and with a rather contented smirk, said, "They're all yours, Mark."

"Thanks, Liz. You really like throwing people right into the lion's den, don't you?" he chuckled. "Well, Hi there, everyone. I'm usually pretty good at putting a person's name with a face from association or description, so let's see how well I can do with my new relatives that I am so excited to meet." Looking over to where his grandfather was sitting, he began, "I know the gentleman sitting next to my favorite grandfather since I met him earlier today, and you'll never know how his sincere welcome this morning thrilled me. It is so nice to see you again, Uncle Noah. I understand that the two of you tried to find me as I scouted the town, but I had a great time and was very impressed.

Next to you, I believe, is your most gracious wife, Eleanor, who will take a call for a spur of the moment dinner without a fuss or complaint. I've heard that she's also a wonderful grandmother to my five newly acquired cousins and has actually had one living with her for a couple of years. It seems, from a few remarks I've heard, that she has the eyes of a hawk and the heart of a saint. Not much goes on around this ranch that she doesn't know about." He took her hand and kissed it as he smiled at the blush coming to her face. "I'm sure looking forward to getting to know you as you remind me of my own grandmother.

Those two were easy. Now, this lovely lady I'll assume is Rachel Becker, the mother of Brad, Mary, and Liz." Taking her hands and pulling her to her feet, he patted her head, which only came to his chest. He then tilted her chin so he could look into her eyes. "Five foot two, eyes of blue, but oh what fun she can be, too," he chanted as he gave her a big smile. "I under-stand you are lots of fun to be around and you're married to a pediatrician in Colorado Springs. I guess your husband isn't here," he added as he glanced around.

Since she is only 5' tall, Rachel put her arms around his waist to give him a big hug and a warm welcome. Mark, however, was glancing over at Christy who was getting just a little nervous as she'd been watching very closely to everything that was going on. Had she told him too much? When he got her attention, over Rachel's head, of course, he had a big grin on his face as his hand moved down her soft, shiny, strawberry blonde hair. It was quite a struggle for him not to laugh out loud when Christy's reply was a shocked look but only a mouthed, "Don't you dare!"

"You are very lovely, Aunt Rachel," he whispered as he gently kissed her forehead and patted her back. "You remind me a lot of my Aunt Kate who often gets teased mercilessly by us guys for trying to keep up with the latest hair styles and colors, but I love your hair today."

Rachel threw her head back to look up at this smiling young man who stood at least a foot taller than she did. She was trying not to laugh as she scolded in a whisper, "Mark, you know you're not supposed to say that to your newly discovered aunt, but thank you. I'm sure I'm going to love you." She reached up and patted his cheek and then sat back down, still giggling. Everyone else, of course, was left to wonder what Mark had whispered to her.

"You ladies are all rather short. They must only grow tall men out here in the old Wild West," he remarked, and that brought a good laugh from all those gathered around.

"That leaves the final two, who should be Joseph and Marge Hayes." As he turned toward the couple sitting on a wicker couch, he smiled and continued, "I have been told you are the ones who live in this original home built by my great, great grandfather, Jeremiah, and that you're the parents of Christy and Brent. You are a lovely, but also gracious lady to open your home to total strangers, Aunt Marge. I understand that you know the ranch and its many functions quite well as you were involved with keeping the books until the last few years when Susan was hired. And Uncle Joseph, you turned down a position in the Law Firm because you had fallen in love with the ranch and wanted to work with your Grandpa Nathaniel. I'm told that the two of you began what it is today, and I'm so anxious to see a lot of it before I have to leave. You're looking very handsome and healthy today, but we were told by Noah about your hospitalization a couple of years ago. We're certainly glad to be able to meet you."

Joseph and Marge were on their feet and embracing him as a long lost son. He then shook hands with Joseph and kissed Marge on her cheek. "Thanks for the most appreciated hospitality," he whispered for only the two to hear.

"Let's see, Brent manages the ranch and lives here, also, with his wife, Susan. I guess she hasn't gotten back from visiting her mother today. I was told I couldn't mistake her since she's the only female brunette in the family.

And then there is Josh Holcomb, the lucky guy, who is staying here until his wedding to Liz in a couple of weeks and then they have a home waiting for them right over there. So, it appears that I still have four members of the family to meet."

Stepping back and glancing quickly around to all of them, he grinned as he asked, "Did I pass my exam?"

"You did a remarkable job, Mark, and we couldn't be happier to find out about our extended family," Joseph replied. "Of course, we're not sure what you whispered to Rachel to cause her to blush and do all that giggling," he chuckled. "Christy must have really bent your ear for you to know that much about each of us, but Christy has always had a keen interest in details and remembers them well. But, to get the chance to welcome a part of our family that we've had to assume wanted no part of us is absolutely overwhelming. It was sad but so good to hear what Lucas had to tell us before you got here."

Mark walked over to an empty chair next to his grandfather. "I just want to say one more thing. I have the most remarkable grandfather here beside me, and I'll never forget the great opportunity he has given me. When asked if I would accompany him on this so called 'wild goose chase,' I didn't have any plans for the summer and was expecting it to be a very dull, unsatisfying one. You can't begin to imagine the thrill it has been for me, just a recent high school graduate, to have this chance to travel so far across our great country and then to discover a part of my family I'd had no idea existed. And that's not to mention the chance to drive that brand new Lincoln Navigator," he chuckled.

"I also want to express my thanks to my Great Uncle Noah, Cousin Christy and her husband, Jon, for the great reception we received when we walked so boldly into the Hayes Law Firm this morning. We didn't know if the name was for the town or for the family, but Christy answered our question rather quickly and excitedly when she went running down the hall calling for her grandpa. It is such a thrill to find you and I want to thank you all for being here and welcoming us. Of course, I think we all wish that Great Grandmother Ruth had been able to know exactly who and what she'd left behind."

They then heard footsteps coming across from the barn and saw Brent and Josh almost running to join them. At the same time, a car was driving into the parking area. Brent stopped and opened the door for Susan and was giving her a brief explanation of what was happening as they approached the rest of the family. "I understand we have some long lost relatives to get acquainted with," Brent remarked as he and Susan started over to where Lucas and Mark had stood up and were waiting. "You probably already know that I'm Brent and this is my wife, Susan. It's great to be able to welcome you to the ranch." His arms were opened to embrace Lucas and then Mark. "I would assume it was quite a long drive across the country to finally find us. I've often wondered how that brave group that settled this town did it."

"Without this young man to do most of the driving, it would've been impossible for me to come find you," Lucas replied. "We've been pretty good friends, during the years he was growing up, and I'm so glad he was willing to put up with me on this trip. Actually, during all the time I was contemplating whether to even attempt it, the only person, other than my wife, that I could imagine being able to tolerate for that long was Mark." He turned and gave his grandson a big smile and a loving pat on the back.

"It sounds like the grandfathers in this family have all been exceptional men, and we grandchildren have been the recipients of wonderful nurturing by them," Brent chuckled as he then presented Susan.

Susan stepped forward for a welcoming hug. "This family gets more amazing all the time, and I'm sure everyone has already informed you that we'll want to hear all about the family you left behind in New York. I can't believe I had actually considered staying at my mother's tonight, but something told me I'd better come home. I had no idea whether it was a good thing or something bad had happened again, but I can see that my ESP or intuition must have been working," she giggled. "It is just so exciting to be able to welcome a part of the family that we knew so very little about."

Brent spoke up again. "I'd like you to also meet Josh Holcomb, who will become a member of the family very soon when he marries Liz. When my dad had his heart attack two years ago, Josh was a lifesaver. He came and managed the ranch so I could stay at the hospital with Mom. He even left college early to do it but, thankfully, he'd had enough credits that he could've graduated in January. He was just finishing the semester to pick up a little more knowledge. He was honored by his professors at graduation because this wasn't the first time he'd helped his fellow man. His school's football team, the hurricane disaster, the Pastor at the college Chapel, and his peers also benefited from his generous assistance, and he has become a great assistant manager for the ranch." He turned and motioned to Josh who had stayed back beside Liz. "Josh, you've actually heard as much as I have about these two special gentlemen showing up today, but come now and meet Lucas Gillette and his grandson, Mark, from New York. They are descendants of Jeremiah and Rebecca's daughter, Ruth."

"It's a pleasure to meet more of this great family," Josh said as he shook hands with Lucas and Mark. "I've heard some of the history of the ranch from several members of the family, and I'll look forward to hearing about the years that have gone by in New York since Ruth decided to go and live with her grandparents. Liz said that you, Mark, are fairly close to her age, so did you just graduate from high school this year or do you have one left?"

"Yes, I graduated this year. I'm enrolled to start college this fall, but I understand Liz is going to be a wife very soon now instead of going on to college."

"That was her dream and also her decision, Mark. I don't want you thinking that I'm trying to keep her from furthering her education."

"Oops, I'm sorry. I didn't mean to insinuate that at all, Josh. I guess it didn't come out the way I meant it. I seem to be doing more of that today than I remember doing most of my life," he chuckled. "I met a young girl in the grocery store this afternoon and really got taken down a peg or two by saying the wrong thing. I'm so sorry if I did it again."

"Let me apologize, too, Mark, because I didn't mean that the way it came out of my mouth either. Maybe I'm a little touchy when I realize people don't know the whole story that this has always been Liz's dream to be a wife and not a college graduate. I have a bad habit of speaking before thinking, at times, so maybe we're both inclined to get off to a bad start by saying things quickly and regretting it later. I certainly didn't get off on the right foot with Liz when we first met three years ago."

Liz had followed Josh over and now remarked, "No, he certainly didn't, Mark. I most definitely thought he was obstinate, a disgusting tease, and a know-it-all. That was until I got to really know him, and now he's the love of my life." With a smile on her face and a kiss on his cheek, she softly whispered as she wrinkled up her nose, "Were you going to clean up a bit before we eat?"

"Yes, My Sweet Mysterious One, I'll follow Brent in and get cleaned up just for you.. Don't you run away now." As he picked her up and twirled her around a couple of times, he was telling Mark how she has been so very, very subtle about getting him to do what she wants for almost three years now, but he loves it. He had then started to give her one of his tiny little pecks on the nose or cheek as he set her back on her feet. Liz, however, was going to be sure that Mark knew how much she loved this guy, so she threw her arms around his neck, even though he didn't smell good, and then proceeded to give him a kiss that had his toes tingling.

"Are you trying to tell me that July 5th isn't soon enough?" he whispered as he was studying her face and saw a slight blush appear.

"I'll see you shortly," she grinned. *I want to tell him about Mark's kiss before anyone else gets a chance to make it sound like I might've asked for it.*

Shaking hands again with the two men, Josh said, "It's been great meeting some very courageous gentlemen who, I imagine, have an interesting story to tell about their trip coming all the way out here. I'll see you again as soon as I go get cleaned up to please my pretty little Princess and probably everybody else," he chuckled. Turning again toward Liz, he could see something in her eyes that he knew he'd have to check into later, but for now he ran his finger down her cheek and headed inside.

Everyone had been watching, however, and just enjoying the tenderness and love that shows so vividly in the faces of the two who have waited so patiently to become man and wife.

Later, after they'd eaten the fabulous dinner the ladies and chef had prepared, they all gathered on the deck to relax. Brent brought out his guitar, which was almost a nightly ritual, and started playing some well known tunes.

"If you happen to have an extra guitar, Brent, you might persuade Mark to join you," Lucas whispered. Mark was sitting across the deck with his other cousins and was unaware of his grandfather's remark.

"Another talent that runs in the family, I see," Brent whispered back. He put his guitar on his chair and announced that he'd be right back. Returning with another guitar in his hand, he walked over to Mark and said, "I understand you have some experience playing one of these instruments, too. How about joining me?"

"I guess my grandpa's been telling tales out of school again, but I do enjoy playing a guitar. I'll attempt to play along with you if you don't get too classical on me. I only know the familiar old songs like they play in Western movies, and a few hymns."

"You'll do fine, then, because that's mostly what I play." For the next hour it was great music for listening and singing along, but finally it was time for some good restful sleep.

CHAPTER EIGHT

Mark could hardly wait to call his dad and mom. He was finally alone after Josh had shown him and his grandpa the available rooms they could pick from. It had been such an exciting day, and even though it was quite late back in New York, his folks were elated to hear about the discovery of an actual family. For them to have been so gracious and willing to even accept the sudden appearance of two unknowns who dropped in out of nowhere was truly an added bonus.

He tried to remember everything that had happened so the call had gone on and on. He even included his tale about seeing this most beautiful girl in the grocery store and then getting tongue-tied when he'd tried to talk to her. They really got a big laugh out of that.

"Just remember," he'd retorted, "your youngest child is of age now and he is paying a lot more attention to the opposite sex than when sports were his only true love. In fact, you guys should see this one very special cousin, Liz, that I met and had the nerve to actually kiss her when I got to guess her name from descriptions that Christy had given me earlier. It's funny I didn't get my face slapped because she's a real knock-out. She has the most beautiful brown eyes, which are so unusual because she has blonde hair to go with them. I'm told they are like her dad's, but he and Brad both have medium brown hair. Her dad hasn't come down from Colorado Springs yet. He's a pediatrician and I understand that he has to make rounds at the hospital tomorrow morning before he can drive down. They actually got everyone except him together in time for a marvelous meal tonight and it didn't seem to bother them at all.

But Liz's smile can make you happy just by looking at her. And, get this, she had just graduated from high school this year, the same as I did, but she is getting married the 5th of July. I told her it was too bad she was a relative because I might have tried to steal her away from Josh," he chuckled. "After seeing them together, though, I'm afraid I would've lost. They are definitely meant for each other. I'm not sure what Grandpa's travel plans are, but I would sure love to be here for the wedding.

I really wish you were here, because you can't begin to imagine what this family is like, and how welcome they've made us feel. It's like we've known each other for years and it's only been one day. I love you guys and I'm so glad you let me come on this trip with Grandpa. You might want to talk to Grandma and see what he told her that I forgot, but I think I'd better say goodnight now or I may fall asleep with the phone still in my hand. I'll call again soon."

The next morning, after a great night's rest in one of the upstairs bedrooms at the Main House, Mark is anxious to see and learn more about this ranch life. It has, so far, been way beyond any imaginations or dreams that he could possibly have had.

Josh had shown them the original master bedroom suite, where he is staying until his marriage, and also told them the story why Jeremiah and Rebecca had included it in their plan. It is located across the back of the original home, before the two wings were added, and had a nice large bedroom, but there was also a smaller room which was used as a sitting room until a nursery was needed when the children came along. The windows had been made extra large in this area, which gave a splendid view of the mountains in the distance and much of his land as he relaxed at the end of the day. A large dressing room and closet had become the master bath room and walk-in closet when all of the bathrooms were added after plumbing and electricity became available.

Outside the master suite, there are two rooms on each side of an extra wide hall with a bathroom to be shared by the two rooms on each side. There had originally been three rooms on each side, but the center one had been taken for the bathroom, extra closet space in the two remaining rooms, and a hall going to the upstairs rooms over the wings. One wing had been added before Nathaniel came home from serving his country in WWI because when he'd informed them that he was bringing his very young wife, Annabelle, with him, that was when Jeremiah had built the wing and he and Rebecca decided to move downstairs. That would leave the master suite for the young couple, and climbing the stairs had also become a little hard on his knees although he'd never admit it.

The early morning breeze coming through the open windows was so stimulating, and as Mark pulled on his jeans and shirt, he remembered that he'd left his new cowboy hat in Jon's Tahoe. *I wonder if he had to go to the office this morning. I probably should wear it if I get to go to the barn.* When he opened the door to the hallway, a door opened almost instantaneously across from his and Grandpa appeared.

"It looks like we've gotten our time schedule synchronized after all those days on the road, Mark. Did you sleep a little better last night without all my rhythmic snoring keeping you awake?" he chuckled.

"I slept very well, but your snoring didn't bother me at all on our way here."

"Well, shall we go see how much we've already missed of this invigorating day?"

"I'm ready except for my new cowboy hat," he chuckled. "I left it in Jon's Tahoe when we got here yesterday. I don't know if they go to the office on Saturdays or not, but Jon told me I should wear it if I'm going to be out with the guys."

"Noah rode out with me yesterday and said that he would ride in with Jon today and get his car. They have a client coming in for a consultation, but he didn't think it would take very long, and then they'd be back."

They'd heard several voices as they'd neared the kitchen and then saw that Joseph, Marge, Christy, Mary and Liz were sitting at the table. Mary and Liz had stayed with Jon and Christy last night, so they had come to the Main House on Jon's way to the office. Of course, they could've walked, but why walk when the car was right there and moving?

"Good Morning," Joseph greeted them as they entered the room. "Did you sleep well with no alarm clock or noise from the other rooms to wake you up? I guess you did have Josh and Brad up there, but it wouldn't be like some of those motels where the noise goes on all night and the beds aren't that comfortable."

"Actually," Lucas remarked, "we didn't rely on an alarm clock on the trip because we were considering it a vacation and we had no strict schedule to follow. I guess we were rather excited about our summer project, although it could've been the noise from the other rooms, because we were usually up and ready to go fairly early each morning. I must say, however, I really enjoyed that delightful fresh cool air coming in the windows during the night and this morning. We'd be relying on air-conditioning back home for that cool comfort by now."

"Well, come on over and have some breakfast. Brent and Josh are doing chores, but they said Mark could join them anytime, if he wanted. Brad will probably be up pretty soon, and he usually likes to help do the chores, too." "Mark," Christy spoke up, "Jon brought your new hat in from the Tahoe before he and Grandfather left for the office a few minutes ago. They have a client who needed to come in for a consultation at 7:30 because he had to be at work by 9:00.. They shouldn't be too long, so we thought we'd get you on a horse today if you're ready for the challenge," she giggled.

"Hold it just a minute before making those riding plans." Marge held up her hands for attention. "There's some shopping to be done, and I thought you girls might do that for us. I was also thinking that Mark might like to spend time with the guys this morning so the riding could wait until this afternoon."

"That's fine, Mom. Mary, Liz and I can go shopping." She then turned to Mark and, without thinking, very slyly asked, "Would you want to go with us, Mark? We'll be going to the large grocery store." She couldn't keep the grin off her face.

"Do you think I should go so soon, Christy?" he asked with a rather concerned and also embarrassed look on his face.

"No, on second thought, I think it'd be better if I checked it out a little beforehand."

"What are you going to check out at the grocery store, Christy?" Mary spoke up in her 'tell me everything' way. "Has something happened already that has Mark involved?"

"Not really. He just needs an answer or two to something that I've promised to help him with."

"That sounds like you're evading my question, Christy, but I won't push it since I see that it's upsetting Mark."

Mark and Grandpa Lucas had fixed themselves a plate of pancakes, sausage, eggs, and a few hash browns. Mark bowed his head for a quick prayer, but then he kept his eyes glued to his plate as he ate every delicious bite. Christy had brought him a large glass of orange juice so she could whisper, "I'm sorry, Mark, I wasn't thinking. Please forgive me." Aloud she just asked if either of them wanted coffee or milk.

"I'd appreciate a cup of coffee, Christy, but I can get it myself," Lucas replied. "Nonsense, Uncle Lucas, I'll get it for you right now."

After bringing the coffee, Christy took Mary and Liz each by an arm and guided them into the living room. "I feel terrible the way I made it sound in there, because I'm not making it easy for Mark at all. He's very sensitive, I can see, and I have to make it up to him. I'm asking you not to pursue trying to get anymore answers about my stupid remark from me or from him right now. Please, you'll know what is going on soon enough, but not right at this moment. Just let me say that Mark went on a tour of the town yesterday afternoon, and it could turn out to be quite an interesting twist to his visit, but it didn't get off to the best start."

Liz hadn't said a word but had been listening, thinking, and even dreaming a little. She knew that Jaclyn Lambre had just started working at the store, and she had actually asked her to be the junior bridesmaid at the wedding. They'd been in the same school during the last two years and had become good friends; so could Mark have seen her at the store and asked Christy to introduce them? If Mark and Uncle Lucas were going to be here for her wedding, it would give her an opportunity to ask him to be part of the wedding party. At the present time, Jaclyn was going to be walking alone during the recessional, but it could be that she could have Mark as her escort. *I'll give Christy time to pursue the situation her way, but I hope my instincts are right.*

"Shall we go see if Aunt Marge has the list ready so we can get the shopping done?" she asked as the other conversation had concluded.

When they returned to the kitchen, Mark was gone, Joseph and Lucas had retired to the deck, and Rachel had come over from Noah's to join Marge for a planning session, and the list had just been completed. Since Christy's car was still over at their house, they'd decided to take Liz's new car and were soon on their way to town. The car had been a nice combined graduation-wedding gift from her dad and mom, but she was still getting used to the difference in handling it.

Laughing and talking, they were enjoying the time together, but as they came around a sharp curve, a doe and her fawn were standing right in the middle of the road. Liz had tried to apply the brakes and slow down so she could safely swerve around them, but they were way too close. Not yet used to the new car, she quickly realized it didn't handle at all like her old heavy one, and she was panicking as they hit the loose gravel at the side of the road. Before she could do anything more, the car skidded off the road and hit a large boulder which caused it to flip over on its top into the ditch.

"Are you two OK?" she asked as she began sobbing. "I'm so sorry."

"We're both all right," Christy remarked after checking Mary who was in the back seat. "Let's see if we can unbuckle these fabulous seat belts that held us so securely and kept us safe. Watch your head as you try very carefully to drop down onto the top. If we're lucky, maybe a door will open so we can get out." As they had gotten unfastened and were trying to open the doors, they heard a car coming down the road. "Please, Dear Jesus, let it be Jon coming home. It sounds like it could be the Tahoe," Christy prayed.

"Can you get your door to open, Christy? Mine seems to be up against the bank over here and won't budge." Liz was frantically pushing on the door toward the field.

"Are all of you OK?" They'd heard the car stop and now Jon's voice was like a miracle coming from heaven.

"Thank God it's you, Jon. Yes, we're OK but we're not sure if the doors will open. The one on the other side is up against the bank and I was just trying to find the handle on this side. Maybe you can open it from out there."

"You might as well relax because there's a huge rock here that will have to be moved before we can open this door. You're apparently wedged between the bank on the one side and the rock on this side. I'll see what kind of tools I can find, but Noah will be coming along any minute so I'll send him on to the ranch for some help."

In minutes, they heard a car and then Noah's concerned voice. "What in the world has happened here?"

They had just started to open the window, but they could feel the car immediately shift as the glass left the frame, so they rolled it back up as quickly and as far as they could. "We'll have to tell you when we're able to get out," Christy called to him.

Noah was back in his car and heading for the ranch while Jon used a hammer and a small shovel to try to move the rock which was against the one door. It had seemed like ages, but it was less than twenty minutes when Josh arrived in his Tahoe with Brad and Mark. They had all kinds of tools with them and said Brent was coming with the tractor. Josh didn't care about the damage they had to do to the car as long as they got the girls out, and they'd finally succeeded in moving the huge rock. They had gotten the one door open, so the girls were out of the car and in the guys' arms by the time Brent got there.

Mark seemed concerned as he asked, "Do you think we should take them to town to be checked by a doctor? They could have injuries that aren't showing up right now."

"You're right, Mark. Let's help Brent get the car out of the ditch and then we'll take them into the doctor's office. Dr. Noland or Dr. Adams will be there even though it is on the weekend. You girls come and get in my Tahoe where there's some blankets to wrap up in so you don't go into shock," Josh ordered and then gave an exasperated sigh when he heard the little giggles. "Just remember, it was July when I was thrown from the horse, and Eleanor had a blanket for me. After that accident, I've always carried blankets in my car."

Brent studied the situation and then decided they would try lifting the car out first with the bucket he had on the front of the tractor. They wrapped heavy straps around each end of the car and through the wheel wells and then fastened them over the bucket. While Brent concentrated on controlling the bucket, the other four guys each had a wheel area to watch for problems. There were a couple of scary moments when a strap started to slip, so they were amazed when they were successful in getting it completely out of the ditch without having to start over. It had a flat tire which was most likely caused when it hit the big rock and flipped, plus the body had taken quite a beating from the flip and landing on several large rocks in the ditch. The five guys were then able to turn the car over and stabilize it with one wheel in the bucket and the straps keeping it from falling. Brent felt he could get it back to the ranch if one of them would ride with him and help keep it steady.

Hearing another car coming down the road, they turned to watch and soon realized it was Dr. Becker arriving from Colorado Springs. He was out of his car immediately and was soon hugging the girls as they climbed from the Tahoe. "It's all my fault," he said to Liz as he held her in his arms and tears were welling up in his eyes. "Your mom begged me not to buy that fancy sports car, but I wanted to give you something special for your graduation and wedding. It isn't the kind of car for country roads, though, and all three of you could have been very seriously hurt."

"Dad, it's not your fault," Liz replied as she hugged him around the waist. "I was most likely going a little faster than I should have been, because I'm not used to the feel of the car yet. But, when I came around the curve, a doe and her fawn were in the road. I guess I tried to slow down too fast so I could swerve to miss them, but we hit the loose gravel which caused us to skid. I thought I felt us hit something before we flipped into the ditch, and I was so afraid it had been the doe or fawn. Luckily, it was that big rock over there that the guys had to move to get us out. We all had our seat belts on and are okay, which is the main thing."

"Well, the next car I get you should be a Hummer so I'll know you'll be protected like in a tank," he chuckled as he still held her tightly in his arms.

"We were going to take them into town to have the doctor check them over, but since you're here, just in the nick of time, would you like the task of doing that?" Josh asked.

"I'll certainly do that. Let's get them back to the ranch so we can make sure there is no remaining shock or severe bruises. I'm amazed how all three of them seem rather calm under the circumstances," he remarked. "It must be those tough Hayes genes."

"It must be, because I think we guys were more shook up than the girls ever were," Jon remarked as he let out a built-up sigh and kissed Christy's forehead. "Their faith in our great God's protective hand didn't hurt, either."

"Not to change the subject, Dad, but we want you to meet our long lost cousin, Mark Gillette. Mark, this is Dr. Becker, or Uncle David, or my dad," Brad chuckled. "I guess we'll have to figure out the exact relationship, when we get around to it, but right now I'd say he's your Uncle David."

"Thanks, Brad, and it's really nice meeting you, Uncle David, although I would have preferred it to be somewhere other than at an accident scene." He smiled although he still seemed a little shocked about the whole incident.

"That's for sure, Mark, but it *is* a delight to meet you. We'll get a chance to talk more when we all get back to the ranch." He embraced Mark just briefly but could feel his body trembling. "Are you all right, Mark? Has the accident made you that nervous, or is there something else bothering you?"

With tears welling up in his eyes, Mark said, "I just can't forget the fact that it was because of Grandpa and me showing up here out of the blue that caused the girls to have to go to the store. It makes me feel responsible and I guess my nerves are a little jumpy."

The girls came running over and took turns hugging their new-found cousin. "Oh, Mark, you had nothing to do with this accident," Liz explained as she held his hand with both of hers. "Almost every weekend, one or two of us go to the store for something we want or need. This was just one of those freaky things that happen, like Josh, a seasoned rider, being thrown off the horse three years ago. If anyone was to blame for this, it was me."

"O.K," he said as he gave her a half-hearted smile and a kiss on the cheek.

"As you know, we three girls have shopping to do, so let's get moving. We need to get our tasks completed." Christy was giggling as she pulled Jon toward his Tahoe. Mark had quietly volunteered to accompany Brent on the tractor, and Liz and Mary went with their dad. Brad was going to ride back with Josh and help with the waiting chores.

CHAPTER NINE

Dr. Becker did a pretty thorough check on his two girls and Christy just to make sure they were all right. The only thing he'd noticed was a slight redness across their bodies where the seat belts had been, and Mary mentioned that her right side had been hurting a little.

"You may feel some soreness and a little bruising in those areas for the next few days. There may also be some stiffness just from the strain of being held by the seat belt while the car was being flipped over and landing in the ditch. I'll write each of you a prescription for a relaxant that will help you tolerate the aches and pains of those muscles when they start talking to you. Just take it a little easy for a few days and you should be fine, especially you, Liz, with that wedding coming up."

They were discussing their trip to town when they reached the deck where most of the family had gathered. "When you girls are ready to go shopping, I'll drive you there this time," Jon spoke up. "In fact, if you'd rather rest, I can go by myself, or maybe Mark would like to ride in with me. Brad is helping Josh and Brent finish up the chores."

"You aren't going to do our job for us, Mr. Holcomb, but we might take you up on the driving job," Christy retorted as she sat down rather slowly. "I do think Uncle David might be right that our muscles will be talking to us for awhile, though."

"I'm at your service, Sweetie. Whatever you feel like doing, I'll go along to help; but I don't want any of you to think you have to keep going if you don't feel like it."

"Did anyone contact the sheriff?" Christy asked.

"Yes, he was contacted and happened to be in the area so he has already been here to inspect the car and will file his report. He was certainly relieved to know that you were all protected with the seat belts, though. When he first saw the looks of the car, he was really concerned. He could, of course, understand the urgency in our minds, that we had to get you out, but we did do quite a bit of damage to the one door. The top was pretty crumpled, too, as there were a few fairly large rocks in that ditch. He said the insurance company most likely will declare it totaled."

"We were so lucky, and it sure taught me a lesson about going around curves," Liz commented. "For two years, while driving back and forth to school, I didn't have a single problem, but this car just handled so differently. Of course, I'd never seen a doe and her fawn in the middle of the road in those two years either. I'm so sorry I put everyone through that ordeal."

"Let's not talk about it anymore. We're all unhurt, and it certainly gave our guests an exciting morning," Christy laughed. "We'd better decide our next move pretty soon, though, because Mom and Aunt Rachel will be needing the groceries we were going after. I can't believe the whole morning is almost gone." Just then, Marge and Rachel came out on the deck to inform them that lunch was ready although it wasn't exactly what they had originally planned. Marge had just finished her announcement saying, "We hope grilled cheese sandwiches, chips, cottage cheese, and a few fresh fruits will suffice," when she saw Eleanor coming across the lawn.

"Oh, oh, here comes a specialty, I'll bet, that will make your lunch extra yummy. Right after you finish eating, maybe Jon will drive for whomever wants to go to the store, and then if you're still planning to go riding, you can do that when you get back. Of course, that could be put off until tomorrow if the girls are a little out of commission. That would give Brent and Josh time to catch up, too. I guess Brad is helping so they should all be along soon."

"Sounds good to me," Jon remarked. "How about you, Mark? Are you ready to eat after the excitement of the morning?"

"I think so, although I'm still more excited about getting on a horse than eating. It was so interesting this morning as I watched the guys working in the barn. They were taking so much time explaining things to me, however, that after the accident I thought, with Brad's help, the three could probably work a little faster without me hanging around. I'll have other days to pester them and find out about running a ranch," he chuckled.

"Well, let's go fill our plates and then we'll see what the afternoon has in store for us, or do you want to wait for the guys to get here?" Jon asked as he glanced over to the older men.

"They actually grabbed some food when they got back with the car, so I think they'll just keep working until they're done," Joseph said as he, David, Noah, and Lucas stood and followed the rest of the family into where the food was.

Rachel met her mother, when she reached the deck, so she could peek into the pan she was carrying. "We were wondering why you slipped away a little while ago, but I guess we all should know by now that you'd come to our rescue." Calling to the others, she informed them that there were now wonderful brownies for dessert. "Thank you so much, Mom," she quickly whispered as she kissed her cheek.

"That's about the only thing you can make in a hurry and still have them come out good enough to eat," Eleanor laughed. "I do have some more fruit in this bag that might help."

"Where's Susan this morning?" Noah asked as they were reaching the kitchen door. Is she still having some morning sickness? I guess we forgot to tell you travelers that we're going to have a little one join us in November or early December."

"She's still having some discomfort, but she had some book work she wanted to get finished this morning, too," Marge answered. "She saw the doctor yesterday, while she was visiting her mother, and everything was reported to be in great shape."

"That's so exciting," Mark exclaimed. "Grandpa and I were wondering if there'd be any little ones to play with. We were trying to calculate how many years ahead of our family you'd be, with Ruth being the youngest, but it turns out there's not much difference at all. Christy is about the age of my brother or one of my two cousins, Liz and I are about the same age and the youngest, so I guess it leaves Brent as the only one who is older around here, along with Jon, of course. The others fill in the gaps," he grinned.

"That's because my dad was so slow in being born," Joseph laughed. "Actually, we understand that his mom had two or three miscarriages before and after she carried him full term, and that was a factor in our lagging behind. Rachel and I did our part to get the family growing, and we could now have two more possibilities for additions to the family if Christy and Liz will just cooperate." He was grinning as he looked over at the two girls.

"Don't try to rush us, Dad," Christy retorted. "I may want to work another year or so, and I'm certainly not going to leave my baby with a nanny or babysitter when I do have one."

"Maybe not a nanny or babysitter, but there's a grandmother and a grandfather, not to mention a great grandmother, who are around here almost constantly. They're just waiting for the chance to take care of a baby or two," Joseph replied rather seriously.

Noah thought he'd seen a smug little smile on Christy's face that just might be hiding something. *I'll have to keep a close eye on that granddaughter of mine now so I'll be one of the first to know when it happens.*

"What about you, Liz?" Joseph then asked teasingly.

"Let's get me married first, Uncle Joseph, but when we start a family will be up to Josh and me. You'll find out when we're ready to tell you. We may want to just enjoy married life together for a little while, like Jon and Christy, but I'm sure God will be with us in that exciting decision, too." She gave her much beloved uncle a 'don't mess with me' smile as she reached the table and began filling her plate.

"I guess I'll have to come back here if I want to see any little babies very soon. At least there *are* possibilities around here. My two cousins back east are only concentrating on their careers in the Army, and my brother and sister aren't even dating anyone right now, so it's very unlikely there will be any little ones in our family anytime soon. Maybe I'll have to be like Liz--marry young and start producing some little grandkids for my parents and great grandkids for Grandpa here." Mark was grinning as he had filled his plate and was now getting a glass of lemonade before returning to the deck to eat.

"Don't go getting ideas in your head too soon, Mark," his grandfather chuckled. "You'll be the breadwinner for the family when you take that step, so make sure you're prepared to fill that position before you think about getting married and starting a family. Just remember that Josh is a few years older than Liz, he got a good education and a good job before he took on the responsibility of a wife and home."

"I was just kidding, Grandpa, but I promise I'll be ready for the task when I commit to the girl of my dreams. I haven't even had a date yet, but I'm going to be looking for a girl like these cousins whose smiles could turn any guy's head. Josh and Jon are sure two lucky dudes finding these two cousins of mine. Someone else will be lucky when Mary is discovered if she hasn't been already."

After lunch was over, Jon was prepared to take the grocery shoppers into town, but Christy noticed that Mary had been very quiet and her food had hardly been touched. "Mary, is something wrong?" she asked as she went quickly to her side. That caused everyone to turn to see what was going on.

Her dad, of course, was at her side immediately when he saw that her face was starchy white. "I must've missed something when I examined you, Sweetheart. You mentioned that your side was hurting so let's go see if I can do a better job of doctoring. We may have to get some x-rays taken. You go ahead, Christy, and get the shopping done. If I need to, I'll call Dr. Noland and see if the clinic has x-ray equipment so we can do a little exploring."

"What about you, Liz?" Christy asked.

"If you don't mind, Christy, I'd like to stay here to make sure Mary's all right. After all, I'm the one who caused all this."

"Mark, do you want to ride into the store with us?" Christy asked.

"I think I'll go back out to the barn and see how the guys are getting along. You two can do the shopping, can't you? I don't think this is exactly the time for me to make another appearance in the store," he grinned.

"I understand, Mark. I've always believed when it comes to making a decision between a girl or a horse, the guy always picks the horse until the girl starts chasing him," she teased as she took Jon's hand and headed toward the door. They heard a little cry of pain from Mary as they got outside, but they knew her dad would take care of her so they'd better take care of the needs of the rest of the family. When they reached the Tahoe, however, they took a moment to hold each other's hands and say a little prayer for Mary and also for their own safety this time before starting the trek into town.

While they were shopping, they looked for Jaclyn but she was nowhere to be found. In the Produce section, however, Christy knew one of the other girls so she asked her if Jaclyn was working today. "Oh, she's working the split shift today, Christy. She'll be back at 6 o'clock and work until 9," she answered. "She'll sure be sorry she missed you, though, because she told me yesterday afternoon that she needed to see you. In fact, she said she might call you because she was afraid there was someone wandering around town who could cause trouble for your family."

"I'd love to talk to her, too," Christy grinned, "because we know who she's referring to but there is absolutely no trouble brewing. In fact, it is the most wonderful thing that could've happened to our family. We've found a part of the family that has been unknown to us for quite a few years. Thanks, Phyllis, for the information."

When they finished shopping and had the groceries in the car, they debated on whether to run by the Lambre's and ease their concern. "It'll only take a minute," Jon said as he headed toward their house. They had just pulled up in the driveway when Jaclyn and her mother came running out the front door.

"Christy, I've tried calling ya'll at your house several times but I could never get an answer. Where have ya'll been? There's something going on, and we think someone may be trying to invade your privacy. It's really hard to imagine that such a young good-looking guy could know so much about ya'll when I've never seen him around here before. He doesn't look old enough to be much more than out of high school."

"Calm down, Jaclyn. We've been at the Main House except to sleep last night, and we know all about the young man who tried to talk to you at the store yesterday. He *is* just out of high school, and he and his grandfather drove all the way from New York to see if they could find some relatives who may or may not have existed. They found us yesterday morning, and when we all got tied up with work, Mark decided to take a tour of the town by himself. His name is Mark Gillette, he is a cousin, and an absolute doll. His grandfather could almost be a twin to my grandfather.

AND, when he decided to come and ask directions, he couldn't see your face until you turned around to ask what he wanted to find. He was completely spellbound when he saw your lovely little face, and he said he couldn't think of a thing to say. He said he was so terribly embarrassed after he'd blurted out that you were beautiful and proceeded to even ask your name. Gosh, I've never had a boy tongue-tied over me, but you certainly did it to our long-lost cousin," she laughed. "He'd like to meet you, if only to convince you that he wasn't lying about knowing and visiting the Hayes family. You really did shock him with whatever you accused him of."

"I'm sorry, Christy, but his opening remarks weren't very convincing that he was an honest and trustworthy guy. Since I've worked only a few days, I thought he was making a play for me, and I was just making sure he knew that I was off limits to a total stranger. He did try to be apologetic as I was showing him the aisle he wanted, but I guess I wasn't in the mood to be receptive. Actually, all I could think about was his using the Hayes name to maybe try to get more information about you. Maybe I'll have to ask the bosses how to handle a similar incident if it should happen again."

"That probably would be a good idea, Jaclyn, although in this little town I'd be very surprised if something like this would happen again, but it's always good to be prepared. Are you getting excited about the big wedding coming up? Only two weeks from today, and I can hardly wait. It doesn't seem possible that my little cousin is getting married because she's just so young, and yet she seems so ready for the responsibilities of marriage. I guess she had a lot of tutoring in that respect while she stayed with Grandma when she was pretty young, and then again during the last two years."

"When it comes to becoming a wife and mother, Liz knows very well what she wants, and she's positive Josh is the one God picked for her," Jaclyn remarked with an odd look on her face. "I hope I can be that sure if the man of my dreams should ever come my way."

"It doesn't usually happen at first sight, Jaclyn, and sometimes it takes a few upsets to prove you can weather the storms that marriage brings with it. Jon and I, as well as Liz and Josh, went through some disturbing trials before we saw the light and were convinced that we had found our soul mates. You have a few years before you need to start thinking about that."

"Not if I could be like Liz, but that's not going to happen," she stated with emphasis.

"And we'd better be getting these groceries home before we have another crisis on our hands, Christy. It was good to see you both, and we'll be seeing you, Jaclyn, at the rehearsal, if not sooner," Jon broke in.

"Do ya'll know how long your cousin and his grandfather will be stayin'?" Carole asked as she and Jaclyn backed away from the car.

"They don't have any definite plans, but we're all hoping they can stay long enough for the wedding. It would be wonderful having some more of our family there."

"Yea, I guess," Jaclyn started kicking at the gravel as she turned toward the house.

"Wait just a minute, Jon," Christy softly ordered. "Jaclyn sounds as if she's dreading that possibility." She was out of the car and quickly taking Jaclyn's arm in a rather tight grip to turn her around and face her. "What is this attitude of yours all about, Jaclyn? Did something else happen yesterday that we're not aware of? Let's get it all out in the open right now so we can correct any wrongs that may have occurred."

"Just forget it, Christy. He actually *is* a part of your family now, and I'll have to accept that whether I want to or not. So, that's that, and I guess I'll have to do some apologizing for my actions, too," she muttered rather disgustedly as she shook loose and ran into the house.

"Carole, do you know what's wrong?" Christy asked as she turned to her newest close friend since they'd brought them from New Orleans.

"I'm not sure. She came home yesterday upset that this handsome guy might be trying to do harm to your family, and she wanted to help. Now, she finds that he is actually part of your family and ya'll are ecstatic about him being here. If I had to guess, I'd say that it is just a little teenage jealousy or embarrassment showing in my daughter's eyes," she grinned. "Don't worry about it, Christy. I'll talk to her and try to convince her that your feelings won't change toward her just because of the way she talked to one of your cousins who is now on the scene."

"Of course my feelings haven't changed toward her just because Mark has come into our lives, but he is most anxious to meet her. He told us that she was quite cold toward him, but he wants to meet and convince her that he was telling her the truth when he said he was visiting the Hayes family. She really sent his hormones reeling for the first time in his life, I think. Could she be a little apprehensive about seeing him again?"

"We'll have to see where that goes, but you'd better run," she laughed. Your husband is getting a little worried about those groceries ya'll have in the car."

"Yea, we have a few more mouths to feed tonight with the Becker family down from Colorado Springs along with the two from New York."

After giving Carole a big hug, she got back in the Tahoe and Jon started backing out of the drive. "Bye now." Christy called and they both waved as they drove away.

When Jon and Christy were driving down Main Street and came to the corner of South Broad Street, they just happened to notice the rescue van coming from the area of the Clinic. Jon quickly pulled into the city parking lot on the corner because they wanted to see if it could possibly concern Mary and what news the driver could give them.

As the van approached the corner, the driver stopped as he apparently recognized Jon's car. That was luck because Jon had just had time to jump out of the Tahoe and start running across the street.

"Dr. Becker and his wife are with their daughter at the Clinic. Dr. Davis was on duty today, but he had called Dr.

Noland before we arrived. Dr. Becker and Dr. Davis thought it was appendicitis, but Dr. Noland is more experienced in surgery. Sure hope that everything turns out well."

"Thanks, Tim. I really appreciate the information."

"Sure thing. Please drive carefully going to the ranch. We heard about the accident the girls had this morning. It's quite a miracle that there were no injuries."

"Yea, it's been quite a day." He turned and ran back to where Christy was waiting to hear what he had learned. They drove back to the ranch almost in silence, both apparently taking some time to pray about the events of yesterday, today, and the ones still to come.

CHAPTER TEN

Jaclyn had immediately gone to her room because she was really confused about the feelings she was having toward this Mark, and all other boys for that matter. She hadn't even known Mark, but she had still considered him a threat when he'd approached her in the aisle of the store yesterday. She then remembered how even a slight glance from a male peer at school this past year had sent her into a panic to where she'd just wanted to run and hide.

She knew she hadn't been able to forget the scary experience in New Orleans, just days before the hurricane had hit their area, but was this a normal reaction? At the time, she'd felt it had been a miracle from God when Jon and Christy had offered to bring her family to Hayes and she could escape that one boy's taunts and threats. She had been almost fifteen when they had arrived here, but she'd looked about twelve. The guys had treated her like a little girl for the rest of that school year, but her appearance has changed considerably the last two years, and she now hates the looks and remarks she receives from a few of the guys.

She'd been so happy when Liz came to finish High School here and they had become close friends. She hadn't liked it, though, when Josh had been around, and she'd wondered why Liz was so crazy about him. She would've much rather spent time with just girls, but there had been very few of them in her classes with whom she'd been able to get acquainted. In fact, there had seemed to be a clique among the girls who had been borne and raised here, and they had even ignored Liz. Of course, Liz didn't mind because she had Josh. *I don't want to even think about this next year without Liz, but at least Grant will be a freshman and I hope he will be a deterrent for me. I guess it's about time to go back to work now, though, so I need to put these thoughts out of my mind.*

When Jon and Christy got back to the ranch, they learned more about why the rescue squad had come to take Mary to the Clinic. Dr. Davis had assured them that they had the operating room, recovery room, and patient's room for care of an appendectomy. He'd told them that he would call Dr. Noland, however, because he hadn't quite completed all the work Dr. Noland wanted him to do in residency, so he didn't have the authority to operate without Dr. Noland being there.

It was almost three hours before Rachel called the ranch to tell them it was over and Mary would be fine. It had been a little tricky for a while because the appendix had been so inflamed they thought it might burst before they could get it removed. David and Rachel had decided that they would both stay at the Clinic with her, and a registered nurse had also been called.

No one had been in the mood to go riding until they'd learned that Mary was going to be all right. Jon and Christy had gone home for a little while, Brent had wanted to spend some time with Susan, and Brad had gone to his room to study for an exam he has on Tuesday. He's taking a couple of summer classes so he can graduate from law school in December. It left just Josh and Liz who graciously offered to take Mark on his first horseback ride.

"We don't have to go riding today," he'd remarked, "but if I could just get on one's back to see how it feels, I'd be more than satisfied for one day."

"Mark, if we get a horse ready for you to sit on its back, you're going to ride a little ways, too," Josh chuckled. "After you help saddle one, you'll understand what I'm talking about. You don't just jump on its back and sit there because the horse is ready to take off."

"I'm sorry, Josh. You can see what a novice I am around horses, but I'm also very interested in learning all about the care of these beautiful animals."

Liz giggled, "You wouldn't have had much fun around here if you'd been one of those city guys who couldn't get their hands dirty, manicured your nails twice a day, and wanted to read or watch TV instead of being outside."

When they headed for the barn, Jon and Christy had returned and decided they would come along, too. Christy's horse, old but faithful Rainbow needed some exercise, and the two older horses that Brent had asked Jon and Josh if they would mind riding over two years ago were in need of some exercise, too. So many things had been going on lately that riding had been put way down on the list of things to do.

Jon and Josh had thought, at one time, about bringing their own two horses from their dad's farm, but it would've been hard on the horses, as old as they were, to make such a change. Consequently, they had been riding these two for some time now. They'd decided today that the very gentle Blackbeard would be a good one for Mark to ride, and then Josh selected the spirited two-year old, Spitfire, for himself. Jon would ride Ramrod, and Liz would be on her favorite mare, Dakota Girl.

Mark was an excellent student as they instructed him about how to slide the saddle pad in place and then lower the saddle onto the horse's back. Blackbeard turned his head to watch, adjusted his stance, but otherwise didn't move. Josh then showed Mark how to tighten the girth strap, but he'd left it much too loose. "I didn't want to hurt him," he'd quickly explained when Josh called his attention to the mistake. He caught on almost too quickly as they let him saddle the two horses for Josh and Liz, and then they were all teasing him for possibly keeping some secrets about having never been on a horse before. They rode around the paddock a couple of times and then hit the trail until they reached the first big pond.

When he dismounted, Mark was quick to realize that riding a horse was far from just sitting in a soft comfortable recliner. He quietly hoped that this was as far as they were going today. Christy and Liz, of course, had loaded their two saddlebags with some goodies and drinks, so they sat in the late afternoon shade and munched while the five horses grazed and also enjoyed the water from the pond. Boots and stockings soon came off and their feet were relaxing in the cool water. It was a beautiful late June day, just a few white clouds drifted across the bright blue sky; and the shade of the trees with the gentle breeze made for a very comfortable stop. They pointed out all the points of interest which could be seen from there, and that made Mark even more anxious to ride and see more. "I can't keep from wondering how Ruth could've left this place," he remarked as he gazed at all the marvels of nature.

They tried a little trotting as they headed back to the barn, and Mark was thrilled. He thought that was easier than the slow lazy walk they'd done on the way out. He also felt he'd had another most exciting day even if he would be sore for awhile.

Most of the family had gone to church Sunday morning. Jon and Christy were to sing a duet so Lucas and Mark had definitely wanted to be there. The rest of the day was to be spent just relaxing, talking, playing some tennis, and then taking a swim to cool off.

Dr. Becker and Brad had gone home Sunday night after they knew that Mary was going to be all right. It was a relief to know that the hectic weekend had finally come to a close.

Mary continued to do well after the surgery and had gone home to Colorado Springs on Wednesday with her mother. Their big van had been just right so she could lie comfortably on the back seat.

It wasn't long until Mary thought she was back to par, and she was determined to still be in the wedding as planned. She'd asked just one thing. She didn't think she wanted all the responsibility of being Maid of Honor so she had requested that Liz ask Christy to take her place. "In fact, that way the two brothers can walk in the recessional with their wives, and I can be held up by my big, strong brother, if needed," she'd chuckled.

Susan had declined to be in the wedding because of her pregnancy, but Brent and his little combo was going to supply the music. Josh's siblings, Jacob and Janice, were going to sing, as they had at Christy and Jon's wedding over two and a half years ago, so again all the siblings and cousins would be involved. Even the newest cousin, Mark, was now going to be a groomsman and would escort Jaclyn during the recessional. A slight problem was that Jaclyn didn't know this yet. As the junior bridesmaid, she'd thought she would be walking alone since there wasn't another male that Josh had wanted to ask to be a groomsman until Mark had come on the scene.

Mark had been absolutely thrilled with all the things he was learning about the ranch as he'd spent almost every morning with the guys doing chores. Liz had taken him to do some shopping on Monday so he now had cowboy boots, and his tux was ordered for the wedding. Josh and Liz had been taking him for a ride almost every afternoon, or whenever the chores got finished. They'd gone a little farther each day, so he could see the beauty of the land and the mountains in the distance. He felt it was absolutely breathtaking, and he loved riding.

Several evenings, different ones had driven around the area with them to see the farms and the residences Mark had noticed the first day when he'd taken the little tour by himself. Of course, Lucas was along on the excursions because he was as thrilled with the ranch and all the surrounding areas as Mark. The first horseback ride for Lucas had been a little traumatic when the horse had accidentally gone off the trail and stepped in a rut that had thrown him off stride and Lucas off balance. Noah had been close enough to realize what was happening so he'd caught Lucas by the arm and kept him from falling, and it didn't deter Lucas from riding again.

Nine days have passed now since Christy and Jon had come to tell Jaclyn and her mom who Mark really was, but that hadn't helped Jaclyn's attitude toward him. Everything had been going well at work, Mark hadn't come back in to send her into a tailspin, but even so, she still wasn't looking forward to seeing him again at the rehearsal just four days away. A big night was being planned then, since it'll be the 4th of July. The rehearsal was to be rather short and sweet, according to Liz, and then there would be a rehearsal dinner at the newly remodeled and enlarged seating area of Copland's restaurant with Josh's parents as the hostesses. After that, everyone had been invited back to the ranch for fireworks to be set up by Brent and Brad.

Who will be there for me to spend time with that night? Jaclyn questioned silently to herself. *My parents will be at the wedding on Saturday, but not at the rehearsal and dinner on Friday night. Almost everyone in the wedding party is either a couple or siblings, but maybe I can sit with Jon and Christy.*

When she'd finished work on Friday, she'd gone directly to her room that she truly loved because she had gotten to pick out her own furniture when the family had come from New Orleans. It was decorated in a sage green and a touch of creamy brown which she'd thought went well with the French Provincial furniture she had found on sale. She'd tried to relax for a little while, but now it was time to get ready to go to the rehearsal.

Christy had come to the store on Tuesday to give her some more details about when she would be picked up, the dress code for the dinner, etc. She'd also told her that Mark and his grandfather were definitely staying for the wedding, and that Mark's grandmother is now flying out for the big event. That certainly didn't help her mood, since she'd wished none of the New York family had shown up here in Hayes. She just felt that a lot of things would change at the ranch if they're going to be involved there now, but surely they'd be going back to New York so Mark could start college. She also suddenly realized there were too many things on her mind now that had her nerves on edge, and she needed to calm down and take a day at a time.

She had been so excited about being asked to be the junior bridesmaid for Liz, and her dress was so pretty she could hardly wait to wear it. But, for some reason, she felt these two strangers were going to spoil the whole thing. She just wished the older of her two brothers, Grant, could go with her for moral support, but maybe she'd just ask to be taken home after the dinner. She repeatedly told herself that she needed to steer clear of Mark and everything would be all right.

Dressed in a pair of bone-colored linen slacks, she'd elected to wear a strawberry-cream colored shirt subtly textured all over with like-hued embroidery. With a vee neck opening just below the laid-back collar, the buttons were then hidden down the front, the sleeves were ¾ length with wide turn-back cuffs, and the waist was embraced with an attached scarf-like belt that had a large buckle fastener and pointed ties. She was waiting when the car pulled into the drive, and she was so relieved to see Christy come to the door.

The pastor was giving a few instructions to the guys when Jaclyn first noticed Mark standing with the others at the arched trellis where the vows were going to be exchanged. She couldn't believe what she thought was happening. She turned to face the three girls who were at the entrance to the house where they would exit. She said, "Liz, I hope you weren't planning to have me walk with Mark in the recessional, because I'm not going to do it. I am supposed to walk alone."

"That was before we discovered we had another cousin who would make a perfect groomsman and give you someone to walk with. What's the problem, Jaclyn? I thought you would be happy to have someone walking beside you. You'll be alone when we're going to the arbor, and that should make you nervous enough," Liz replied.

"Well, I'm not happy. I wanted to walk alone both ways so everyone could see my dress, and I certainly don't want to walk with Mark. I'm just not going to do it!" she said very emphatically and walked away.

"Do you want me to talk to her?" Christy asked.

"Thanks, Christy, but No. This is my wedding and I'll settle this to my satisfaction, not hers." Liz had a very determined look on her usual smiling face as she walked to where Jaclyn was now standing and glaring toward the guys. "I'm sorry you're upset with my decision to have my new-found cousin take part in my wedding, Jaclyn, but he is going to be one of the groomsmen and he is assigned to the position that will have him walking beside *you* when we exit. Are you going to accept that, or are you going to act like a spoiled brat who apparently wanted to be the main attraction in her first ever bridesmaid dress?"

"I just can't walk with Mark, Liz, and I can't understand why ya'll have to have him in your wedding when ya'll hardly know him," she replied rather sarcastically.

"This happens to be *my* wedding, Jaclyn, and I'll have whomever I please in it. It is not your decision to make. Your only decision to make is whether or not you'll take part as you've been asked. I wanted you to be a bridesmaid because I thought we had become good friends these last two years in school and that it would be a nice opportunity for you. However, if you can't accept the position I've offered, then I'll have no other choice but to replace you. I have two friends in Colorado Springs who are coming to the wedding, and either one would love to take your place and be a bridesmaid. One of them would fit into your dress perfectly."

"Ya'll wouldn't, or couldn't, get someone else at this late date, and ya'll know it!" she snapped. "Ya'll just want to scare me!"

"Is that your decision then, Jaclyn? You can't walk with Mark so you aren't going to be in my wedding? If that is how you feel, I'll go make a phone call right now."

"Ya'll are really serious?"

"I'm not going to beg or pamper you, if that is what you're waiting for, and I'm not changing my mind about Mark being in the wedding. I *can* get someone to take your place, Jaclyn, so it is up to you to say Yes or No right now. So, what's it going to be?"

"I want to be in ya'lls wedding, Liz, but I have a terrible fear about being around guys. I don't know why, but I'd much rather be around girls. I'll probably be awfully nervous, but I'll try to make it that far with him."

"Are you saying you're a lesbian, Jaclyn? Even if you are, I've never heard of one so afraid of a guy that she couldn't at least be a friend or walk beside one. A lesbian isn't afraid of men; she just doesn't want to *sleep* with one."

"I don't want to talk about this anymore, Liz." Looking toward the arbor, she then said rather apologetically, "I guess they're waiting for us to finish this rehearsal," and she started back to where Mary and Christy were waiting.

"You'd better listen closely and do what you're told then, Jaclyn, or you'll be out of this wedding yet. Do you understand?"

"Yes, Liz, I understand and I'm sorry I made such a fuss. I really didn't mean to upset ya'll when I objected to walking with Mark."

Everything went smoothly until Jaclyn walked stiffly beside Mark without taking his arm as they walked together during the recessional. The pastor had followed them, quietly said something to her, and then slipped her hand into place on Mark's arm. She knew the pastor was watching, but she jerked her hand away as soon as they reached the house. She didn't look at Mark or say a word, but she breathed a little easier when he'd excused himself and walked over to where the Pastor was talking to the guys. She then saw Liz staring at her, and she knew she'd better change her attitude quickly or she'd definitely be out of the wedding she wanted to be a part of so badly.

Realizing they'd be leaving for the restaurant in a few minutes, she decided she would force herself to look happy, be congenial with everyone, even Mark, if she had to be near him, and get through the rest of the evening. She actually put a rather convincing smile on her face as she approached the girls.

CHAPTER ELEVEN

Liz had taken Christy aside to ask if she and Jon would see that Jaclyn got to the restaurant because she wanted to talk to Mark. Mary and Brad had gone with their parents; Noah and Eleanor had taken Lucas and his wife, Esther, who had arrived from New York that afternoon; and Joseph and Marge had ridden with Brent and Susan. Tom, Frances, Jacob and Janice Holcomb had gone on ahead to make sure everything was ready, and the Pastor was picking up his wife at home before joining them. As everyone entered the private room at the Copland restaurant, they took their assigned seats around a beautifully decorated table. Not being aware of the conflict which had taken place, Tom and Frances had seated Mark and Jaclyn next to each other as they had Josh and Liz, Christy and Jon, and Brad and Mary. Liz prayed there would be no bad scene.

Liz had explained to Mark about the confusing conversation she'd had with Jaclyn so he was expecting the worst. "I'm sorry, Jaclyn," he whispered to her as he held the chair while she was seated, "but I promise I won't bite. I guess we were the only two without partners, so it was obvious that we'd be seated together."

"That's all right, Mark," she said very softly but without much feeling. Forcing a smile, she turned toward him and continued, "I understand it couldn't be helped. I'm just so excited to be involved in such a happy event, aren't ya'll? I have only been to one wedding before in my life, let alone being a bridesmaid in one. I couldn't pass up this opportunity no matter what I had to do or put up with."

"It was certainly a surprise to Grandpa and me when we not only found a family that was so welcoming, but one that was also having a wedding. So, yes, I'm very excited to be a part of this wonderful occasion." He noticed that Liz was watching them, so he smiled and gave her a wink to assure her that all was going well, or so he hoped.

Their conversation was halted when Tom lightly tapped his glass to get everyone's attention. "We are here tonight to again celebrate two families being drawn even closer by a marriage that is indeed a miracle we all feel was in God's hands from the beginning. When you consider that a young rebel who was determined to live his life as he pleased, could meet the most conscientious young lady who had God leading her life without question, it sort of sends a case of shivers up your spine. There isn't time to relate all the good and bad things that have happened to this young couple on their three year on and off love affair, because our food would be ice cold, but we are so thankful for a marvelous outcome, and thus, this wonderful event starting tonight and ending with the wedding and reception tomorrow--not forgetting that there will be a honeymoon after that," he chuckled.

"Shall we have a short word of prayer so we can start eating this enticing food that has been especially prepared for us this evening? Dear Father in Heaven, thank you for all the special people in this room tonight. We ask that Your hand will continue to guide Josh and Liz as they will soon begin a life together as husband and wife. Bless each and every one of us, and we certainly thank You for bringing Lucas, Esther, and Mark from New York just in time to help celebrate this occasion with us. May we always be in your loving care. Amen."

After the meal was finished, Jon, Brad, Brent, and Christy all took turns relating some incident that had happened which was either funny or sad in the lives of Josh and Liz. It was a fun evening, but it was finally dark enough that they could go to the ranch for the fireworks display that Brent and Brad had set up. Jaclyn had relaxed and thoroughly enjoyed the dinner and the tales that had been told, and she forgot all about asking to be taken home.

As they were leaving the restaurant, Mark smiled at her and asked, "Would you mind if I rode back to the ranch with you in Jon and Christy's car? I thought maybe Josh and Liz might want some time to be alone. I understand that they can't see each other after the fireworks until the wedding late tomorrow afternoon."

"Is that really a strict rule about getting married?" Jaclyn asked as she studied his face to determine if he was serious or teasing. "There are just so many different types of marriages these days; I don't know how they could control that. What about the ones who elope or are married by the Justice of the Peace?" Mark was so amused about how serious Jaclyn had gotten about his remark that he just couldn't control his grin. "I really don't know if it's compulsory, Jaclyn. It's just a tradition that has been handed down through the ages, and a lot of couples observe it. In today's life styles, I really doubt that a large percentage of couples stick to the rules, but I did hear Josh and Liz remarking that they couldn't see each other after the fireworks tonight."

"I like that tradition, but I doubt that I'll ever get married the way I feel right now about guys and their daring actions."

They had reached the car and Jon and Christy were waiting. "We wondered if you both would be riding with us. That was a wonderful dinner, don't you think?" Jon asked as he gave a subtle wink to Mark.

"I'm stuffed, but I'm really looking forward to the fireworks," Mark replied and then glanced at Jaclyn to see if she was going to comment.

"I loved the dinner *and* all the stories you guys told about Josh and Liz. They must've had quite a time getting together, both happy and sad. I'm glad it all turned out well for the two of them."

Mark opened the door for Jaclyn to get in. He'd noticed she hadn't used ya'll in that last remark. Could she be relaxing a little like Christy's remark had suggested earlier? She slid clear over to the other side, so he sat fairly close to his door, too. He didn't want to cause any more problems and was just happy she'd agreed to ride with him at all. When they'd reached the ranch, the deck was reserved for the older couples, but there were folding chairs and heavy quilts that could be put on the ground for the younger set.

"I'd love sitting on the ground to watch the fireworks," Jaclyn really surprised Mark by saying as she picked up a quilt and started toward the edge of the group. "Would you like to join me, Mark, since I guess we're still the odd couple?" she giggled

"I'd love to join you if it's all right with you." Again he'd realized there'd been no ya'll.

She patted the place beside her and Mark sat down quickly before she had a chance to change her mind. "I guess you haven't seen fireworks here at the ranch before, either, since it's your first trip here. It'll be my first time, too. I've heard that the two guys only do this for the weddings. We didn't move here until after Christy and Jon were married, and Brent and Susan didn't get married here at the ranch. I don't know if there were any fireworks to celebrate their wedding, or not. I suppose Brad and Josh could've arranged something, but I understand their wedding and reception was in a church so it would've been a little difficult for anyone to set up a fireworks display. Do you have any brothers or sisters, Mark?"

"I have a brother and a sister, but they are both still in college. My brother is in law school and my sister just finished her sophomore year of college. Neither of them have any plans for getting married in the near future. I understand you have two younger brothers. Do they get along with their big sister?"

"Pretty well. Grant will be starting high school this Fall which will be nice for me although he has two or three good friends that he'll probably spend his time with. I was so lucky that Liz came to Hayes for the two years of high school because most of the girls in this school are rather snooty and ignored both Liz and me. My little brother will be in 7th grade, but he has several good friends to chum around with, too. I guess I'm the one who doesn't know how to make friends."

Some of the fireworks had started and they stopped talking to watch for a few minutes. During a break, Mark had remarked, "You'll do fine, Jaclyn. Just show them that gorgeous smile and they'll have to like you." He grinned and then wondered if that had been the wrong thing to say to her. When she didn't reply or tell him to get lost, he decided to ask her about something else she'd said as they'd approached Jon and Christy's car. "What did you mean by your remark earlier that you'd probably never get married because of the way you feel about guys? Can you elaborate on that a little?"

"I don't know if I can, exactly. Something happened two or three days before the hurricane hit New Orleans which threw everything into a turmoil. It was pretty traumatic for me as well as a little embarrassing, and since then I haven't wanted to even be close to a guy. I was still quite small for my age, but a few of the bullies at my school knew that I should be close to fifteen because of the classes I was in. They were older, and the big football player who thought he was God himself, decided on a Thursday afternoon that he was going to show me what happens to a guy when he....ah wants something. He pulled me behind a vacant building and tried to touch me in places he said would make me swoon." She jumped suddenly as a big boom lit up the sky, but then some beautiful displays followed which brought oohs and aahs from everyone. Mark, however, was watching Jaclyn's face and saw the tears welling up in her eyes. He was hoping she would be able to continue telling him about the actions of that jerk because he wanted to know exactly what she'd gone through. No wonder she'd acted as she had at the grocery store and at the rehearsal. He waited to see if she would continue, but when she didn't, he asked, "Jaclyn, did he hurt you?"

"No, I jerked and slapped his hand as I tried to get away from him, but he grabbed my arm with one hand while he was unfastening his jeans with the other. He turned my head and made me look when he brought it out, and then he said he was going to demonstrate how it thrilled all the girls. I was wearing a skirt that day and he started to reach toward the hem. I kicked him as hard as I could as high as I could, and then I ran away when he doubled over and let loose of me. I guess I'd landed my foot in the right place. The next day I was so scared after school because I was alone on the way home, and at school he'd told me I was going to pay big for kicking him. He must've had a football practice that day, though, because I did get home safely. I was actually thanking God not only for the weekend but for the hurricane as it began destroying our city because I didn't have to go back to school."

"I'm so sorry you had to go through that. No girl should be harassed in that way. Did you report the incident to the principal or to your parents?"

"No, Mark, and I don't know why I've told you. You just seem so easy to talk to, but I'm surprised I could tell you, a total stranger, when I couldn't talk to my mom about it. I just thought God had answered my prayers when Jon and Christy arrived and brought us here to Hayes. Recently, though, I've realized I haven't been able to shake this feeling that other guys are just waiting to attack me. Since my body started changing the last couple of years and the guys have started whistling, ogling, and smiling, I've really become paranoid. Liz has been a lifesaver the past two years, but I'm going to be alone this next year and I'm pretty scared not knowing what it's going to be like at school or even on the streets."

Without even thinking, Mark put his arm around her shoulders, and to his surprise, she leaned toward him until her arm was touching his side. He slowly inched a little closer so she didn't have to lean so far, and they watched the rest of the fireworks without moving or saying another word. He knew now, however, the reason for her actions toward him that day in the grocery store, and it made it even more important for him to get to know her.

Of course, Jon and Christy, Josh and Liz, and Grandpa and Grandma Gillette had all noticed what was happening. They didn't know the gist of the conversation, but they felt Mark was definitely growing up, was performing a miracle with Jaclyn, and it was looking hopeful that there would be no embarrassing problems during the wedding tomorrow.

When the fireworks were over, Jaclyn sat up straight and quickly apologized, "I'm so sorry I used you as a back brace, Mark, but I didn't even realize I was doing that. My mind must not have been registering except on the beautiful formations in the sky."

"No need for an apology, Jaclyn. It was truly my pleasure to be your back brace," he chuckled as he picked up the quilt.

Jaclyn grabbed the other side and they soon had it all folded nicely, but they were standing quite close to each other as the last fold was made. Mark couldn't keep from grinning as he bent down and kissed the tip of her nose. "Just a thank you for helping me with this uncommon task," he whispered.

"You're--uh--welcome, I guess," she sort of whispered back as she stepped away. An adorable smile was on her face which convinced him that he had made some progress toward at least a friendship with this darling girl who had his heart pounding like the Energizer rabbit does on his drum. "I suppose--uh--I'd better--uh--find out who's--uh--taking me home," she stammered as she tried to move farther away.

"Are you going to let me ride along and walk you to your door?" Mark asked as he was carrying the quilt toward the deck.

"That's--ah--not necessary, Mark. It would be all right, though, I guess--um-- if that is what--um--you'd like to do."

Jon and Christy were waiting by the deck and they were soon on their way. Mark, of course, realized that Jaclyn wasn't hugging the side of the car this time so he inched over a little, got settled comfortably, and then reached over and took her hand in his.

At first, he thought she was going to jerk her hand away, but he kept his touch tender and patted her hand with his other one without a hint of any aggressiveness. He was thrilled when she let him continue holding it while Jon and Christy kept the conversation going about the dinner and fireworks. They were at her home much sooner than he had hoped.

"I'll get your door, Jaclyn, so sit still a second until I get around there," Mark whispered to her as he opened his door and hurried around to her side of the car. He held her hand again as she exited the car and as he walked her to the door. "Thanks for a great evening, Jaclyn, and I'll see you tomorrow afternoon," he said as he slowly opened the screen door.

"Thanks, Mark. I really did enjoy everything once I got my head on straight. I realize now that I should've taken the time to notice how much you looked like Brent before I acted so terribly rude in the store that day. I'm sorry and I look forward to seeing you tomorrow, too." She then quickly slipped inside the house.

CHAPTER TWELVE

"Hey, Romeo. What in the world did you do to that girl to make her turn to putty in your hands?" Christy was smiling and her eyes were glistening in the lights from the dash as she waited to get an answer when Mark climbed back into the Tahoe.

"You're too inquisitive, Christy, and I think my talk with Jaclyn tonight was a rather personal matter that I don't feel right about disclosing. Let me just say that she experienced something in New Orleans that no young girl should have to go through, and she has been too embarrassed to even talk to her mother about it. Why she talked to me, I have no idea, but I was honored and feel I shouldn't betray her confidence."

"Wow, that's really something, Mark, and I'm very impressed. No more questions on the subject, I promise you."

"Thanks, Christy, you're really special and I feel so blessed to know that I have a cousin like you. My sister, the only female in our age group back home, I'm sorry to say, hasn't been very outgoing or caring where other's feelings are concerned the last few years. From what I've heard about the Whites lately, I think Deb might have some of their genes because she is likely to do anything to get what she wants. Maybe she'll change one day, at least I hope so."

"I'm sorry to hear that, Mark. You aren't the ornery little brother that she's had to put up with all these years, are you?" she chuckled.

"I suppose I have been in a way. Mom told me that Deb had wanted a baby sister, and she was pretty upset when I arrived. I guess I was lucky that Steve would play with me or I probably would've felt like an unwanted child."

"It was sort of like that around here. Brent had wanted a baby brother, and I'm told that he threw a tantrum when they brought me home. When I started smiling and cooing at him, he softened a little, and then when I started walking and following him wherever he went, I guess he realized he was stuck with me. It wasn't long, though, until he became aware that I was sort of fun to have around and then he became my protector, my teacher, and my confidante. He's been a wonderful big brother and a great help when my insecurities popped up."

"You don't act like you could've ever had insecurities, Christy, but I guess this is the end of our conversation for tonight." Jon had just pulled up at the Main House. "Thanks, Jon, for letting me talk to your sweet wife on the way home. It has sure been fun finding out how interesting girls can be after thinking only about sports. I guess I'll see you both tomorrow."

"It was my pleasure, Mark. I'm learning more about my wife all the time just by being quiet and listening. Get a good night's sleep because tomorrow is going to be a terrific day."

"Yea, I'm really looking forward to it, and I'm one very lucky guy to have gotten the opportunity to help Grandpa find all of you this summer. Goodnight, now." He patted the top of Christy's head as he jumped from the Tahoe and ran toward the house.

"That is one outstanding kid, and he makes you feel like you've known him for years. He has the compassion to listen and try to understand people's problems, but he also has the strength to say no when he feels it should be kept confidential. He'll make a great lawyer some day," Jon remarked as they drove on over to their house. "Now, I wonder what the girls are up to at our house. Will I get to sleep at all tonight," he chuckled.

"I'll try to calm them down at a decent hour, Sweetie, but it's such an exciting time to be involved in a wedding, especially if you're a girl. I remember the night before our wedding when Mary, Liz, Susan and I were together. Mom finally came upstairs and had to strongly urge us to get some sleep. This time we have Liz, Mary, Janice and me, but I won't be sleeping with them. I have a much better bed partner now," she giggled.

"Thank you, Mrs. Holcomb, I appreciate that complement. By the way, why wasn't Jaclyn included in the overnight shindig? Will her feelings be hurt again when she learns she was left out?"

"No, she was asked to come, but she decided she'd rather stay at home and come with her parents and brothers tomorrow. Of course, that was before she got so chummy with Mark tonight."

"Well, I'm glad it wasn't an oversight or a snub." He'd pulled the car into the garage and walked around to open her door. Putting his arm around her waist, they walked together to the door and on into the kitchen where they found the girls in pajamas and drinking a soda.

"Where is everyone else sleeping tonight, anyway?" he asked.

"Upstairs at the Main House, we have your folks in Josh's rooms," Christy calmly explained. "He insisted they take that because he had moved most of his belongings to the new house yesterday. He's sharing the room with twin beds with Jacob for the night. Uncle Lucas and Esther are in the one he has been staying in because he didn't want to move. Mark is in the same room he's been using, and Brad is in the last one in that area. David and Rachel are at Grandpa and Grandma's and we have all these lovely girls with their one very handsome male protector," she smiled lovingly as she patted his cheek.

"Thank you, Christy, for the rather prejudiced but another nice complement and I'll try to live up to your expectations of protector. Are you girls going to retire pretty soon so I don't have to prop my eyes open to watch over you?" he pleaded.

"I'm ready," Mary spoke up. "It's been a rather tiring day for me and I'd think Liz would be in need of sleep, too, with the honeymoon coming up after the wedding tomorrow. She's been waiting a long time for that particular night, and I'm sure she doesn't want to fall asleep," she giggled.

"Don't worry about me, Big Sister. I've been sleeping late for a week so I'll be more than ready for that exciting first night. Josh will probably be the one to fall asleep because he and Brent have been especially busy this last week."

"I wouldn't really count on that, Liz," Jon chuckled. "Josh has a lot of stamina, as well as determination, when it comes to something he really wants to do. You should remember that from that long ago night on the dance floor."

"You *would* have to remind me of that again, wouldn't you, Jon? That was back when I didn't think I could even tolerate him, let alone marry him, but times do change," she smirked.

Everyone was laughing as they started upstairs to make sure things were in order for a spectacular wedding ceremony. Two of the four were yawning as they climbed the stairs, so Jon was encouraged that he would get a good night's sleep after all. Of course, he hoped that Christy would be coming to bed shortly because it was almost impossible to get to sleep if she wasn't beside him now. Actually, it wasn't long until he felt her slip into their bed, he pulled her into his arms, kissed her goodnight, and they were soon asleep.

Jaclyn checked in with her parents, giving them a quick report on the evening, and then went to her room. She couldn't understand all of these strange feelings she was having about the evening with Mark. She'd been all prepared to have a horrible time trying to be halfway decent to him after Liz had given her the ultimatum to agree to her terms or step aside. She couldn't really blame Liz, either, because it was, after all, Liz's wedding. She realizes now that she had been a very selfish egotistical egghead by almost insisting that Liz tell her new found cousin that he couldn't be in her wedding.

What really had her confused, though, was how easy it had been to talk to Mark. He seemed to just pull the words out of her until she'd even told him about the incident back in New Orleans that she hadn't told to anyone else. She'd certainly felt his concern, when he'd put his arm around her, but even now she couldn't remember how she'd gotten over against him. She could only remember having the most wonderful time at the dinner sitting beside Mark, watching the fireworks while beside Mark, and then walking to the door with Mark who was holding her hand as he'd done in the car. *He's the most remarkable guy I've ever known*, she was thinking as she crawled into bed, and of course, her dreams were of Mark holding her in his strong athletic arms.

Saturday was busy as everyone was completing their tasks as soon as possible so there would be plenty of time to leisurely dress and prepare for the wedding. The yard had become so beautiful the last two days as the nearby Nursery had delivered the big urns of shrubs and flowers and arranged them in a semi-circle which formed a spectacular ceremony area. Other containers lined the outer edges of the seating area. Fresh flowers would be put in the ivy that covers the trellis shortly before the wedding begins.

At 4 o'clock, a white limousine pulled up to the west side of Jon and Christy's home, although out of sight of the ones now congregating for the wedding. White chairs had been placed on both sides of the red brick path leading from the Main House to the arbor, and a garland of white tulle was fastened with yellow roses to small stakes along both sides of the path. The whole area looked spectacular.

Quite a few of Liz's previous school friends and close acquaintances of the family had driven from Colorado Springs for the event. Friends and relatives from Oklahoma were there, as well as four members of the college football team who had come to support Josh as he said his vows. At least he hoped they had come to support him, but who knows exactly what those football players would have up their sleeve.

Jon had left the girls earlier to be with the guys and help keep Josh steady and calm as the hours ticked away. Surprisingly, though, Josh had seemed as cool as a cucumber. His day had included chores as usual and then he'd relaxed on the deck of the new house until time to get dressed for his wedding for which he'd waited two long years. His only concern was that the house not get messed up for Liz to come home to.

At 4:20, Brent and his little combo, set up to one side of the trellis, began playing a medley of romantic tunes while the three sets of grandparents were seated by Brad and Mark. Noah and Eleanor were seated in the front row on the left side of the path, leaving room for Rachel and David Becker. Lucas and Esther had been seated earlier in the second row beside Joseph, Marge, and Susan.

The Holcomb and Shelley grandparents were in the second row on the right side of the path. Since Janice and Jacob would be singing and were sitting on the other side of the trellis from the combo, Matthew Riley, who had been declared another member of the family since he'd started dating Janice, was seated with the grandparents. It was now time for Josh's parents to be escorted by Mark to the first row on the right of the path.

Just before 4:30, Rachel Becker, the bride's mother, who today was a true blonde-haired beauty, was on the arm of her son, Brad, as she was escorted to her seat beside Eleanor and Noah. Brad and Mark then took their places as groomsmen beside Josh and Jon.

The limousine pulled alongside the house with the door adjacent to the path. Calvin Becker, Liz's cousin, opened the side doors and extended his hand to Jaclyn as she emerged in her strapless buttercup dress styled with a fitted bodice and slightly flared knee-length skirt made of polyester chiffon with a handkerchief hem. She wore yellow high-heeled sandals and she carried a small bouquet of Shasta daisies accented with baby's breath and greenery which was cupped in a lace holder with a bow and streamers matching her dress. It was then Mary in an identically styled buttercup dress, shoes, and also carrying a bouquet of Shasta daisies. It was quite a contrast--Jaclyn being a dazzling brunette and Mary being a gorgeous true blonde.

Christy then emerged also wearing an identically styled dress in buttercup, and she was carrying just a slightly larger bouquet of the Shasta daisies. They had all taken their places and turned toward the limo when the combo raised the tempo for the wedding march.

Everyone stood as Liz slowly emerged from the limo with that beautiful smile on her face. Her sparkling eyes took a quick look straight toward Josh before she then turned to smile at her father as she took his arm and they started down the red brick path. Her white strapless gown of taffeta was snugly fitted down over the hips and then flared slightly as it descended into a long train. A row of fabric covered buttons, down the back of the bodice, concealed the Velcro which fastened the actual opening. Her veil was attached to a small lace cap, and her bridal bouquet was five large white lilies surrounded with lush greenery and long flowing white streamers. She wore the earrings Josh had given her as a wedding gift which were small rings of white gold set with tiny diamonds dropping from a single diamond at her lobe.

Janice sang The Hawaiian Wedding Song, after the pastor had finished his few opening remarks, and Jacob sang The Lord's Prayer as they later knelt on a padded bench in prayer. They were finally husband and wife, and their kiss showed the elation in their hearts of finally reaching their long-awaited wedding day.

The reception was being held in the banquet room of the Copland Restaurant so there would be air-conditioning, and a band had been hired so Brent could be with Susan and the rest of the family. Wonderful food was available, and the dance floor was usually full after Josh and Liz had started the activity.

Mark was thrilled to find that Jaclyn had stayed beside him after the recessional and had ridden with him to the restaurant in Lucas and Esther's car. Since her parents had been at the wedding and was also going to the reception, he'd thought she might've elected to ride with them. They got some food and found a table with Jon and Christy. When he'd asked her to dance, she hadn't hesitated but he soon discovered she was a great dancer and he wasn't at all. He'd always been too interested in sports to worry about learning to dance. As he struggled to not step on her toes, he was thinking. *I'd really like to have this mean something, between Jaclyn and me, but how can anything happen between the two of us when we're going to be clear across the country from each other. What was I thinking when I fell for her the first time I saw her?*

Just then a tap came on his shoulder. He turned to see Brad standing there with a big grin on his face. "Could I possibly have a dance with this lovely lady that you're trying to monopolize? We have met before so I'm not a complete stranger to her."

"I guess if it's all right with her, Brad. She's a marvelous dancer, and I'm afraid I may have been a little clumsy here and there so she may have some sore toes. I didn't take dancing very seriously, because sports took up most of my time, and I'm paying big time for it now. Do you want to dance with Brad, Jaclyn?"

"I think it's the correct thing to do when someone cuts in, Mark, but I'd like to dance with you again real soon." She gave him a big smile as she turned to Brad.

Mark watched as Brad maneuvered all the right steps so smoothly, and he had Jaclyn tight enough in his arms that they were probably feeling each other's heart beating. *Gosh, should I be doing that? I feel like going out and taking her back, but she looks as if she's having a great time. She doesn't look like she's afraid of guys tonight. Had that incident been made up just to make me feel sorry for her? Girls sure make life more confusing, but I think I like what they add, too.*

Looking around the room, he saw Liz standing and watching as Josh was dancing with her mother, Rachel. *Now, there's a woman who can change her appearance about as quickly as snapping your fingers,* he grinned as he headed toward Liz. *Maybe I can hold Liz in my arms once, at least, before she scoots out of my sight with that husband of hers.*

"Hey, Liz, has your husband deserted you already for an older woman? She's a rare beauty, too, so you'd better keep an eye on her," he smiled rather mischievously.

"That mother of mine is something else, isn't she?" she laughed. "She has always been the life of a party so I didn't expect anything different here tonight. I had a dance with my dad, but he's not as much into dancing as Mom is. I think he went to get a cool drink after we'd finished the fast dance they were playing. We should've picked a slow number," she laughed.

"Would you be good enough to dance a dance with me? I'm afraid I may step on your toes, though, like I did Jaclyn's. It's no wonder she jumped at the chance to dance with Brad."

"Are you up for the jumpy one they're playing right now? It's probably a lot easier than the slow ones because you just twist and jump, swing your arms and head, and look at your partner now and then. Nothing to it," she laughed. "Let's give it a try."

Mark glanced at the other couples who were laughing and hollering and, as Liz had said, just doing a lot of moving around, alone. It didn't look too complicated, so he grabbed her hand and headed to the dance floor. Before he knew it, he was having the time of his life, watching Liz and the others and then trying to copy their movements. He couldn't believe Liz could make all those movements in that wedding dress, but the train had somehow been taken off and she was having no problem as she kept time with the beat of the music.

"That was great, Liz. Thank you so much," he told her as they walked over to where Josh and Rachel were now standing. He quickly put his arm around her and gave her a nice little kiss on the lips after he'd softly whispered, "I hope this is permissible right in front of your husband." He then looked at Josh and murmured, "You are such a lucky guy."

"I know that, Mark, but let's watch those little kisses you've been stealing, actually on the very day you arrived, I hear. I've waited too long to let her slip away now," he chuckled as he put his protective arm around her. "My special kisses are coming a little later."

"I wish it were possible for me to steal the complete Liz away, but I do approve of the man who won her heart. I still get to claim her as my special cousin."

Josh and Liz were then summoned to cut the cake. They fed each other a small bite and then each took a sip of wine from the same little glass. After that little task was done, it wasn't long before the lovely princess and her groom mysteriously disappeared since they were going to Hawaii for their honeymoon. No wonder the Hawaiian Wedding Song had been sung

Mark was looking around to see if he could find Jaclyn, but she was still dancing with Brad so he headed toward Mary who was sitting alone. She looked a little tired and pale as he sat down beside her. "Are you feeling O.K., Mary?" he asked "or have you worn yourself out by dancing too much so soon after your surgery?"

"I tried a couple of dances with Brad, but I do feel a little weak and clammy. Don't go telling my family, though, because I really don't want to spoil the night for them, especially Liz. I'll be O.K. if I can just sit here and rest for awhile."

"Josh and Liz have already slipped away, but I'll be happy to keep you company."

"That would be nice, Mark, but I thought you were Jaclyn's escort for tonight."

"I think your brother is doing a better job at that than I was, especially on the dance floor. I'm not very good at this dancing bit, and Jaclyn seems to love it."

"Well, Brad can certainly entertain her in that area. He loves to dance and most likely knows all the dance steps there is to know. He was the guy all the girls wanted to dance with when he was in High School. That's why it's so strange that he hasn't really dated much and has never had a steady girlfriend. He's almost finished with his Law School courses, and still no girlfriend. Did anyone tell you that Liz asked him to come down and be Jaclyn's date for the Christmas Dance and Spring Prom the last two years?"

"No, I didn't hear that bit of news. No wonder they looked so good together out there on the dance floor---they've had previous practice. I can see now why it wasn't hard for her to accept his cutting in for a dance earlier. Are there any serious feelings for each other that you know of? I certainly don't want to cause any problems between them."

"I don't think so, Mark. He hasn't even hinted that he had any interest in her. I guess he'll find the right girl some day." He glanced at her with a smile on his face, but suddenly saw that her eyes were closed and she was trembling. He looked around the room to see who he could alert, and he saw Jon and Christy just coming off the dance floor. He tried to get their attention, but luckily Rachel had been standing close by and had seen him motion to Jon and Christy with a concerned look on his face. She walked over to see if she could help, but then immediately saw Mary in trouble.

"Go find David quickly, Mark. I'll stay here with Mary." Just as he started across the floor, he saw Mary slump onto her mother's shoulder.

He found David coming to ask Rachel for a dance. "Mary isn't feeling well, Uncle David, and Rachel is with her. She slumped onto her mother just as I left to find you."

Jon and Christy had seen Mark take off on a run and then looked to where Rachel was holding Mary in her arms. They'd gotten there just before David and Mark arrived, but then stepped aside. In just seconds, Dr. Becker asked, "Christy or Jon, if you have your cell phone with you, please call 9-1-1 or go find a public one. We've got to get Mary to the hospital in Colorado Springs and Dr. Dan Wilder. She is so pale, I'm afraid she may be hemorrhaging internally, but I'm not sure why. I don't trust anyone else doing surgery on her except Dr. Dan Wilder. Maybe she wasn't healed enough to have been out there dancing those fast dances. I guess I should've warned her more strongly about exerting herself that much, but I assumed she was healed by this time." He was scolding himself as he murmured, "It proves the old saying that a doctor should never treat a member of his own family. I just pray that Dr. Wilder will be available."

"Did I hear my name mentioned?" A tall handsome man with reddish blonde hair and flashing blue eyes was standing just a few feet away looking over the situation. A somewhat tall but lovely brunette lady was by his side.

Dr. Becker turned around and gasped. "Dr. Wilder, how in the world could you be here just when we need you so badly?"

"Do we have a serious problem, Dr. Becker? I'm here because my wife and I were at the wedding and reception at Josh's request. We've seen each other several times since he's been at the ranch and my parents are living here again. May I be of service?"

"Oh, thank God. This is my daughter, Mary, who had an emergency appendectomy by Dr. Noland at the Clinic two weeks ago. At that time, we were here in Hayes to meet some of our family from New York. I guess I failed to warn her strong enough about dancing too soon, but she should have been healed. I'm afraid there may be some internal bleeding now."

Dr. Wilder was already on the phone talking to Dr. Noland and securing the Clinic for x-rays and surgery. Dr. Noland would meet them there in minutes. The siren could now be heard as the Emergency Van was on the way from its headquarters only a block or so away. He turned to his wife and asked, "Are you ready to be my nurse, Mauni?"

"Of course, Dan. I'd love to assist you in surgery." The smile they shared would have convinced anyone that their love was sincere. They'd gotten married just six weeks before Jon and Christy, but she had given birth to their second little boy in April. It is rumored that she has endometriosis and will have to have surgery in the near future, so they're trying to get a nice-sized family completed before that happens.

Dr. Wilder had been keeping a close watch on Mary's vital signs and appearance, as best he could without any equipment, but he could tell it was quite serious. Everyone had stopped dancing and eating and were quietly standing around. He turned and asked them to all join hands and pray. He led in one prayer and then motioned to Joseph, who had at one time also been his patient, and quietly asked him to take over the praying because the Emergency van had arrived.

Everyone was thankful that Josh and Liz had gotten away before this happened since they felt nothing should interfere with the honeymoon and happiness of that darling couple. They also knew that if Liz got word of her sister being ill, she would be back immediately to be by her side.

CHAPTER THIRTEEN

Jaclyn had come to stand beside Mark, and he soon realized she had a strong grip on his arm. He could feel her trembling so he took her hand in his and put his other arm around her shoulders. He then decided to take her from the scene as they were now putting Mary on the stretcher to carry her to the Van. Putting his hand to the small of her back, he guided her over to where the food was, just to get a less disturbing place to talk.

"I'm sorry this had to happen to upset you, Jaclyn," he said as he took her in his arms and held her close to his chest. It felt so good to feel her heart beating against him.

"It just brings back so many memories of the wounded and dead after the hurricane in New Orleans," she whispered as if she were reliving it in her mind. "Everyone was in a panic because there was no place to go, and nothing to eat. We did have a few clothes and a small cooler of food that Mom had grabbed before we had to leave our home, but it's so hard for me, anymore, to see someone ill, or hurting, or in need."

"From what I've heard, Mary has the best doctor in the area taking care of her, so we can be thankful for that. Maybe we could talk about something else so you can relax just a bit. I could try to dance with you again, but I guess it would have to be without music." At that exact moment the band started playing a soft romantic ballad. Jaclyn giggled as she started swaying to the rhythm.

"Do you have a magic wand or something, Miss Lambre?"

"No, I just had a wish to continue being held in your arms. I guess we could've danced without the music, but this makes it acceptable to all who happen to see us."

"Wouldn't you rather be dancing with Brad? You two looked awfully good out there together on the dance floor, and I understand you've had some previous practice."

"Oh-oh, someone has been talking, I see. But yes, Brad was my escort to a couple of dances the last two years. Liz asked if he'd do it when I didn't have a date. She didn't want me to miss the dances. Brad is a good dancer, and I enjoy dancing with him, but I can't seem to talk to him like I can to you. You've helped me get over my insecurities and fears about guys in just the few short hours of being near you. I can never thank you enough for that, but are you trying to get rid of me now?"

"No, I'm not trying to get rid of you. Since I have helped you, though, does that mean that you'll let me see you some more before I have to leave to go to college? Man, I wish I could attend college out here in Colorado. You couldn't keep me away from you if that were the case."

"I'm afraid there isn't a college that close by, Mark, that would let you be close *all* the time, although Pueblo isn't too far," she giggled. "There are telephones and e-mail, though, so we could keep in touch, and I'd love to do that."

"Would you really be willing to do that, Jaclyn? I understand Josh and Liz kept the lines of communication open with telephone calls and e-mail, and look where they are tonight." He ran his fingers down her cheek and then eased them over to tilt her chin up so he could look into her eyes. *Man, I hope I'm doing all this right. Liz didn't complain and I guess I've seen enough kissing in movies, so I'm going to give it a try.* "I'm going to kiss you, Jaclyn. I hope you don't mind."

"I was hoping you would, Mark. It'll be my very first kiss and I'm so excited but also a little scared. Brad didn't even kiss me the night of the dances."

"I'm not very experienced in kissing, either, so we'll just play it by ear like that old song said something about 'doin' what comes naturally." He was smiling as he kept his hand on her chin, and then bent down slowly until he could place his lips so softly on hers. He paused to see if there was going to be any refusal, but when she put her hands up around his neck and pulled him closer, he continued with a kiss that was really meant to please. Just a few seconds later, his tongue was touching her lips without any conscience thought on his part, but when he tried to get her to open her mouth, she pulled back.

"I don't think I'm ready for that, Mark," she whispered, but her hands stayed around his neck and she placed her lips on his again, so soft and so sweet.

"Oops, I'm sorry," they heard someone say, and they pulled away from each other to see who had caught them. Of course, it was Brad.

"I was going to ask Jaclyn if she wanted to dance again, but I see she's found a lot nicer pastime. Don't let me interrupt, but I think I heard a few people remark that they were thinking about getting some more to eat before leaving."

"Thanks, Brad, I guess we got carried away a little. Maybe we should fix a plate of food so we have a good reason for being over here. What do you think, Jaclyn?"

"That's probably a good idea, Mark. Are you hungry, too, Brad? The food does look delicious," she remarked as she grabbed a plate.

"I think I'll pass. Enjoy, you two." He turned and slowly walked away.

Mark could see the pink in Jaclyn's cheeks as she stood looking but not selecting any food from the table. He'd also noticed the rather sad look on Brad's face and now he knew he might've stepped in where he didn't belong since he'd learned about their involvement at the dances. He'd have to check further into this new situation and then decide what he should do.

"Surely you can find something you like," he calmly remarked as he joined her. He put a few relishes on his own plate and then deliberately put a piece of celery and a small slice of carrot on hers. "How about some hot wings or maybe some shrimp?" he asked as he continued to add items to his plate. She went over to the cheese and fruit trays where she got two or three pieces of cheese and a few grapes. She came back to where he was making a beef sandwich in a miniature bun. It apparently looked good because she started making herself one, too. They had just finished when two or three couples came to the same table, so they quickly got a drink and sat down at one of the small tables where they could watch the dancers.

"We're safe for the moment," he whispered with a big grin on his face. "That is unless I get the urge to kiss you again." He took a big bite of his sandwich, and then just looked at her and chuckled. "You are so cute when you blush."

"Stop it, Mark," she scolded. "You'll have me scared of all boys again because I'll be afraid of what they'll do or say to get me to blush. Just eat!" She had tried to be real serious, but the look on Mark's face had gotten her to giggling.

He sure loved Jaclyn in this mood, but what are her real feelings for Brad?

They hadn't heard anything from the Clinic by the time the band had packed up and was leaving. Lucas called Mark over to where they were sitting with Joseph and Marge, but Jaclyn had stayed back. "Brent and Susan left earlier because she was getting tired, and Brad is going to hitch a ride home with Jon and Christy. Esther and I can ride with Noah and Eleanor if you would like to take Jaclyn home in our car. I don't think she lives too far because her parents said she could walk home when she was ready when they left a little while ago. They thought she was having too much fun to make her go home with them. We can wait for you, though; if you're not sure you can find the ranch alone."

"Are you sure you want to let me do that, Grandpa? I saw her house last night after the fireworks, but I'm not sure I could find it again. Jon was driving so I wasn't paying too much attention. I'm confident I can drive to the ranch, but that is your new car."

"You drove it most of the way for us to get here, Mark, so I'm not worried about the car. I just want you to realize that Jaclyn is only seventeen and I trust that you'll know how to behave as a gentleman should. She apparently has felt safe with you yesterday and today, so don't do anything to spoil it. O.K.?"

"I understand completely, Grandpa, and thank you. I'll see you at the ranch." He shook his grandfather's hand and kissed the cheek of his grandmother before turning to go back to Jaclyn. But where was she?

Brad was standing near the door waiting for Jon and Christy who were saying goodbye to the last of the guests before leaving. Mark walked over to him and asked, "Brad, do you know where Jaclyn went? Grandpa just gave me his car keys so I can take her home."

"She left just a couple of minutes ago. Said it was time to go home. I assumed you'd said your goodbyes."

Mark's mind was whirling. Why would she leave without saying goodbye? Where does she live and how far does she have to walk? He saw Christy and Jon coming across the floor and ran to them. "Jaclyn left while I was talking to Grandpa. I don't know where she lives from here, or which way she would go. Can you give me directions?"

"It's only six or seven blocks to their house, Mark. Why don't you ride with us and we'll go see if we can find her," Jon replied as he put his arm across Mark's shoulders.

"Grandpa let me have his car so I could take her home, so I'll need to drive it to the ranch. I want to see Jaclyn tonight, Jon, because she promised to have a date or two with me before I leave for college."

"O.K. then, you follow us and we'll lead the way to her house. Let's go."

They soon saw her on the south side of Main Street just getting ready to cross to the east side of Lakewood Drive. She wasn't walking too fast in the high heels she was wearing, but when she got to the other side and turned south, they noticed a car that had been creeping along beside her had also turned and was now on the wrong side of the street. Jon quickly pulled to that side of the street, too, and stopped at the curb. Of course, Mark was in the car right behind him, and Jon, Brad, and Mark were out of the cars quickly, walking toward her, and they could hear the loud voices of some guys who were inviting her to join them. "Don't use her name," Jon quietly warned as a door of the car was opening and a young man was starting to get out.

Jaclyn was so scared her legs would hardly move, but she was forcing them to keep her going. She just couldn't stop and give in. She had seen more lights shining behind her, and she was sure she was going to be raped multiple times like the girl in a newspaper article she'd read recently. *There are too many for me to fight off or kick this time. Oh, why didn't I ask someone to take me home since it was getting so late?*

The car door had opened and she was almost ready to collapse when she thought she saw some flashing lights back on Main Street. The guy was almost to her, but she moved so she could glance around to make sure the police were going to turn this way. She glanced at the other three guys coming toward her, but the lights prevented a clear view. *They do look familiar, but could it be possible? I'm probably just hallucinating.*

Then, all of a sudden, she heard Jon's voice. "You'd better get back in that car unless you want the three of us to take you down," he'd ordered with authority.

The guy had stopped his hand in midair, as he'd just reached out to grab her. He turned to look at the three coming toward him and saw the police car at the corner. "We're five to your three, and you're all in tuxedos," he'd just boasted as the squad car turned the corner. He looked back at her, and at that moment Jaclyn kicked off her high-heeled shoes and didn't stop running until she was in Mark's arms, but she couldn't hold back her hysterical sobbing.

"Oh, No," the guy groaned. He'd guessed her age, when he'd gotten a good look at her, and he knew they were in big trouble with the police car almost to them. "She's just a kid, you guys, a gorgeous one, but a kid just the same." He'd just started to get back in the car but then turned to say something to Jon. "We weren't doing anything but having a little fun. She sure looked older, though, all dressed up like that. If she's been in a big fancy wedding, or to a gala party, how come she was going home alone?" He glanced at the squad car that was stopping and grumbled, "Man, is she hooked up to a radar system, or have a direct line to the cops?"

"Shut your mouth before you get us in more trouble than we're already in, you darn fool," one of the guys inside the car was yelling. "Get back in the car!" another shouted. Of course, the policeman was out of the squad car and heading their way.

Mark still had Jaclyn in his arms and had started back to the car, but the officer called to them with an order as he'd reached the car with the guys. "I'd like to talk to ya'll, Young Lady, and also to the three gentlemen who seem to have rescued ya'll. I'll be there shortly. Ya'll can wait in your cars where it'll be more comfortable, if ya'll like, but don't get any ideas about just leavin'."

In minutes, another officer came running through the trees from the station to assist. The town only has the one squad car, but there are two officers on each shift. Of course, it had been Christy who had called them when they'd seen the car creeping alongside Jaclyn.

The second officer, who had actually taken the call and relayed it to the squad car that was cruising Main Street, came to Jon's window and immediately recognized him as a lawyer from the Hayes Law Firm. He'd also recognized Christy, whom he'd known all his life and had gone to school with. "Good evening, Mr. Holcomb. Hi, Christy. I'm Officer Greg Hiatt, Sir. I assume you've been attending the long-awaited wedding and reception of Josh Holcomb and Liz Becker this evening. Would you like to explain your involvement in our rather unusual Saturday night ruckus?" He then handed him the shoes that Jaclyn had kicked off.

After introductions were made, Jon, Mark, and Brad told the officer how Jaclyn had decided to walk home when Mark's grandfather had called him over to talk to him. He was actually offering his car for Mark to take Jaclyn home, but that, of course, wasn't clear to her and she didn't want him to think that she was expecting him to see that she got home. They weren't actually a two-some but had been paired together when she was a bridesmaid and he was a groomsman. Since Mark was from out of town and didn't know where Jaclyn lived, they were all trying to find her and get her home safely before going to the ranch. They certainly hadn't expected to confront a carload of guys trying to lure her in with them.

When the 1st officer reached Jon's car, the carload of guys had turned around and was headed north on Lakewood Drive, as fast as they dared, toward Route 50. Stooping down to peer in the window, he glanced at Jaclyn in the back seat, still in Mark's arms. "We're terribly sorry about this, Miss, but ya'll shouldn't be out walking alone this late at night when ya'll are all dressed up for a fancy party. I suppose ya'll have been to that big shindig at the Haven of Rest Ranch tonight," he sort of smirked as he noticed them all in formal attire.

"Where we have been is not the subject here, Officer," Jon spoke up. "People have always had the right to get home safely in this town, and it's upsetting to think we might have a carload of out-of-town troublemakers invading those rights. Who were they, anyway, and why were they here?"

"We happen to be the law here, Mister, and we're certainly able to handle the few little disturbances that occur in this town," he retorted.

The other officer, however, quickly tapped him on the arm and motioned him away from the car. He tried talking quietly to him. "That is Jon Holcomb with the Hayes Law Firm right over there, and he's married to Christy Hayes, you know, like the name of the town. She's the granddaughter of the one and only Noah Hayes, who owns that Law Firm and who knows what else in this town. I don't think you've met either of them yet, since you've worked nights since joining the force, but you'd better watch what you say or do right now. Otherwise, you may not have a job long in this town."

Turning back to Jon, he said, "Mr. Holcomb, this is Officer Wilks, and he's just been here on the force for less than a year. I think he'll be glad to tell you what you want to know."

"It's nice to meet ya'll, Mr. Holcomb," he said rather forced. "The driver of the car was the owner and was from Pueblo. Everything checked out. He said they'd just been out doin' a little cruisin' tonight. They'd never been down this way before, and they have promised they won't come down here again. There was no drinkin' or drugs involved, and they all swore they hadn't been lookin' to hurt the young lady. They're all attendin' college at Pueblo, but they'd found jobs for the summer so were stayin' and workin' instead of goin' home."

"Thank you for the information, Officer Wilks. If you've been in Hayes for less than a year, may I ask where you came from? I noticed a very distinctive southern accent."

"I come from Mississippi, Sir. After the hurricane, my family went north to Kansas to stay with some relatives, but the town didn't need any more policemen. I'd been takin' odd jobs here and there and just happened to hear someone mention that Hayes, Colorado, was lookin' for an officer. I was on my way that afternoon and was so happy when they hired me. I'd been on the force in Gulfport for over eight years, but my wife and son are here with me now."

"Very well, welcome to Hayes. The young lady is from New Orleans and also a victim of the hurricane. She has made a new home here with her family. This was very traumatic for her, so it might be wise to patrol the streets more diligently, especially on Friday and Saturday nights during the summer when school is out. I may have a talk with the Chief about that. If you're finished with us, we'll get the young lady home safely."

"Goodnight, Sir," both officers remarked as they stepped back from the car.

Jon had heard the whispered reprimand, of course, and was chuckling after closing the window. "It's nice to know that Noah and the Law Firm have such high authority in town."

"What did you expect, Jon? You're working with the descendants of the man for whom the town was named," Christy giggled.

Jon gave her a rather unimpressed look and a grin, and then turned to Mark. "Since you have Jaclyn to show you the way, I guess the rest of us don't need to go any farther. Do you want Brad to ride with you to make sure you get to the ranch?"

"I can find my way to the ranch, but if Brad wants to ride along, it would be all right, I guess. It'd give me someone to talk to on the way home."

Brad couldn't quite smother a snicker. "I think Mark can handle the situation just fine, Jon, and I'd like to get back to find out about Mary, if that's O.K.?"

"Sure thing, so we'll probably see you tomorrow, Mark. Be real careful on that Ranch Road because the deer are pretty bold around here after dark. Goodnight, Jaclyn, you were lovely today and did your job well. I'm sure we'll be seeing you soon."

"Thanks, Jon, for everything, and I'll certainly be praying for Mary. Goodnight, Brad. Thanks again for all the dances, and Christy, thanks for your patience and concern."

"We're just glad we got to you when we did, Jaclyn," Christy remarked. "I guess our little town is going to be changing right along with the rest of the country. Thanks for being a part of the wedding. I know Liz was glad you helped make it a wonderful day."

Jon waited for Mark and Jaclyn to get in the other car, and the squad car also waited until both Jon and Mark had pulled away.

CHAPTER FOURTEEN

"Well, Jaclyn, you are now the navigator to show me the way to your home again. I wasn't watching very closely last night, but Jon told me that it wasn't too far so I assume there's a turn to be made soon."

"Let's turn left on Wilderness Road, which is just past the church. Then you turn north, or left again, at the first corner on the left which is just past the Wilder Elementary School. It will be Colman Drive. The first street you'll come to, across from the school, only goes to the right and is Wilder Road. That's where the very impressive home of Dr. and Mrs. Paul Wilder, the former dentist, is located. After you pass their house, the road has several curves and then meets up with Lakewood Drive on the way to the State Park. It's a pretty drive and the land was originally all Colman property. His grandfather must've staked out about the same amount of land that Jeremiah Hayes did, but apparently in an area that the town needed to grow to the place it is today.

I think Dr. Wilder retired several years ago and he and his wife moved to Florida. They did some extensive traveling, I'm told, but when their son, Dr. Dan Wilder, told them he was going to get married, they came back north, re-established a relationship that had been strained for years, and have become a very close-knit family. That marriage was in September, 6 weeks before Jon and Christy were married three years ago this coming October. They now spend a lot of time in Colorado Springs, because of the grandchildren, but they are both wonderful citizens of our little town.

As you know, Dr. Dan Wilder is the doctor taking care of Mary tonight although his home and practice are in Colorado Springs. I imagine his parents are babysitting while he and his wife were attending the wedding and reception. Dr. Becker knows that he is the best in the area and was amazed when he showed up at the reception, like a miracle sent from God.

I understand that he was the one who took care of Josh three years ago, on the 4th of July, and they struck up quite a friendship, apparently. Josh and Liz had just met that weekend, and then Josh had been thrown off a horse when the whole group went riding. Liz had, at first, thought she couldn't even tolerate him, but then she'd spent hours sitting in his hospital room while he was unconscious with a head injury. That was the beginning of the long and difficult road to their beautiful wedding today."

"That's a great story, Jaclyn. Maybe you should write a book about all the people you have learned about here in Hayes, but right now you have me completely confused. I think I've passed both Wilder Road and Colman Drive, but I couldn't remember what you'd told me to do. You've been throwing so much information at me all at once, I couldn't concentrate on where I was supposed to turn. Should I have turned right on Wilder Road or left on Colman Drive?"

"I'm sorry, Mark. I get carried away when I start talking about the Hayes family or others in this neat little town. It's been so exciting to learn just a little of the Hayes family history, and there seems to be a great story about how each couple met and the problems they faced along the way, but the town has a history all its own, too."

"Do you want me to turn around, Miss Lambre, or do you want me to continue out into the real wilderness? It looks like we're about to the end of the homes, but the road does keep going. Maybe we could park out there for awhile and do some history making of our own," he chuckled as he finally pulled into the last driveway and turned around.

"I'm beginning to wonder if I really am safe with you, Mark Gillette. Maybe that first impression I had of you in the store *was* right," she giggled. It wasn't long until she said, "You turn *right* now at the next corner, Mark, which is Colman Drive. I understand that was Mrs. Wilder's maiden name, and her father was a prominent financier who owned the bank here for years. Just go slow now so you can turn to the right again into Daniel Circle. Our house will be the second one as you keep to the right around the beautifully landscaped island. You can't miss taking a look at that since the entire neighborhood spent a whole weekend in April busily digging, planting, and pruning to make Daniel Circle one of the prettier areas in town. If you haven't guessed, Daniel was Mr. Colman's first name, and Dr. Dan Wilder, I presume, was named after his grandfather as was our cul-de-sac. Our home is right here."

Mark pulled into the driveway and shut off the engine. "You've really learned a lot about your new home, Jaclyn, and I'm proud of you. Very few high school students, that I've known, would be interested in why a street was given a certain name or what the person did that caused him to be honored in that way. I'm interested in learning all I can about Hayes, too, the town and the family. Maybe you could help me on those dates we're going to have before I leave for college. Of course, we could try Wilderness Road again to see where it goes if we keep following it, or do you already know all the good parking spots the local kids use on their dates?"

"Since our kiss earlier tonight was my first, I must say I've never been on Wilderness Road with a guy. I do know that the road turns north about five miles out of town. It passes a farm house or two, and then it ends when it reaches Main Street. Our family has driven around a lot to get familiar with the area so I do know quite a few of the roads that lead out of town. I certainly hope we get to do more than learn street names and family history, though, if you're going to be around for awhile."

"Oh, I think we'll get around to a little more than that," he chuckled. "I'm learning real fast how much fun it is to spend time with pretty girls. How about if you lean over here so I can hold you right now?"

"I didn't mean it that way, Mark. I just meant that I hope we aren't going to sit around and learn statistics every time we're together. They have a marvelous tennis court at the ranch, a relaxing pool, as well as the horses to ride. Do you think we could do some of those things?"

"It sure sounds good to me, but are you going to let me hold you now and maybe enjoy a second kiss?"

"My parents are going to be wondering what has happened to me, and I do have a long and rather scary story to tell them yet tonight," she remarked as she reached over and patted his cheek.

"O.K., we won't dally too long tonight, Miss Evasive, but I'm looking forward to some nice long kisses tomorrow night. Will you go to the movies with me?"

"Are you sure you haven't had enough of me? I was terribly rude to you at the rehearsal yesterday, I got upset when Mary was in pain, and I was hysterical when those guys were after me. I'd think you'd be ready to say 'Goodbye, Jaclyn'."

"Never! You made up for snubbing me at the rehearsal by being extra nice at the dinner and while watching the fireworks, and your kiss earlier tonight was more than enough payment for whatever I did to help calm you during the upsets that certainly weren't your fault. So, may I pick

A Summer's Adventure

you up at 7 o'clock? Maybe we should make it 6 o'clock so we can get a bite to eat at the Cafe before the movie starts at 7:20."

"If you're sure you want to see me again, I'll be ready. I have to work four hours, but I'll be off at 3 o'clock so I can certainly be ready by 6:00. Do you think you can find my house again?" she teased.

"Sure, I turn on Wilderness Road, go to the very last driveway in town, turn around and come back, turn left--no, right on Colman Drive, and right again into the circle called Daniel.. Got it down perfect except how do I find Wilderness Road?" He was laughing as he gave her a hug, messed up her hair with his fingers, and then started to get out of the car.

"Don't I get at least one kiss tonight before you send me off to bed?"

"No, you had your chance and passed, so the one at the reception is all you get although I might give you a little peck on the cheek at the door." He hurried around to open her door, but she was pouting and wouldn't move. "Do I have to pull you out of that car and carry you to your door, Miss Lambre? The neighbors might get a kick out of seeing that, but I don't know how your parents would feel."

She was grinning as she reluctantly got out of the car but then looked around and saw that all the houses in the circle were dark. "Yep, they all stayed up and watched for me to come home," she smirked.

Mark reached for her hand and then very gently kissed each finger as they walked to the door. "I saw that in a movie once and I must say it isn't at all bad," he chuckled.

"I just can't believe how quickly we've gotten acquainted and are so relaxed with each other, Mark. I would've never, ever dreamed, after my experience in New Orleans, that I could be with a guy and be as unafraid as I am with you. You are a very special person, and I'm so glad I got to meet you."

When they reached the porch, however, she turned toward him and tried to be silly by acting out her goodbye. "Well, my Romeo and my hero, I guess this will have to be a Farewell and a Goodnight, until we meet again tomorrow night at 6:00 p.m."

"You're being rather dramatic, Jaclyn, but I shall be dreaming of you and awaiting the pleasure of getting some long, sweet, passionate kisses as I'm building up my endurance in my chamber at the Ranch where I slumber." He then bowed as an actor after a great performance that had rocked the crowd.

"Oh, brother, now who's being dramatic?" she giggled as she started toward the door.

Mark quickly pulled her back to face him, tilted her chin so he could look into her eyes as his head was bending down and his lips were coming closer and closer to hers. She was all excited as she waited for another kiss like the one at the reception, but then "Just a peck," he murmured as he passed her lips and just lightly kissed her cheek. "Goodnight, Jaclyn," he was chuckling as he opened the front door and gave her a little push on the small of her back to send her inside. "Sleep tight and hold me in your dreams," he whispered as he quickly closed the door and walked on air to the car. He had to sit still for a couple of minutes to be sure he was thinking clearly before starting the engine and heading for the ranch.

He'd decided to go back down to Wilderness Road which he would then take over to Lakewood Drive although he'd seen an intersection to his right that he thought would most likely have been Lincoln Blvd. After he'd turned right onto Lakewood Drive, passed Lincoln Boulevard, and was approaching Monroe Street, though, he felt that the car which had pulled off of Lincoln Boulevard was driving much too close behind him. He could tell in the rear view mirror that it wasn't the car with the guys from Pueblo again, but he was sure, when he'd turned onto Main Street, that this driver wanted his attention. He'd rolled his window down as the car pulled alongside him and started yelling.

"Hey, New Yorker, I'm warning you, you'd better leave my girl alone. I saw you with her when she was being bothered by those other out-of-town guys and I saw you parked in her driveway. She's going to be completely mine this next year, now that Miss High and Mighty is out of the picture, and I want her fresh and untouched, if you know what I mean. You'd best be gettin' out of town before you find yourself wishin' you had."

Mark didn't want to tangle with this creep, whoever he was, especially outside the city limits in his grandfather's car. He was so glad he'd taken the tour of the town that first day, because he quickly made his move. He slowed down slightly as he approached Broad Street and the other car zoomed past the intersection and on out Ranch Road. Mark made a quick right turn onto N. Broad Street and then a right again onto Garfield which would take him back to Lakewood. Another right took him to Main Street and then a left to the police station. He hated bothering the officers again, but he couldn't take any chances with his grandfather's car and in a strange town. If he'd been home in his old pickup, it would've been a different story. He would've given the guy a run for his money because he would've known the layout of the area and another dent in his truck wouldn't make much difference. Of course, he could also handle himself in a fight, if needed, because he'd had training in martial arts.

Officer Hiatt came to the door and, of course, recognized the car and Mark. "What is the pleasure of seeing you again so soon, Mark?"

"I really hate to bother you, Sir, but you know I'm driving my grandfather's car and I'd hate to have it get scratched up by a guy trying to play a big shot. I don't know who he is and I couldn't get all the license number, but I'm pretty sure it was a light cream or silver colored Kia or Toyota. Anyway, he started following me on Lakewood Drive after I'd taken Jaclyn home, and he warned me to leave her alone or else. He said he planned to make her his own, now that Miss High and Mighty Liz Becker was out of the way, and he wanted her clean and untouched, if I knew what he meant. I didn't want to tangle with him out on the Ranch Road so I decided to come here and report it. Oh, that looks like the car right now," he remarked as he'd glanced in the rearview mirror when he'd seen car lights going by slowly.

"I suspected it would be that one because he is the only boy in town who can get into trouble without even trying. His folks have been considering sending him to a special school, and this will most likely make the final decision for them. Let me get the squad car and I'll follow you home. I could call the Sheriff, since it's outside the city limits, but I may be able to turn around before I have to drive clear to the ranch. Hold on for just a couple of minutes."

Mark could see the inside of the office and thought the officer had actually made two calls, not just one to the squad car. He wondered if he could've possibly called the guy's parents. *Maybe I should take off for home real soon,* but then he chuckled to himself. *You can't get rid of me that easily, whoever you are.*

When Officer Hiatt returned to the car, he was smiling. "You must've given him a bit of a scare, Mark, because he just got home and his parents will see that he has no car for the next month. I think it's safe for you to drive out to the ranch now unless you still want one of us to follow you."

"I'll be fine, Sir, and I thank you so much for your help. I hope I don't have to bother you again unless it's for a good cause."

"Goodnight, Mark. It's been a pleasure to meet you. It's certainly been a rather unusual day for our little town. I hope the rest of your stay in Hayes will be pleasant and without any more disturbing incidents."

"I'm sure planning on it being that way. My new found family has been way beyond anything I could've dreamed of, and I'll hate to leave when it's time to go off to college."

"Well, good luck. Are you just starting college, or are you an upperclassman?"

"I'm just starting so I still have a few years of schooling ahead of me. Goodnight, Sir."

Mark was on the Ranch Road when thoughts started racing through his head. *Just how much do I really know about Jaclyn? Is she as innocent as she seems, or has she been seeing this guy and just decided a change for the summer would be fun? Can she be playing both Brad and me for fools? Her sad story about the guy in New Orleans sounded so real and her eyes were full of tears while she was telling me. She's really not that good at acting, is she? I'll have to talk to Christy and also to Liz when she and Josh get back from their honeymoon. I'm sure Liz would know if there was anything going on between Jaclyn and this guy last year at school and also about the relationship between her and Brad.*

I wonder how long Grandpa plans on staying. I hope I have time to find answers to all this before I have to leave. It's going to be hard enough with college adjustments and maybe a long-distance relationship without suspicions filling my brain.

Will Grandma be riding back with us? I haven't heard anything about her plans on going home. It would be sort of fun to have her along. I remember when the two of them used to take me on their occasional short trips, usually just a day, but sometimes overnight. They were really characters when they got started on their storytelling and teasing each other.

Mark finally glanced around and realized nothing looked familiar. "Now what have I done?" he asked himself. He pulled over to the side of the road, got out and studied the area.

He didn't see a thing that he had seen before. *Surely I'm on the right road. I didn't make any turn except the curve where the girls had their accident.* He turned to look back the way he'd come, and then he thought he could see some house lights very dimly back a ways. He also thought they were illuminated about the way the houses at the ranch are situated. More lights were shining from the one in the middle than the one to its right, and there were a few more lights farther to the southwest. *That could be Jon and Christy's. At least I hope I haven't got myself completely lost and end up sleeping in the car tonight.*

He got back in and carefully turned around. He drove slowly now and kept his eyes on the road as he headed back. He was soon at the familiar entrance, and he breathed a sigh of relief. He also whispered a big "Thank You, Father," as he drove under the unique Haven of Rest sign that he'd learned has welcomed people to the ranch ever since Jeremiah first installed it so many years ago.

Mark was surprised to see so many lights still on as he drove in, but it wasn't too late yet, he guessed, even though he felt he'd been through several weird situations already at the reception and afterwards. First it was Mary becoming sick and upsetting Jaclyn, and then it was Jaclyn leaving and being harassed by the guys from Pueblo. He'd certainly enjoyed the time alone he'd had with her after that, but not the confusing confrontation with the guy who told him to go back to New

York and leave her alone. Missing the entrance to the ranch had completely thrown him into doubting his sanity.

When he reached the kitchen, he found almost everyone sitting there looking worried, and most of them had a cup of coffee which meant sleep had most likely been put on hold. He soon discovered that the concern was about Mary and that a few decisions were being made at the clinic about how to proceed. They were all waiting to hear from David or Rachel.

They quickly informed him that after x-rays and a Cat scan had been taken, it had been determined that Mary's condition was much more serious than originally thought, but it had nothing to do with the appendectomy. Dr. Wilder had felt that there wasn't enough medical equipment here in Hayes, and Dr. Noland had agreed. It was then decided to have the hospital helicopter from Colorado Springs come after her. It was always possible that there could be complications that needed a specialized staff with a fully equipped OR and ICU as quickly as possible. Patients of Dr. Noland were often sent to Colorado Springs for just that reason.

Just then Christy and Jon walked in the door, and the phone began ringing. Joseph motioned for Jon to answer. It was David reporting that the helicopter was almost ready to land. "Only two can be in this helicopter with a patient," he informed them, "so Dr. Wilder and I will go with Mary, and Rachel will be at the ranch shortly to pick up Brad. Tell him not to worry about our belongings because some of the others can bring them tomorrow if they want to drive up and spend time with us. We need all the prayers you can recruit, and Rachel will definitely keep in touch."

Jon could hear the sound of the 'copter landing and then cutting its engine. "They'll have her on the way to Colorado Springs a.s.a.p." he said as he turned to Brad. "Your mom will be here shortly to pick you up. Don't worry about belongings. Some of us will take them when we drive up."

"Thanks, Jon. Did he mention what they had found?"

"No, he was in too big a hurry. Maybe Rachel will take time to tell us."

Brad had gone to his room to get a few of his things, and Rachel had arrived at the door by the time he returned. "I don't know what to tell you except that Dr. Wilder says she'll probably need surgery immediately. The doctors were discussing procedures for blocked carotid arteries or possibly a heart valve problem. We have to get going so I'll call you as soon as I know anything more. Please keep your prayers going for God's help, and ask for prayers at church tomorrow if you can. Are you ready, Brad?"

Nodding, Brad headed for the door, and they were gone.

Everyone joined hands while Joseph led them in prayer. They then decided it was time to get some sleep, if possible, because tomorrow would be another long, nerve-wrecking day. "We are sure sorry all these things are happening while we've been blessed with the three of you just joining us from New York, but we're thankful you can add your prayers to ours for the success of the surgery as well as the safety of our traveling newlyweds."

"We're very thankful to be here and to add our prayers, Joseph, but I do think we should try to get some sleep. We'll see you in the morning."

CHAPTER FIFTEEN

Mark found it very hard to settle down. Too much had happened today, but he was so glad the wedding had gone well and Josh and Liz were now on their honeymoon without the worry of Mary's illness. Of course, he knew Liz would be terribly upset when she learns she wasn't here for her sister.

Mark's thoughts then took a turn to his relationship with Jaclyn. *Why does everything have to be so complicated? How can we possibly think that we're dating when we'll be clear across the country from each other? And what about Brad? Do those two have feelings for each other that they're not revealing just because of my sudden interest in her? Brad's too nice a guy, I suppose, to even consider informing me to keep my hands off a girl he's interested in, especially if there are no definite attachments.*

Maybe Jaclyn and I will have to consider it just a short summer romance and go our separate ways. But can I? It doesn't really make a lot of sense, but she has so quickly become a part of my life that I don't want to lose. Maybe it's just because she's the first girl I've ever paid any attention to. Will the next four years in college change that so maybe I shouldn't let this summer bother me? Just let it be a nice short summer attraction and then concentrate on my college education. He pounded his pillow, plopped down his head, and tried to relax, but there was still one big problem--he couldn't make his pounding heart agree as he drifted into a restless sleep.

He moaned when the alarm started beeping right close to his ear, but he was out of bed and dressed in a matter of minutes. He'd been helping with chores every day for the last couple of weeks before the wedding and had then volunteered to help Brent while Josh was gone on his honeymoon. Brent had accepted without hesitation, so it was exciting to think he was really going to be working on the Haven of Rest ranch, riding the range like a real cowboy, and helping his cousin in ways he had never dreamed possible.

When he reached the kitchen, he was really surprised to find his grandma standing at the stove fixing sausage and scrambled eggs. "Well, Grandma, don't you look right at home here in the big ranch kitchen?"

"Well, it's one thing I can do to help this family while they're so upset about Mary. Of course, Joseph wanted to go to the hospital and give support to his sister, and Marge does the driving for him these days, so they're gone. Noah and Eleanor are driving up there after they go to church, but I assume that Noah may have to come back to the office before Joseph and Marge are ready. I understand Susan is going to see her folks right after church and will stay overnight because she has an appointment with her obstetrician tomorrow. So, I'm now on duty for the day fixing meals for you hard working ranchers," she grinned. "Here's your plate, Mark. Brent went to make sure that Susan was awake and then he'll be back to eat. Are you excited to be able to help Brent with the chores while Josh is gone?"

"It's going to be a blast. I just hope I don't mess up, but there's a lot to learn around a ranch, and I've only had a couple of weeks to train."

"You'll do fine, Mark." They both turned to see Brent coming into the kitchen with a big smile on his face. "I won't dock your pay or send you back to New York if you happen to forget something. Chores are not a minute by minute operation. Horses and cattle seem to be over-whelmingly patient which is very fortunate around this family," he chuckled. "Thanks, Esther," he said as he took the plate that she handed him, kissed her cheek, and went over to sit with Mark at the table.

"Thanks, Brent. I intend to do my very best, but I know I'm far from being a gifted and trained partner like Josh."

"Josh is one of a kind, that's for sure. I was so fortunate to get him at a very stressful time here at the ranch when Dad was in the hospital with his heart attack. It's still hard for me to understand the strength and will-power he demonstrated in that relationship with Liz as he was saddled so quickly with all the responsibility of running the ranch, too. Even though they had become really close, he had actually walked away from her two and a half years ago so she could enjoy her high school years without any distraction from him. He admits he was in love with her, but they both went and had a relationship for a few months with someone else during the separation.

It was amazing that they had both failed about the same time Jon called to see if Josh would be willing to leave school and come up here to help out. He'd had enough credits to graduate mid-term, but he'd elected to stay the second semester to pick up some additional knowledge.

Liz had been trying for a couple of years, at least, to get her parents to agree to let her come down here to finish high school. She'd never liked high school in Colorado Springs and would have been happy to quit after her sophomore year, but her dad wouldn't agree to that. Her one dream had always been to become a wife and mother," he chuckled. "She'd always had a love for the ranch and Hayes, so when her parents finally gave in to her wishes that summer, she became completely dedicated to finishing her high school years. I wonder, though, if Josh may have been the driving force behind that, too. He knew the importance of an education, and he didn't want her to miss out on those happy, carefree years.

She continued to get all A's because she wanted to convince her mom and dad that they had made the right decision by letting her come down here to finish school and to be near Josh.

Josh hadn't missed a beat in running the ranch all the time I was at the hospital with my dad and mom, and we now work together as close as brothers. He had also been very close to his big brother, Jon, and it is so evident that he is thrilled to still have him close by."

"Thanks, Brent, for telling me. I hadn't heard that part of their relationship, but I did hear Liz say that God played a big part in bringing them together from the day they met. I understand that Josh was thrown from his horse and Liz spent hours at the hospital while he was unconscious."

"That's right, Mark, and it would take too long to tell you that whole story. We have animals waiting to be fed before we go to church. Are you ready to tackle your new chores?"

"Yes, Sir, let's go. Goodbye, Grandma. We'll be back to go to church if I don't goof up too much." Giving her a kiss on the cheek, he followed Brent out the door.

Grandma watched with pride as the two young men walked side by side toward the big barn. *Dear Lord, please give Mark a wonderful experience here, learning about the life of all these wonderful relatives who have wondered for years about the lost sister who was led astray by a greedy grandmother. I hope Ruth is watching from up there and finally knows how much she was loved and missed. Thank you for giving Lucas the time and the courage to take the tiny bit of information he had and follow through on this adventure, and thank you for Mark who was willing to be his grandfather's partner in this successful search.*

"Good morning, Sweetie." She turned then to watch Lucas enter the kitchen and come to give her the usual morning hug and kiss.

"Sit down, Dear, and I'll bring our breakfast to the table."

"I guess our grandson has started his first day of real ranch work. He has had the most excited expression on his face ever since our arrival here. I don't remember him ever being so enthused about things, even his involvement in all his sports. Of course, some of that could be the addition of that sweet little girl, Jaclyn," he laughed.

"You're absolutely right, Lucas. Our grandson is having the experience of his life this summer, and it's all because of your determination to try and find this missing family of yours. I'm so proud of you for not giving up on the dream you've had all these years. It's just too bad Ruth didn't get the chance to come home and learn the truth."

"I'll never be able to fully forgive myself for not taking the time to bring her back here after she finally let it be known that there might be family in Colorado. Life seems to deal some hard knocks for folks sometimes, but we certainly found a marvelous extension to our family tree, don't you agree?"

"I most certainly do. I just feel so bad that Mary has had to experience this upset, what-ever it turns out to be."

"Well, it appears that Dr. Wilder is a very experienced surgeon, so we'll just need to pray that God is leading him to find the problem and to solve it."

"I thought I heard you talking to James this morning. Is everything all right back home and at the office?"

"Yes, he says he could use me, but he has been able to handle it. He has put Stephen to work doing some research and filing, so everything is going well. He wants us to stay as long as we don't wear out our welcome," he chuckled.

"He actually hopes we can all meet someday, either here or there. I'm really glad that he's showing an interest now in this adventure. He and Kate had both been rather nonchalant about the possibility of there being any family way out in Colorado."

"Oh, I hope we can accomplish getting them all acquainted, Lucas. Do you think some of these might want to come to New York?"

"Well, it's where the family started west from. I thought Noah might be interested to see where his grandparents grew up and went to school."

They had just finished putting the dishes in the dishwasher when Noah and Eleanor walked in. "We're sorry you had to be pushed into service, Esther, but we really do appreciate your willingness to help. I don't remember a time we had so many things go wrong about the same time," Noah remarked. "If you don't mind, I'll have a cup of coffee and maybe Lucas will join me on the deck. It's a beautiful morning. Did Mark join Brent this morning to help with the chores?"

"He was beaming like he'd just won first place in something," Lucas chuckled as he refilled his coffee cup and the two headed out the door. "You ladies come join us unless you have female talkin' to do."

"We'll be out shortly," Eleanor answered as she grinned at Esther. "Those two are so much alike it's frightening at times."

"I'm so glad someone else has noticed that. I was beginning to think I was seeing double," Esther replied. "Lucas and I were just talking about maybe some of you wanting to come to New York. He thought Noah might like to see where his grandparents grew up and went to school."

"I think Noah already has that on his schedule of things to do, at least in his head. Let's join them and see what's on their minds this morning. Of course, we'll be leaving right from the church to go to the hospital, but I think we'll be coming home by noon tomorrow. Noah has a late afternoon appointment with a client he really needs to see."

Mark glanced around the church hoping to see Jaclyn, but then he remembered that she would be working four hours today. *If she's getting off at 3 o'clock, that means she went to work at 11:00, and that would've made it impossible for her to come to this service. She may have come to the early one, though, or her family could attend one of the other churches. We didn't mention anything about going to church yesterday so that's a topic to be discussed on our date tonight. It's really important to me that the girl I date is a Christian and attends the church services as much as possible.*

Mark had always been very much involved in his church back home, and God was very real in his life. He had been enjoying the services here, too, especially the Sunday when Jon and Christy had sung their duet. Today a Dr. Neil Davis and his wife, Susan, sang a beautiful hymn and the sermon was impressive and thought provoking. *Maybe I'll ask Christy if Jaclyn and her family attend here. It might save an awkward moment later.*

After the service, they all decided to go to Copland's restaurant for lunch. Esther had offered to fix lunch at the ranch, but everyone agreed that the restaurant would be a lot faster and much less work for their guest. Noah and Eleanor could then be on their way from town, instead of from the ranch, which would save several miles of driving.

Brent and Mark had a few more things to do around the barn, and then Jon and Christy joined them for an afternoon ride. It was a gorgeous day with a few white clouds and a great breeze, and they had a clear view of the mountains in the distance. They rode to the lake that has the cabins which are used when the guys go hunting for pheasant and deer or for a day or two of fishing.

The water was cool and it coaxed all of them to take their boots off and go wading, but before long someone slapped their hand on the water and sprayed a fine mist over the others. Of course, that started a big water fight, and when they finally stopped, everyone was soaked, even the horses that had entered the water to cool off and get a drink. The four sat on the bench that had been cut from a huge log until they were almost dry. They enjoyed some snacks that Christy had brought, and then they rode back to the barn. Mark had never had so much fun, but it got him to thinking about how quickly he'd be leaving for college. He'd thought at first that the summer would be an eternity, but now it was slipping away all too soon.

He'd gone to clean up, so he'd be ready for his date with Jaclyn, and then he'd joined his grandparents who were relaxing on the deck. Brent, Jon and Christy were now at the pool, but Mark thought he'd pass that today. Maybe Jaclyn could come out and join him one day soon, and then he'd truly enjoy the pool. *It'll be great to see her in a swimming suit,* he mused. *Boy, I really am sounding like some of those guys on the team that I thought were a little crazy. How many years did I waste with my mind always on sports?*

CHAPTER SIXTEEN

When Brent had heard about the threat to Mark after the wedding, he'd suggested that he use the ranch truck on his date tonight. Mark had told him about the officer calling the parents and that the car was taken away from the kid for a month, but Brent still felt it would be best to be in the truck because there could be other boys not too happy about a New Yorker moving in on their territory. "Jaclyn will understand why you don't have the big new car with New York plates when you tell her what happened. We'll get the truck all cleaned up so you'll be right in style since a lot of young guys are driving trucks these days." The extra hands had been put to work and the truck was shining and spotless inside and out when he pulled into Jaclyn's driveway. When she opened the door at 6 o'clock sharp, there was no remark about the truck, but Mark thought his eyes were going to pop out of his head. She was so cute with her hair pulled back into some sort of comb-style fastener that looked like a butterfly, but small tendrils of curls were falling to outline her face. She was wearing a mini skirt with a soft knit top fashioned with a modest vee neckline, a knotted surplice front and tiny cap sleeves. She wore a pair of white leather thongs on her very small feet.

"Wow, you look great, Jaclyn. Are you ready to go get something to eat?" "Yes, but I was just wondering if I should take a sweater along in case the theater is cold like it can be at times. What do you think?"

"I think I can keep you warm if the theater is cold," he chuckled. "Is that a promise, Mark, or a threat?" Jaclyn asked.

"On my honor I will try to do my duty to keep you warm and comfortable if the theater becomes cold," he pledged with his hand over his heart and a big grin on his face. "Of course, you can take a sweater if you'd like. The truck may not be as warm as Grandpa's car would've been if it cools down later." On their way to the truck, he told her about his experience on the way home last night, and that was why Brent had suggested that he drive the truck.

She was really upset that he'd been put through an ordeal like that because of her, but she *had* picked up her sweater before closing the door behind her.

They stopped at the cafe because Jaclyn just wanted a small salad and iced tea. Mark ordered a chicken sandwich, French fries and a cola, and then Jaclyn tried to sneak a few fries off his plate. That resulted in a hand slapping duel all in fun, but they did finally get around to discussing a few things, too. Jaclyn, of course, asked if he knew anything more definite about Mary. Then Mark asked about the church attendance and discovered that she and her family attend the Catholic Church but that she had come to the Community Church several times with Christy. She actually confessed that she'd enjoyed those services much more than she did the Catholic services because so much of the Catholic ones were in Latin. She felt that she'd also learned a lot more about Jesus and his work on earth at the Community Church. After that, they talked about some of the things they could do at the ranch in the days ahead before he leaves.

Since they had just eaten, when they reached the movie they'd decided to just share a bag of popcorn with their two drinks, but the movie was so good that their attention was fully on the screen. About three-fourths of the way through the movie, though, a blast of cold air hit them as the air-conditioner apparently turned on. Jaclyn was suddenly cold and shivering, but realized she'd left her sweater in the truck. Mark put his arm across her shoulders and pulled her close to him. He'd kissed the top of her head and then her forehead, but he couldn't resist also finding her mouth. He was so thrilled when she responded, and he wrapped both arms around her. He could feel her heart beating against his arm as he tried to keep her warm, but his own body was doing strange things. *Get a hold of yourself; you are only trying to keep the girl warm,* he tried to convince himself over and over, but his male hormones weren't listening. He tried to concentrate on the movie until he got himself under control, but he was sure glad when the air shut off and he could bring his arm back and feel comfortable again.

Knowing he had to get up early to help with chores, and Jaclyn was scheduled to work in the morning, too, they decided it had been a long enough date when they left the movie. He did park in front of her house for a few minutes, and the bench seat made it easy to pull her over close so he could get a few kisses. He may not have thought about girls too much when he was playing sports, but the guys had made sure he'd seen some of the sexy magazines they had in their lockers. During one kiss, he got the chance to put his hand on her thigh at the bottom of her mini skirt, but she'd grabbed his hand and brought it back to her waist. His hand then moved slowly up her side, but he was only just above her waist when her hand quickly brought it back to her waist.

Having a girl in your arms is a lot more fun than a hard and unyielding basketball or football, and I have one more move that I read about when I sneaked into Stephen's room and looked at the magazines my big brother just thought he had hidden well. His right hand was now holding her tightly around her back while he was playing with her hair and caressing her face and ear with his left. He then moved his hand down to her neck as he continued one kiss after another until he thought he had her under his spell like the instructions had said. He quickly slipped his hand inside her blouse and his fingers had almost reached her bra when she jerked away and slapped his face really hard.

"Ouch! Jaclyn. It didn't say you'd do *that* in those magazines I found in my brother's bedroom."

"Just what were ya'll trying to do and prove, Mark? I thought I was safe with ya'll, but I see guys must all think along the same old line. I'm going in the house." She tried to quickly pull away, but he still had his arm around her and held her so she couldn't move.

"I'm sorry, Jaclyn, please let me try to explain."

"Ya'll don't need to explain, Mark. I understand all too well, I'm afraid, what runs in all boys' minds. I thought ya'll was different, and I even told ya'll about my experience in New Orleans, but I see that ya'll are after the same thing he was although a little more subtle. Just let me go, Mark, and I mean for it to be right NOW!"

She was out of the truck by the time he was around to her door, but he took her arm and walked her to the house. "May I call you to plan something at the ranch," he begged as he held the screen door open for her. "I'll make sure we have others there with us so you won't have to worry about me doing something wrong again. O.K? I'm so sorry I got carried away, Jaclyn, but please don't let that other kid get near you," he warned. "I think he is *really* crazy."

"Don't worry about that, Mark. I think I'll have Mom or Grant walk with me when I go to work, if I can't ride with Dad, and then one of them can meet me when I get off. I don't want anything to do with that creep, but I'll be sure to do some deep soul searching before I accept an invitation to the ranch from ya'll, too. I wish Liz were here to talk to. Goodnight, Mark."

"Please forgive me, Jaclyn. I'm really sorry I did those things, but I do have some very strong feelings for you although we haven't known each other long. I don't understand what it all means, but I know I want to get to know you better." He could only stand and watch as she unlocked the door and disappeared inside.

"Oh, Dear God, what have I done now?" he moaned. "I guess I have a lot more to learn about girls and dating if I plan to ever succeed in the romance department."

Grandpa Lucas was still sitting on the deck when Mark parked the truck and then was walking slowly and dejectedly to the house. "Well, Mark, how'd the first date go? Come and sit with me for a little while and let's sort of plan what our next move should be. I guess your grandma is thinking about flying home next weekend if everything goes well with Mary and all is back to normal around here."

"I was wondering if she was going to fly back or maybe decide to ride back with us. It would be fun to have her along, but I know it would be a hard trip for her. Do you remember the trips when the two of you used to take me with you? It seems like only yesterday at times, but I guess it's been at least four years now. I got too involved with sports in high school to spend those great times with you. I really missed them, and I suppose that's why this trip has meant so much to me. Of course, the discovery of relatives has to be the ultimate prize at the end of the rainbow this time."

"I'm glad you've enjoyed this trip, Mark, because it has been something out of a fairy tale, that's for sure. How could we have ever dreamed that we would find the most perfect relatives who were so willing to accept us? Also, for you, it appears that you have found a little romance along the way. So, back to my original question. How'd the first date go?"

"I'm really not sure, Grandpa. I've had very little practice in the dating game, and I think I might have ended my little romance by acting like a fool tonight. I actually got my face slapped and a promise that she'll have to do a lot of soul searching before she'll even accept an invitation from me to come out here. I'd asked if she'd like to spend some time here and even guaranteed that we wouldn't be alone, but she was noncommittal."

Grandpa couldn't help chuckling. "Well, Mark, getting your face slapped a few times is just part of learning the rules of romance. Girls as young as Jaclyn usually need a very slow introduction to kisses and a few little touches. After they have dated for a year or two, that sort of thing becomes expected. I imagine this was Jaclyn's first date, just as it was for you, so I'm sure if you were experimenting at all, she was shocked and angered. Can I assume that you've been snooping in your brother's room lately and perhaps found the magazines that get well used, it seems, when guys get to college?"

"How do you know about those, Grandpa? Actually, a few members of the team had a magazine or two in their locker that they were proud to pass around."

"Well, I was in college, Mark, and I also dated a few girls who had never been on a date before. Of course, I dated a few of the more experienced ones, too. Your grandmother just happened to be one of the innocent ones, but she had a wallop that sent me halfway across the room when we were kissing and my hand wandered a little too much. I fell totally in love with her that night, but it took almost two months for her to accept another date with me. Those are memories I'll never forget!" he laughed as he remembered those days of long ago.

"There is one big difference, Mark, that you should remember, and that is that the new magazines of today are much more graphic and vulgar than they were when I was sneaking a look at them, and I wouldn't advise you to follow many of the ideas they like to portray. Just remember that a girl is always to be cherished and protected from all the hurt in the world, and I sure hope you've had the chance to learn that as well as enjoying a simple little touch that may have gotten your face slapped."

"I wish I'd talked to you *before* I had this date instead of after, but maybe I can get her to forgive me before two months are up. I won't be here that long."

"That's true, Mark, and maybe it isn't supposed to be a lasting thing. I understand that Liz asked Brad to come down the last two years to be Jaclyn's escort to the Christmas dance and also to the Spring Formal. I noticed how well they danced together at the reception, so could there be something going on between them that they don't even realize yet?"

"Jaclyn mentioned that she loved dancing with Brad, but she couldn't talk to him like she could to me. She thanked me for helping her get over her fear of guys. She even told me about an incident that happened in New Orleans that she hadn't been able to talk to her mother about. I really felt privileged that she could confide in me."

"I think Brad may be coming down for a few days, when Mary is out of danger. I think he wants to get a little more acquainted with you. Maybe you should keep your eyes open if and when the two of them are together. Not that I want to put a damper on your love affair, but with you in New York and the two of them around here, there *is* a possibility of a fading love."

"Thanks, Grandpa. I'll try to take all this into consideration as I try to straighten out the puzzle of life. I guess I'd better go up to bed now and try to get some sleep before those early morning chores beckon. Are you coming up soon?"

"I'm going to sit here a little while longer. I can't get enough of this fresh Colorado air and the huge expanse of sky you can see with the stars and that big gorgeous moon shining down to lighten up the whole area. Goodnight, Mark. I hope you can sleep well. I'll see you in the morning."

Mark got ready for bed and then lay on his back looking out the windows where he could also see the moon and stars twinkling in the clear sky. *What a wonderful place to live,* he mused, *but my life, future and family are apparently in New York. Could it ever be a possibility that I might live out here one day and work at the Hayes Law Office with Jon and Brad? Of course, Noah is there now, but by the time I get through four years of college and also law school, it would seem logical that he'd be ready for retirement. But, on the other hand, Grandpa will also be retiring and leaving Dad and Stephen in charge. So, who would I rather be working with---Dad and Stephen or Jon and Brad? Three Gillette's or a Holcomb, Becker, and Gillette. Oops, I forgot about the other partner, Mr. Adams. That might be too many attorneys for this little town, but that's also too many years away to worry about.*

He thought a little more about his conversation with Grandpa concerning romance and the chance of getting your face slapped if you didn't behave. It was hard to imagine that his grandfather had ever had his face slapped, especially by his own sweet, always smiling and so understanding grandmother. He was soon beginning to yawn, however, and he knew he should try to get some sleep. *Morning will be coming and the excitement of helping Brent on the ranch is happening right now. That's a lot more fun to think about than seven years from now, or even trying to understand my new interest in girls.* He closed his eyes and had soon fallen asleep.

A dream included getting his face slapped, but there had also been a wonderful hug and a kiss from the girl who looked so much like Jaclyn.

CHAPTER SEVENTEEN

Noah and Eleanor returned the next day with word that Mary had come through the carotid surgery quite well. They had also found a heart valve problem, but Dr. Wilder was pleased with the prognosis. However, he wants her to stay in the hospital a day or two before going home.

The days went by faster than Mark realized, and it was soon Thursday afternoon. He hadn't called Jaclyn, and the Brad thing was still bothering him. When he'd finished the chores that he'd been assigned, he caught Brent taking a break. He grabbed a can of soda and joined him. They discussed a couple of things that Brent wanted to get done tomorrow and Saturday, and then Mark asked if he would help him with a problem he needed an answer to.

"Of course, Mark. If it's something I can help you with, I'd be happy to contribute my limited expertise," he grinned.

"Well, it isn't anything mind boggling," Mark chuckled, "but I was wondering if you might possibly know how Brad feels about Jaclyn. I understand Liz asked him to come down and be Jaclyn's date for the dances at school over the last two years, and it just might be that I'm intruding where I shouldn't have trod."

"Oooh, that's a little tricky, Mark. I do know that Brad escorted Jaclyn to the dances the last two years, but I never heard anything about what their feelings were toward one another. My cousin has been noncommittal when it comes to girlfriends, although he loves to dance and didn't miss any of the dances at the high school level that I'm aware of. Liz has remarked about his solitude and that he told her once that he needed to find a girl down here or he might as well stay at home with a good book. He had realized that it was pretty much all couples anymore, and he felt like he was an outsider. I understand your concern, Mark, but have you and Jaclyn even discussed what you might do to keep in touch when you return to New York and start your college studies? Is she possibly considering it just a summer fling?"

"We mentioned at one time that we could e-mail and telephone each other like Josh and Liz did when they were separated, but I'm beginning to think that would grow old after a while, especially when there's not much chance of me getting back out here to see her for maybe two or three years. I don't want to make her feel she has to devote all her time to me. I don't know what college will be like, who I'll meet there, or what activities I'll want to become involved in. I was involved in several sports during high school, and I might want to investigate something along that line in college."

"With all those probabilities, Mark, if you want my honest opinion, I would keep this relationship on a friendship only basis. You're both really too young to be getting serious so soon anyway. Now, I know that Liz got married right out of high school. She *was* 19, though, and Josh was five years older, but Liz was an exception for knowing what she wanted to do with her life long before she met Josh. Getting an education should be the first priority for a guy, however, so you have a chance for a good job. Have I made it any easier for you or just made it a little more confusing?"

"You've given me some things to think about, as my grandpa did the other night, but I was wondering if there was a special reason why Liz was 19 when she graduated."

"Yes, and she was one furious little girl when she was held back from starting first grade. She'd been looking forward to being in school with Mary and Brad, but she had a rare case of pneumonia that almost killed her, and it took several months for her to regain her strength. She'd always loved the ranch and begged to come down here and stay with Noah and Eleanor most of that time. That's one reason they are so close and she again stayed with them to finish her last two years of high school. She also got to date Josh for those two years instead of a long distance relationship, although I doubt if that would've changed the outcome with the way they felt about each other."

"Wow, I guess my next step is to call Jaclyn and see if she'll even talk to me. I made a little mistake on our date, and she was pretty upset when she went into the house."

"Oh, oh, did you get your face slapped?" he chuckled. "Oh, to be young again and get to go through that experience one more time."

"Why didn't either you or Grandpa talk to me *before* I went on that darn date if you knew what I was going to be facing?"

"And spoil all the fun of learning it first hand? No, Mark, that would never do," he chuckled as he got up, patted Mark on the shoulder, and strolled down toward the horses. "Want to go check the fences with me?"

"Of course, but I'm not going to talk to you anymore about my date. You and my own grandpa both got too big a laugh out of my stupidity."

"Mark, it wasn't your stupidity we were laughing at. It was remembering our own experiences that were amusing. Those days were a little humbling, I admit, but I wouldn't go back and change them for the world. Just be sure to keep them tucked in your memory bank for one of those wonderful 'good old days' stories someday when either your son or grandson asks why his face got slapped by a young girl on their first date."

"That sure sounds like a million years away. Should I keep a diary?"

"I don't think you'll need anything written down to remember the first time you got your face slapped. It will most likely raise its ugly head several times before you find the right girl to spend the rest of your life with, however."

After dinner that evening, Mark helped clean up the kitchen and then went up to his room. He thought he'd call Jaclyn and see if she'd like to come to the ranch on Saturday or Sunday afternoon. Brent had told him that they'd be done with the chores and the other tasks by 1 o'clock at the latest each day.

One of her brothers answered and then yelled right into the phone, it seemed, to tell her she had a call. His ear was still ringing when she answered, but she seemed happy and he was encouraged, but only until she'd had a chance to hear his voice. "I didn't expect it to be you," she remarked after he'd said hello and quickly apologized for not calling sooner.

"I'm really sorry, Jaclyn, but you know I'm helping Brent while Josh and Liz are gone, and it was slower with me not knowing all the tricks of ranching. I called to see if you might be interested in coming out here either Saturday or Sunday afternoon. Brad may be coming down, and I was wondering if you'd have a girlfriend you'd like to bring along. If not, then maybe Grant would like to come. We can go riding for awhile and then maybe swim before we go and have dinner."

"Did you say Brad may be coming? I *have* met a girl at work and we've been sort of taking our breaks together when we're working the same shift. I could ask her if she'd like to come along with me. We both work from 8 to 1 on Saturday."

"Jon and Christy might join us, too. They both love to go riding. The office has been extra busy this week, so I hear, which will make them eager to get out on the trails."

Can I call you tomorrow night, Mark, and we'll make final plans when I know if my friend can come? She has a car so we'll have our own transportation."

"You're really upset with me, aren't you, Jaclyn? I talked to both Grandpa and Brent, and they informed me that they'd both been slapped when they first started dating. My own grandma was one of the girls who slapped Grandpa, and he said he fell hopelessly in love with her that night. She made him wait almost two months for their second date, but it all worked out for them. I'm still really sorry I upset you, but I hope we can have another date before I have to leave for home and college. I have learned a lesson, Jaclyn, and I'll be on my best behavior if you'll just give me another chance."

"We'll see, Mark. I'll call you tomorrow night. Until then, I'll just say Goodnight."

"Goodnight, Jaclyn." *Whew, she's really upset, but maybe not as much as she was when she slapped my face. At least she didn't ya'll me on the phone. I think I'll let Brad ride next to her. He's a better rider than I am, and maybe she won't try to make me take a tumble if she's riding beside Brad. Even better, maybe we should let the girls ride side by side and Brad and I will ride together. Of course, we could always ride single file, too. That would really solve the problem. Oh, for heaven's sake, what is this girl doing to me?*

Brad came driving in late Friday afternoon. He'd just finished up his classes for the summer and wanted to do some things that were relaxing and fun. After they'd eaten, and Brent and Susan had gone to their wing of the house, Mark asked Brad if he'd like to go for a walk with him. As they strolled down around the pool, Mark told him about the possibility of Jaclyn and a girlfriend coming out tomorrow or Sunday to go riding and swimming, and Mark definitely saw a bright sparkle in Brad's eyes.

"Maybe we can go to the Pub and Grub to eat and do some dancing." Mark tried to be discreet as he continued to watch to see if the appeal to hold Jaclyn in his arms would show in Brad's eyes or face. *Yep, an interest was definitely there.*

"I love dancing and especially with Jaclyn," he said. "Did you know that Liz asked me to be Jaclyn's date for the Christmas and Spring Formals? That was really a lot of fun-- but it was just a courtesy date," he was quick to add.

"Yea, someone told me that after I'd seen you two dancing at the reception. You do make a nice looking couple, Brad, which makes me want to ask you a very personal question.

I want the absolute truth, too, and I don't want any hems and haws about it. Are you at all interested in pursuing a relationship with Jaclyn? She and I had a date Sunday night, and I got my face slapped for trying to touch her a couple times where I shouldn't have. She is really upset with me, but I sensed an interest in coming out here when I told her you'd be coming down for a few days. I'm really sorry if I stepped into a situation without checking everything out, but Christy didn't say anything, and Jaclyn *is* somebody who could turn a guy's head."

"O.K., Mark, you want the truth, so I'll tell you the truth. I hadn't thought a thing about Jaclyn being anything more than a friend to my sister until I saw the two of you together at the rehearsal dinner, the fireworks, and also at the reception. My normal 'take it or leave it' attitude plummeted a good 20 degrees that night after the wedding, especially when I saw you kissing,. I wanted to come and grab her out of your arms. Of course, I knew I hadn't said anything to cause her to think I had any romantic feelings toward her, so I had to walk away. I then almost accepted Jon's suggestion that I ride home with you that night, but I controlled myself. She shouldn't have any reason to think you're up to some mischievous trick to hurt her or me."

"You didn't completely answer my question, Brad. Could those reactions just be a case of a little jealousy or possessiveness, or would you be interested in dating Jaclyn? You plan to come down here in December, after you graduate, and then there'll be a chance for two more dances before she graduates in May or June. You also know I'll be in college in New York, so I wouldn't be able to come clear out here just for a dance. As my grandpa pointed out the other night, I'm going to be in New York and the two of you are going to be here in the same town, so it's reasonable that a connection could easily develop between the two of you. I have six or seven years of college in front of me while you're going to be graduating and starting a good job. So, before I let myself get anymore involved, I need to know if Jaclyn is the girl you feel you would like to get close to and date."

"If you put it that way, Mark, I guess I'd have to say that she passes every criterion I've ever wanted in a girl. I haven't actually dated anyone, but I really would like to give it a try with Jaclyn. What are your feelings, though? Are you sure you can just walk away and chalk it up to a short summer romance?"

"If you're serious about Jaclyn, you have first choice since you've already dated her at least four times when you escorted her to the dances."

"Let's see how tomorrow afternoon and evening go. We have a new girl to meet, too."

They had taken off their boots and sat dangling their feet in the water of the pool when Brad suddenly gave Mark a shove and he went tumbling into the water fully dressed. Not to be outdone, Mark quickly turned around and caught Brad's foot, so they were both in the water and soon splashing big sprays at each other and laughing like two crazy kids.

"What in the world are you two up to?" a familiar voice and a chuckle was heard as Jon and Christy dove into the pool from the other end. They soon surfaced close to where the guys were having the water fight.

"Just being a little crazy," Brad laughed. "I haven't had this much fun since we were in our early teens. Do you remember all the water fights we used to have, Christy?"

"How could I forget? You and Brent against Mary and me for several years, but when Liz finally joined us, she was really sneaky. She would dive way deep, especially at night, and then come up behind you guys and almost drown you. She really came out of her shell when she was about twelve or thirteen."

"You two had better pull those wet pants off before they drag you clear down to the bottom," Jon chuckled. "We won't be embarrassed if you swim in your boxers. It's done quite often around here, and it's not much different from swim trunks anyway."

"Two small but distinctive differences," Mark laughed. "There's no cord to tighten 'em around your waist and they're a little fuller and thinner with nothing too protect your privacy if the water lifts the boxer legs a little too high."

"I guess we could all go skinny dipping," Brad chuckled. "We did that a few times, too, as we were growing up. Remember, Christy?"

"Brad Becker, you were sworn to secrecy about those little childhood experiments. I wondered at the time if we should trust you," she laughed.

"Another little piece of information about my angelic wife, I see, that puts her into an almost human light. I guess Liz shouldn't be the only one to be called mysterious," but he was grinning as he pulled her into his arms for a kiss. "You're still my special angel, though, even if your halo has slipped a little." "Another topic of conversation, you lovebirds, is what Mark and I were discussing before you invaded our privacy. We were having a conversation about Jaclyn. It appears that Mark wasn't a perfect gentleman when he took her on their date Sunday, and she had to slap his face." A big moan was heard from Mark. "Anyway, there were several things that we were discussing. Mark wanted to know, first of all, if I had any romantic tendencies toward the girl; second, his grandpa told him that things might change a bit between her and me when I come here in December to start work; and third, Mark is going to be far, far away in old New York.. It's a little tricky, you see, with the two of us realizing that we sort of like the same girl."

"It's only if Brad is truly interested. I'll just quickly bow out," Mark replied.

"I guess I should take some of the blame for that," Christy spoke up, "but I hadn't seen you show any interest toward her, Brad, so when Mark had seen her at the store and asked if I knew her, I saw no reason for him not to get acquainted. I'm really sorry because I should've at least told him you'd taken her to the school dances. But, getting back to this other interesting situation, Mark, what is this about getting your face slapped?" she grinned.

"Oh, nothing much. We were kissing and my hand just wandered a little. She was quick to stop that by slapping my face, but she's still not very happy with me."

"Oh, I see. The inquisitive youth," she giggled, "and on your first date. My, my."

"Can we change the subject, please, unless you have a good idea how I can step aside without her being suspicious of a family rejection of some kind here?"

"I'd think it would make it a little easier if we knew whether she has any feelings for Brad. Then, if you're sure you can really step aside, Mark, I think it'd still be better if you continued to be involved for awhile, like a long distance friendship. Maybe there'd be a way the two of you could make her think she was doing the actual choosing, not you guys. I understand that you and Jaclyn have talked about trying to keep in touch with an occasional phone call and e-mails, so you could do that without causing any suspicions to surface. I don't think Brad would object to that, would you?"

"No, I think that's a good idea, especially through December. When it's time for the dance, they could talk about it and maybe Mark could even suggest or agree that I might take her again since I had before. After the dance, I'll start asking her out on dates, and then we can see how she might want to proceed with whatever feelings she may still have for Mark. Of course, I hope she'll tell him she's in love with me," he chuckled as he splashed water in Mark's face and took off toward the other end of the pool.

Mark was soon in hot pursuit, took a dive under the water and came up very close to Brad's legs. He grabbed his boxers and pulled them off with very little effort. Then, not even seeing it coming, Mark's boxers were slipped off by Jon who had come quickly alongside and jerked them off in one quick yank. Lucky for them, the sun had gone down and it was dark enough to prevent too much embarrassment in front of Christy who was now sitting on the edge of the pool and getting a big kick out of it all.

Mark then looked at Brad, gave a little sign, and they immediately grabbed Jon and tried to reciprocate by one holding him while the other untied his swim trunks. Jon was a little stronger than they had imagined, but they finally got them off. "Mommy," Jon yelled, "these roughnecks are being all mean to me!" He tried to really sound upset but couldn't keep from laughing.

"You roughnecks stop being mean to my little boy," Christy declared with a laugh of her own and a not-too-motherly sounding voice, either, but just then another male voice was heard approaching the wooden deck surrounding the pool.

"What in the world is going on down here that is causing so much laughing and even someone yelling Mommy?" Lucas came to stand beside Christy who was laughing so hard she couldn't say a word. She heard a few splashes and knew that three grown men had taken a dive but she wondered just how long they could stay under water.

"Hi, Uncle Lucas," she was finally able to get out between gasps of trying to catch her breath, "I think we have some grown men acting like little boys in the pool, and I'd say they're a little embarrassed at the moment because of your arrival. They were just trying to coax me back in by crying for Mommy. Do you swim well?"

"I think I can hold my own in a pool. I even won some blue ribbons somewhere along the way when I was in school just those few years ago," he chuckled. "What are they up to, skinny dippin'?"

Christy was quickly on her feet, took Uncle Lucas by the hand, and pulled him with her into the pool. He'd apparently had an idea what was coming so slipped his shoes off before they reached the edge. She'd known he was wearing all washable clothes so she didn't hesitate to get him wet along with the guys. She didn't realize, though, that he'd come with his trunks on expecting to go for a swim.

The two of them were at the shallow end of the pool and Lucas stood there, just staring at her, with a very wide grin across his face. "Christy, you are the most daring and the most darling young lady I have met in my life, and I love you so much. This water feels absolutely enticing."

About that time the three guys surfaced with their trunks and boxers back in place, and they started tugging on the shirt of this 75 year old grandpa. He stood there laughing like a little kid as his shirt was thrown onto a lounge chair. They were starting to pull on the elastic waist of his sport pants when another grandfather appeared. "Oh-oh," Lucas moaned, "I've probably just lost the respect of my senior cousin and host."

Christy was quickly out of the pool and walked over beside her grandfather. She gave him a big smile as she took his hand. He'd had this treatment many times before so was now always prepared when he came to the pool. His rubber thongs were kicked off as he let her pull him into the pool.

"I see you got yourself initiated, Lucas, by being a little too inquisitive. I didn't learn too well the first time, but after that I've come prepared. The water's great tonight," he said as he slipped his knit shirt over his head and the knit pants quickly went to join it somewhere on the deck. "You ready to do some swimming?"

"That's what I came down here for, but I didn't realize I was going to be pulled in and undressed. I have my trunks on, but are all of you just in boxers?" He'd noticed Brad and Mark's ballooning out a little but he couldn't quite see what Jon or Noah were wearing.

"I think Brad and Mark are the only ones who didn't come prepared tonight," Noah replied, "but this kind of thing is done on the spur of the moment so one or two are usually caught unprepared when they get pulled in."

It didn't take long for the guys to yank Lucas's elastic waist sport pants off and then take off swimming before he could grab them. They all swam and fooled around for another hour or so before they finally got towels from the bath house, dried off, and headed back to their respective houses in their still wet boxers and trunks. Their other clothes were left in the bath house to dry. Lucas was feeling lucky that Esther had gone up to bed early, but Noah wasn't the least bit afraid of what Eleanor would think. She had been pulled in on a few of the dunking games over the years, too.

When Mark got to the house, he saw a message on the counter and then realized that he had not been here to take Jaclyn's call. "Another black mark against me?" he grinned as he read the message.

"Mark, I'm sorry I missed you. Your grandmother said you were outside with Brad. I'm glad he'll be there. My girlfriend, Teri, and I will plan to come out tomorrow afternoon if it is still alright with you. We'll plan to be there by 2 o'clock. You had mentioned riding and then swimming so we'll come prepared. We'll also bring some clothes for later since your grandmother said she thought you had made some plans in town, too. It sounds like fun. See ya. Jaclyn"

"Well, Cousin, it sounds like we have a couple of girls to entertain tomorrow afternoon and evening. Are you up to it?" he grinned, but as he looked at Brad he noticed he had a puzzled look on his face. "What's wrong?" he asked.

"Are we going to pair off? If so, how's that going to work? I'm not too good at those so-called blind dates."

"I'd thought it might be best if we let the girls stick together and we stick together while out riding and driving to the restaurant. After we get to the Pub and Grub, we'll dance with both of them and make it a rather buddy, buddy night. Is that O.K. with you? Of course, after one dance with me, they'll probably both want to dance only with you, but we'll work it out."

"That sounds good. Do you think they'll want to drive Teri's car to the restaurant so they don't have to come way out here and then drive back to town fairly late?"

"That might be an option, but we'll cross that bridge when we come to it, too."

"Cool. I think I'll hit the sack now. That last exam this morning was a tough one, and then driving down here for an unexpected romp in the pool has really worn me out. I've got to get my rest now so I can dance, dance, and dance tomorrow night because my new-found New York cousin can't dance."

"Yes, Mr. Astaire, let's get ready to dance," Mark laughed as he twirled around and then nearly lost his balance as his feet wouldn't co-operate with his brain. "Poor girls, I really do feel sorry for them when it's their turn to dance with me."

"You're sure a carefree sonofagun, aren't you? I wonder what kind of a lawyer you'll make with that attitude. Of course, both Grandpa Noah and Jon are certainly fun loving, and your grandpa was really a great sport tonight. Maybe it's me that needs to think about how to change my attitude and outlook on life."

"I think a good lawyer has to be able to ride with the tide, so to speak, but let's leave that discussion for another time, Brad. I'm sleepy, too."

"I wonder why that would be," Brad chuckled as they headed upstairs for some good shut-eye. The lights were still on in the room where Lucas and Esther sleep, and the guys could hear soft voices and a little laughter.

"I guess Grandma wasn't asleep after all," Mark whispered as the two said goodnight and disappeared into their individual rooms. Mark was sure his grandmother would get a big laugh out of Grandpa getting pulled into the pool and actually stripped of most of his clothes. He had been prepared for a swim, though, since he'd had his trunks on. The great time they'd had was more than he and Brad had considered when they'd just gone out for a walk. It was sure tempting now to just fall into that comfortable bed, but he realized his boxers were still a little too damp. He took time to take them off and pull on his pajama bottoms. For once, he wasn't too anxious for the alarm to go off in the morning.

CHAPTER EIGHTEEN

Brad and Mark were both up early Saturday morning to help with the chores and then to get ready for their guests. Esther was still doing the cooking because Joseph and Marge had been in Colorado Springs all week. They'd been giving Rachel help with hospital visits and also the care of Mary when she'd gotten to come home. Mark very lovingly put his arms around his grandmother and softly whispered, "Would there be a chance that you might fix a few treats for us to take on our ride this afternoon?"

"I think I can manage that, Mark, but it might be time for you to learn to do some of that yourself. You're going to be on your own in college this fall, and neither your mother nor I will be there to feed you," she retorted with a chuckle. "I hope you aren't expecting Deborah to do those extra things for you."

"That would be the day. I could do it, Grandma, but I'm not very familiar with this kitchen and where all the things are. Do you want to show me, or would it be easier to do it yourself this time?" he smiled as he put a big kiss on her cheek.

"I'll do it, but you know I'm planning to go home tomorrow afternoon. According to the latest plan, Joseph and Marge are coming home sometime today. I still haven't been able to pin your grandfather down to when the two of you will be back home. Has he confided in you?"

"No, not really, but I had assumed that we'd start home around the 1st of August."

"I think we'll take off from here on the 28th of July, just so you both will know," a deep voice announced from the doorway. "Good morning to you, Mark and Brad, and also to My Lovely and Wonderful Sweetheart."

Lucas couldn't keep from grinning as he patted Mark and Brad on the shoulder and gave his wife a big hug. "Does that answer your question of the day? I thought maybe the conversation this morning would be about another event that you might be intrigued to hear more about, Esther. You were a little too sleepy last night to hear the whole story."

"I got enough of the story to realize that you and Noah were acting like a couple of very young unsophisticated lawyers who would probably surprise your clients beyond words, at least in New York. It probably wouldn't faze these down to earth, wonderful and friendly ones around here, now that I think about it. Why can't we sometimes take our hair down and enjoy a few of the really off beat things back home?"

"Why, Esther, My Dear, you surprise me! Do you want to be pulled into the pool and do some skinny dippin' with us? I'm sure we can arrange that later today after the young ones have gone off to town to dance. We could get Noah and Eleanor and have ourselves a good old-fashioned swimming party and really live it up." He then threw his head back and laughed heartily when he noticed that his lovely wife's face had turned a blushing red.

"Lucas, you should be ashamed of yourself. You'll embarrass Mark and Brad when you're talking like that."

"After last night, I don't think much would embarrass those two," he chuckled.

"Who's being embarrassed around here?" They all turned to see Brent coming into the room laughing. "I heard enough of that conversation to realize what must have happened at the pool last night. Not much can embarrass this family of ours, Esther. We all love to share our silliness, our happiness, and even our sorrows with each other, and it usually doesn't matter when or where. I'm glad the guys were able to enjoy themselves."

"Well, breakfast is ready so you'd better all eat so you can get your chores done," she mumbled quietly as she turned back to the stove and started dishing up all the great smelling food she'd been preparing.

Mark slipped out of the kitchen and ran up to his room. He was only gone a few short minutes, but he didn't explain when he came back down and no one asked. He ate quickly to catch up and then the three guys took off for the barn after either giving Esther a hug or a kiss on the cheek.

Susan had come and was standing in the doorway watching the affectionate display by the guys. "I think someone has been doing a splendid job of feeding our working guys in the mornings from that display of thanks. I'm so slow these days that they would most likely starve if they waited for me to feed them. Marge has always been there for them, but you have been a Godsend when she wanted to be up there helping Rachel. We're all going to miss you a lot, Esther, when you leave."

"Thank you, Susan. I just hope and pray that the rest of your pregnancy goes well and you have a very healthy, happy baby. Can I fix you something?"

"No, but thank you, Esther. I have a special diet that my doctor suggested, so I fix it before I join the real world each day. It has seemed to help with the morning sickness, and I'm extremely grateful for that. I'm going down to the ranch office now and try to do some daily bookkeeping, so I'll see you guys later. Lucas, I thought I heard some laughing when you all came in last night. It couldn't be possible that you got caught with the pool rascals, could it?" she giggled.

"Yes, I sure did, and that took me back quite a few years to when I was young and foolish, but having so much fun. I'm going to try to get Esther involved in some of that silly foolishness, too, before she leaves tomorrow."

"You'll enjoy it, Esther, if you like the water at all. Get Noah and Eleanor to go with you. They indulge quite often, actually, but mostly late at night when they think we're all in bed asleep. With my sleeplessness the last two months, I've observed the happy lovebirds as they walked back to their house carrying their clothes and smooching all the way. I sure hope Brent and I can still do that when we've been married over fifty years. See you two later."

"And you thought I was out of my mind, Esther, when I told you what I'd been doing last night. We definitely have a date at the pool tonight, Sweetheart, with or without Noah and Eleanor, and it'll be even more fun when I get you back to bed." His eyes were twinkling like stars in the sky as his fingers lifted her chin for a kiss, and he so loved the blush that he could still bring to her cheeks.

"You are so naughty, Lucas," she said as she gently pushed him away, "but you've always had a way to make life quite interesting, too. I'm actually looking forward to being able to see what this pool experience is all about. We might have to install a pool in our backyard at home," she chuckled as she went back to cleaning up the kitchen. With Lucas there to help, it went rather fast except when they stopped for a kiss or two. They were relaxing on the deck when Noah and Eleanor arrived to visit.

"Esther thinks we may need to install a pool in our backyard at home, Noah. Do you think we'd get enough use out of it in New York? It certainly couldn't be used as long each year as it can be here."

"Maybe you should consider building an indoor pool, Lucas. Would there be a way to add a room to your home? If you could have it heated in the winter and quite a few windows that could be opened in the summer, it might make a great recreation room for the two of you.

Of course, you might have quite a few more visitors than you do now," he chuckled.

"I may talk to an architect and see what we might be able to do. Having visitors come to go swimming might be a plus because it would discourage the bridge players," he chuckled.

"Esther might be a little disappointed, but I'd be delighted because I'm not a very good bridge player."

"You don't enjoy playing bridge, Lucas? I thought it was your idea that we join that weekly boredom. If not, let's definitely look into a pool," she exclaimed.

Jaclyn and Teri were right on time when they arrived that afternoon. The chores were done and Mark and Brad had showered and changed clothes so they would smell a little fresher for the girls. Mark was at the car to welcome them and to take the bouquet of flowers that Jaclyn handed him. "I hope those are all right, Mark. You seemed to be in such a hurry when you called that I didn't have time to ask if there was a special kind of flower your grandmother liked. This is Teri Handley by the way."

"Hi, Teri. Welcome to the ranch. These flowers are great, Jaclyn. Thank you so much for answering my S.O.S. Why don't you both come on in while I give them to my wonderful grandmother? Brad is talking to her about the final months of law school and then, hopefully, coming down here to work with Noah and Jon. I'd thought that was all settled, but I guess I jumped to another conclusion without checking it out first. I don't know why he didn't correct me. That's not the first time I've done that since I got here either."

"My understanding," Jaclyn replied, "is that he has talked to Noah a lot over the last few years and he'll either be working at the law office or at the ranch. It might even be that he'll work part time at both. From what he told me, when we were at the dance in May, he truly loves any of the possibilities as long as he's here in Hayes and can spend time at the ranch. It seems their entire family thrives on this ranch."

"I can't find fault with them for that. It's such a fabulous ranch and the little town is so unique. I wish I could stay here, too."

"It would be great if Brad's father would definitely decide to come here and open his own pediatrics office. We could sure use a doctor specializing in children's health with the town growing like it has for the last few years. They felt so fortunate when Dr. Davis came to help at the Noland Clinic, and I think that was just before my family got to come here. I also heard that Dr. Wilder was the one who introduced him to Dr. Noland after he'd met Neil and Susan one day as they were driving by their house, heard an explosion, and then saw their house on fire. Dr. Wilder actually saved Susan and their baby when he coaxed them from a second floor window."

"There's certainly a lot to learn about this little town." They'd reached the house and Mark held the door for the two girls to enter. Jaclyn had met Esther and Lucas at the wedding so she introduced Teri to them and to Brad. Mark noticed the great big smile Jaclyn had for Brad, and although it tugged at his heart, he knew it would be for the best if that was to become the serious relationship.

A Summer's Adventure

"Hey, Grandma, I had Jaclyn bring you some flowers which are from us guys. You know we appreciate all you do for us around here, but we wanted you to have something to really show how much we love you."

"Oh, Mark, they're beautiful. Thank you, Jaclyn, for doing that for the boys. They will be wonderful on the table tonight because we just got a call from Marge saying they'll be here by supper time."

"That's cool. It'll be great to see them again." Turning back to Brad and the girls, he then asked, "Are you all ready to go riding? Brad and I have the horses picked out and ready to be saddled, so we can be on our way shortly." They all headed for the door after saying a goodbye to the grandparents. Esther slipped the saddlebag full of food into Mark's hand as he again kissed her cheek. "I love you so much, I hope you know that," he whispered and gave her his big happy smile.

"Just be careful on those horses. They are big animals and we've heard what Josh went through when something jumped in the tall grasses. Keep a good hold on the reins."

"Yes, Grandma," he chuckled. "We'll be extra careful so none of us will land in the hospital like Josh did. Just remember, though, his prize for going through that tumble and concussion was Liz. I'd say that wasn't such a bad deal."

"I'd think there'd be easier ways to get a girl to pay attention than getting thrown off a horse, Mark. Just use that sweet personality and dazzling smile of yours," she whispered and grinned as she shooed him out the door. He ran to quickly catch up with the others.

The ride was going well, but it was a pretty warm afternoon. They enjoyed their stop at the pond, wading in the water, and eating the goodies and drinks that Grandma Esther had put in the saddlebag. They debated about riding farther, but finally decided that they'd rather ride back to the barn and then take advantage of the pool. Brad and Mark had succeeded in keeping it a group outing, and the girls acted as if they had possibly decided on the same plan. It was a relaxing and fun afternoon. They'd played a volleyball game in the pool with a beach ball, did some racing in different strokes, and then stretched out on the lounges to soak up some sun. Of course, both girls were very good swimmers and the time had passed quickly. It was soon time to get ready for dinner and dancing.

The two-room suite upstairs was available for the girls to clean up in. Brad and Mark were using the two rooms on one side of the hallway so they shared the bathroom between those two. Of course, Lucas and Esther were still using one of the rooms on the other side of the hallway so the boys were trying to leave the bath on that side just for them.

They were almost ready to leave for the restaurant when Joseph and Marge got there from Colorado Springs. After the greetings, introductions, and receiving the latest update on Mary, they took off. The girls had decided to drive Teri's car back to town, so they met the guys at the Pub and Grub. Since Brad was the only one old enough to order a drink, they by-passed the bar and went directly to the restaurant area where the dance floor was also located.

After they'd ordered their food, Brad asked if anyone would like to dance while they were waiting for it to be served.

"I'd love to," Jaclyn replied quickly and the two of them headed to the dance floor as a slow romantic song was playing.

"I'm not a very good dancer, Teri, but I'm game to give it a try if you are." "Actually, Mark, I'm not a very good dancer either, but if you want to take a chance of me stepping on your toes, I'm game, too."

Mark took her hand in his and was soon holding her rather snugly with his arm across her tiny back and moving to the rhythm of the music as Liz had taught him to do at the recent wedding reception. Teri seemed to move effortlessly and they both surprisingly avoided the other's toes.

"Hey, we aren't doing too badly for our first dance, are we?" Mark chuckled and then glanced down into her beautiful green eyes as she tilted her head to look up at him.

"No, we're doing pretty well, but with you holding me as tightly as you are, I can't do much but move when and where you do," she giggled.

"That's a trick I learned from watching some of the dancers at a reception I attended recently. Would you like for me to let you loose? I'd really hate to, you know, because I'm really getting into the feel of you in my arms."

"Well, since there is still some of this song left, I'd like to finish that, at least." "Good," he murmured as he pulled her even closer. He could feel her heart beating at a pretty rapid rate, and he knew his was responding, too. Her small but well formed breasts that he had, of course, noticed in her swimsuit, were against his chest. *This is a very pretty girl,* he was thinking, *although her coloring and hair are just the opposite of Jaclyn's.* Teri's hair was cut quite short and it framed her face with little ringlets of blonde curls. She had the cutest nose and small appealing lips that he wanted to put his lips against, but he decided to resist that urge. *This dating game isn't bad at all, but I think there could possibly be even more girls I'd like to meet at college before I make my pick since it appears I've definitely lost Jaclyn.*

Without even realizing it, they had danced to three songs when they finally noticed the server was heading toward their table with a tray of food. They saw that Brad and Jaclyn were also making their way back in that direction.

The conversation was non-stop as everyone seemed to have questions for each other about what was going on in their lives. They learned that Teri had just moved here with her parents from a little farming town in southern Illinois, and she had graduated from high school in May. Her father had been hired as the new principal of the Hayes High School as well as coach of the football team. Teri is now enrolled at her father's Alma Mater and in a couple of weeks would be heading to her grandparents' home in Youngstown, Ohio.

Mark almost choked on the bite of food he'd just put in his mouth. "We won't be that far away from each other," he muttered as he finally swallowed the food and took a drink of water. Brad was chuckling at the apparent interest Mark was showing in Teri's direction, and Mark gave him a 'watch it, buddy' look. "Well, it's certainly not as far as Colorado," he quietly remarked with an exasperated sigh.

"Where are you going to college, Mark?" Teri then asked.

"I'm enrolled at Amherst."

"Oh, that's really a great school. I had a Sunday school teacher who had gone there, and he was always giving it very high ratings."

"Yeah, my whole family has gone to Amherst which includes my grandpa and my grandma, my dad and mom, my brother and my sister, and now me. I think my aunt and my great grandfather and grandmother went there, too, but my uncle and two cousins went to West Point."

"That's quite a testimonial for the school," she grinned.

The conversation continued to give Teri the information on Brad and his plans for the future, and then Jaclyn remarked, "Well, it's obvious where I'll be this next year, but after I graduate from high school, I don't know where my future will take me. I doubt if it'll include college because my folks lost everything in the hurricane, and it has been quite a struggle to get back on their feet. If it hadn't been for Jon and Christy and Mr. Hayes, I don't know where my family would be now."

"College isn't for everyone, Jaclyn," Teri commented. "If there were more kids in my family, I most likely wouldn't be going to college either. I just happen to be an only child and an only grandchild on my dad's side, so my grandparents are paying most of my college tuition. I want to be a teacher and that means a lot to them since they were both professors and, of course, my dad was also a teacher before he became a principal. He has always loved small towns, but that isn't where the higher paying jobs are in education."

They had ordered pie ala mode for dessert, and after Brad and Mark had a few more dances with the girls, they decided it was time to call it a night. They awkwardly stood at Teri's car, not wanting to say goodbye, but finally Brad took Jaclyn in his arms and kissed her cheek. He then did the same to Teri. "They're all yours now, Mark," he chuckled as he started walking toward his car.

"Brad and I will call you two and try to get together again before we all have to leave for college, except Jaclyn. It's been a fun time and has given me nice memories to take with me, but I guess I'd better say goodnight before Brad goes off without me." He had hesitantly taken Teri's hand in his but then kissed it and did the same to Jaclyn's. He was embarrassed as he turned and quickly took off toward Brad's car, but thoughts were certainly racing through his head. *I am so confused. I now realize I like both of the girls, but I don't have any idea of what to do about it. Surely I'm not going to fall for every girl I hold in my arms, but does just a nice friendship give you these feelings of not wanting to leave them?*

Mark hasn't dated very much, has he?" Teri commented to Jaclyn as they pulled away from the restaurant. "His kiss goodnight on our hands was certainly a lot different from most guys these days, but it was rather sweet. Of course, Brad kissing our cheek wasn't exactly the usual thing these days either," she chuckled.

"Mark asked me to go to the movie with him last Sunday, and I think our date was the first for both of us. It was rather awkward, but he is a remarkable guy and that night I got a nice gentle kiss. Of course, what do I know about kissing? I only know he made tingles go all over me. It was funny how he resorted to kissing our hands tonight," she giggled.

"Since you were dancing with Brad more than Mark tonight, I wonder what your true feelings are toward Mark. When he mentioned that we wouldn't be too far away from each other in college, I got the feeling that he might like to continue a friendship, or possibly even something more. That is, unless I'm stepping where I shouldn't be at all."

"Mark means a lot to me, Teri, because he was able to help me get over a fear of guys after an experience I'd had in New Orleans. We've remarked about the distance that's going to separate us, but there are e-mails and telephones to keep in touch. It just doesn't seem too logical, though, when he has so many years of college left. Brad, on the other hand, is almost finished with his schooling and will be working here in Hayes, but I don't have the rapport with him that I have with Mark. I really don't know how to answer your question, Teri. It is really so confusing."

"I think I understand, Jaclyn, so let's just leave it at that for now. I'm not thinking about anything serious during my first year of college, and I felt that Mark was having the same kind of thoughts. There's plenty of time to discover everyone's true feelings. It's getting late and we both have to work again tomorrow."

CHAPTER NINETEEN

In the church service on Sunday, the pastor's message had been based on the many miracles of Jesus, which Mark enjoyed very much. Several familiar hymns had been sung and the anthem was a wonderful version of The Ninety and Nine.

After the service, goodbyes were said to Esther, along with a few tears, since Lucas and Mark were going to take her to Colorado Springs where she would catch her plane back home. Lucas had decided they would have lunch at the restaurant up on the highway, which he and Mark had stopped at on their way to Hayes from Pueblo that eventful Friday because they'd felt they might still be too early to invade the small town. It wouldn't be as emotional for any of them, either, as it would've been if they'd stayed in Hayes.

Lucas sure hated sending her home alone, but she'd done quite a bit of flying over the years, when she'd gone to see her parents, so she knows her way around the airports quite well.

She has a stop-over in Minneapolis and Buffalo, but James, Ann, Stephen, or Deborah will be there to pick her up when she arrives in Jamestown.

Her flight left at 4:12 so it was after 6:30 by the time Lucas and Mark got back to Hayes. They slipped into the cafe for a quick meal before going on to the ranch, and Brent had just started to play his guitar to entertain the family when they arrived. A guitar was quickly handed to Mark and the music really began. When Noah and Eleanor finally got up and started home, he remarked, "We were just making sure you got home safely. We're going to miss that sweet wife of yours, Lucas, and I'm afraid this means it won't be long until you and Mark will be leaving us, too.

"I think we'll stay another week, if we haven't worn out our welcome, and then I do need to get back to work and Mark has to get ready to start college. I thought I might go to the office with you tomorrow and see what kind of monkey business you guys get into out here in the West," he chuckled.

"Be glad to have you. We'll see you in the morning then. Will Esther be calling to let you know she's home safely?"

"Yes, she should be home by 9:30 or 10:00 Colorado time, so I'll read and not call it a night until I hear from her. Sleep well, you two."

It was actually after 11 o'clock when his phone finally rang. Lucas had been pacing the floor for the last hour. "Hello, Lucas," he heard her tired and agitated voice coming over the line. "There was about an hour's delay in Minneapolis but now it appears that there could be a wait here in Buffalo of several hours. I guess someone forgot all about the six of us going on down to Jamestown and a commuter flight was apparently not scheduled. I talked to James and we decided that I'll just take a cab on home when I get in. It's ridiculous to have him stay up for such a foolish mistake, or whatever it is. Actually, they told us very little except that there was a chance that there could be a considerable delay because a plane had not yet arrived to take us on to our destination."

"I'm so sorry, Sweetheart. I was getting quite concerned when it was after 11 o'clock here and I still hadn't heard from you. I hope you can sleep later in the morning."

"Well, it's after 1:20 here now so I'm sure I'll sleep later in the morning if none of the family calls just to make sure

I'm home," she chuckled. "Oh, Sweetheart, they're calling out something about a flight to Jamestown, so I've got to go. I don't know what this is all about, but I'll give you all the details when I call you tomorrow, after I get up, that is. Maybe the plane was just late in arriving. Bye, Dear."

"Goodnight, Sweetheart. I'll say a prayer for a safe trip. I love you."

Richard Adams was really nervous as he waited for Noah to arrive at the office the next morning. He'd been out of the office the day Lucas and Mark arrived, but he'd heard all the wonderful news of the lost being found. He had just been biding his time because he hadn't wanted to put any more pressure on the family dealing with the new arrivals, the wedding, and then the sudden illness of Noah's granddaughter, but he had some exciting news of his own that he had to share with Noah.

He was again a little hesitant when he realized that Lucas had come to the office today with Noah, but he was determined to get this done. He hadn't seen any early appointments on the schedule so he made his way toward Noah's office. He was a little apprehensive as to how Noah might take the news, but he didn't think it would be any big deal, especially since Jon had been doing a great job. He rapped on the door that stood ajar, and Noah immediately invited him in." Good morning, Richard, what are you up to this morning? This is Lucas Gillette, and he wanted to come with me to see what kind of monkey business we carry on around here. So, what can I do for you?"

"I'd like to talk to you about something that I feel is quite important, Noah, if you have time. Good morning, Sir,

I'm sorry I wasn't in the office the day you and your grandson sent the Hayes family into quite a celebration."

"Is this about a client, Richard, or is it personal? Should I send Lucas over to see Jon while we have this talk?"

"I don't mind if Lucas stays, but it does concern my future with the firm."

"Oh, well, have a seat and let's hear what you have to tell us."

"If you remember, I had been on a short vacation the week that Mr. Gillette and his grandson arrived. I had been visiting with different members of my family, but especially an uncle who had asked that I meet with him. I think I've mentioned, over the years, about this uncle who owned a small law firm in northern Colorado. Well, he wants to retire around the first of the year, and he's offering the firm to me, almost free of charge, as I'm the only other member in the family who is practicing law. You know my son had enough credits to graduate from college early and is now attending law school. He's ecstatic that I'll have a place for him to practice when he's finished with his studies. I realize that I have only a small investment in this firm, but I was wondering if you'd be willing to buy my share to help me get started with a few changes I would like to make in my new firm."

"Richard Adams, this is the most exciting news since our relatives walked in here from New York, but I guess that hasn't been so extremely long ago. How were you able to keep such a wonderful happening quiet all this time--it's been almost six weeks."

"It hasn't been easy, Noah," he chuckled. "If I hadn't been so busy with that one case, I probably would've found myself at your door much sooner. So, do you think we can work out some kind of a deal?"

"Of course, we can work out a deal. It's amazing how God works everything out for us, isn't it? I'd been wondering if we'd have enough business to include Brad when he graduates in December, and here you are opening up a space for him. When were you going to walk out on us?"

"My uncle wants to be retired about the middle of December so he can make plans to take his wife and married children on a cruise over the holidays. His thought was to close the office for vacation, and then I would open it after the holidays. Of course, that is up to me. I can keep it open if I'd like, but a nice leisurely vacation sounds pretty good to me, too. I'll most likely spend some of that time making the changes I want in the office, though, before I buckle down to a full-time one-man office until my son can join me."

"We have a little while to work out the details then. I'll get Susan started on some of the paperwork, and then we'll get an audit done. You've done a marvelous job for the firm, Richard, and we'll see that you are rewarded for your service. Of course, we'll miss you, but this is an opportunity you couldn't turn down."

"Thanks, Noah. I have a client coming this afternoon and I have some preparing to do, so I'll let you show Mr. Gillette how you spend your day. It was nice meeting you, Sir." He was up and out of the office before anymore could be said.

"We certainly have an awesome God, don't we, Lucas? What could we possibly do to top a miracle like that?"

"I think it's great that it will be a one family operation, Noah. It's unusual, though, that there will be three different surnames on the plaque when it's all family members."

"You're right, but I'll take them anyway I can get them," Noah chuckled.

The intercom broke in just then and Noah answered. "Mr. Hayes, there are two men out here who are ready to come to blows about something, but I can't understand what.

. . . . .

"I'll be right there, Amy," he interrupted. "Come on, Lucas, I may need you to help prevent a duel right out here in our waiting room."

When they opened the office door and started toward the front of the building, they could hear the loud yelling and arguing between two men who they could see were dressed in overalls, short-sleeved shirts, and straw hats--one somewhat older than the other.

"Hey, hey, hey," Noah called, "Let's calm down here and discuss your differences like grown, civilized men, shall we?"

Noah took the arm of the older man to try to calm him, and then Lucas quickly grabbed the younger man's arm from behind as it appeared he was preparing to land a punch either on the man Noah was holding, or on Noah himself. He was yelling, "Don't insult me by referring to me with the same description as him."

"All right," Noah remarked, "Let's discuss your differences like a grown man and a little boy, and I don't really care which is which. If you can't behave, we'll just call the police over here and you can talk through the bars of a cell. Now, which do you want?"

"I'll talk to you," the older man quickly spoke up, but the young one just stood rigid in Lucas's hold and glared at everyone.

"Where's that young one who works here?" he finally asked. "He's got more sense than any of you old guys. I talked to him the other day at the cafe, and he said he'd be glad to check it out if I wanted him to."

Noah turned to ask Christy where Jon was but she wasn't at her desk, either.

He then looked at Beth and asked, "Do you know where Jon and Christy are?"

"They're both over at the Court House checking out some records on a case. They also thought they might do some checking into the complaint of one farmer against another for letting some cattle get into his meadow. Ooooh," she moaned.

"So, you have already talked to Jon about this problem, I see. Are you wishing to retain him as your lawyer, or do you want to discuss it with each other and come to a conclusion that will satisfy both of you?"

Before there was an answer, the door opened and Jon and Christy walked in. "Well," Noah exclaimed, "just the one we've been looking for, it seems. These gentlemen decided to bring their quarrel to our office and almost came to blows. We just learned that the one had talked to you the other day at the cafe. Do you have any advice or answers for them?"

"I just may have, Noah. Christy and I decided to run out to the property to see what the circumstances were, and we were able to give it some perspective. Let's all go back to the conference room, if you don't mind, so we can get comfortable." He led the way back to the room at the back of the building and motioned for every one to take a seat.

"Now, as I said, Christy and I went out to the two farms. We found a fairly large gap in the fence where the cattle apparently got out of the pasture. Normally that would be a sign of neglectful farming. However. . ."

"See, I told you it was all your fault, you old goat," the young man shouted. "Just a minute, I'm not finished," Jon stopped him by holding up his hand.

"Normally, I said, this would be a sign of neglectful farming. However, when I looked at the other sections of fence as far as I could see, they were in excellent shape, so I took a closer look at the fence at the gap sight. Christy and I both feel that the fence had been cut, not old and neglected, so we want to ask you, Mr. Stellar, if you've taken a count or inventory of your stock since they're back in protective quarters?"

"Yes, I actually did, Mr. Holcomb, and I can't account for two of my cows that were about ready to calve. I've been out looking for them every day because I thought they may have bedded down in a soft patch of grass along the creek, but I haven't seen hide nor hair of them. I hadn't given a thought to maybe they'd been stolen."

"We'll get back to that problem in a few minutes, but Christy and I then went to the other farm and found the gate to the meadow wide open and a young boy, about 10 or so, was riding his small cycle all around the edge of the meadow. We motioned for him to come over to us.

He was very helpful when we asked if he knew about the claim of cattle getting into the meadow. Without hesitation, he said it was his fault. He said he was allowed to ride there so he wasn't on the road. He'd been out there several times, but one day he had forgotten to close the gate. When he went out the next day, he saw the cattle and immediately reported it to his father. He said he told his father right then that he had mistakenly left the gate open and apologized for the trouble it had caused.

So, in my most humble opinion, Gentlemen, I think the guilt of this incident is pretty much shared by both of you. Although I don't think the damage of the fence was your fault, Mr. Stellar, it is your fence and it should be repaired quickly and satisfactorily, and a father of a young boy, Mr Sanford, needs to start listening to his son instead of trying to make someone else pay for a son's mistake. It also might be wise for you to check on exactly what your son is doing occasionally and make sure all is well at the end of the day. If you are still going to file a complaint, Mr. Sanford, then the Judge will hear your case when he comes to hold court in a couple of weeks. You may set up an appointment if you'd like our firm to represent you.

Are there any questions?" Not waiting long, he continued. "If not, I'll charge you both a fee for my time doing the inspection this morning. I hope you can become good neighbors who will try to work out problems calmly and non- judgmental in the future. It would be nice if you would start by helping each other settle this one. Maybe you could take time to mend that gap in the fence together and then a reasonable compensation for the damage to the meadow would help mend the hard feelings. That's all I have to say. You may see the girls in the office to settle your account, Mr. Sanford, but I'd like to talk with you, Mr. Stellar, if you'd like some help in finding your cows or the culprit who took them. I'll be right back and you may wait in here if you have a few minutes to discuss it with me. If not, you may come along and see the girls in the office." Jon held the door for Mr. Sanford, but Mr. Stellar remained sitting, so he quickly went to his office where he entered information in the computer that the girls would need.

"Well, what do you know about that?" Lucas exclaimed as he and Noah returned to Noah's office. "You've got an attorney for sure in that boy when he can have the answers before a complaint has even been filed."

"I saw the quality of his expertise in his resume and then I was completely sold on him when we'd finished our interview," and Noah proudly added. "I snatched him up quickly even if it was against my sweet granddaughter's protests."

"And I was finally smart enough to accept his love and his proposal," Christy giggled as she headed to her desk and the other work that was waiting for her. She stopped just long enough at her husband's office door, however, to blow him a kiss. He smiled and mouthed an "I Love You" but he was now heading back to talk to Mr. Stellar.

"I love him so much," she murmured as she continued down the hall, "and it might be about time to see if I can let him know just how much in a very meaningful way. He has been so considerate, and patient, and loving as I've wanted to continue my career, but I'm hoping I can surprise him with the one thing he wants so badly." She could hardly contain her giggle as she sat down at her desk and studied the papers in front of her.

She'd noticed that Amy and Beth had gone for a break shortly after she had come to the office area, so she quickly picked up the phone and dialed a number. An appointment was then made that concerned a note she'd had on her calendar. Another note made her flinch, however, as it reminded her that she hadn't finished typing the deposition she had taken on Friday. She needed to get that done pronto, so her mind was soon on what had to be done today. It wasn't unusual for her to be humming softly while she was typing, but she actually surprised herself when she realized it was a well-known lullaby today.

CHAPTER TWENTY

Brad and Mark made plans to take Jaclyn and Teri to see the new movie, Hancock, that was showing at their theater Tuesday night. They expected Josh and Liz back home from their honeymoon sometime tomorrow so they didn't know what the rest of the week would be like at the ranch. Since Mark and his grandpa were heading back to New York next Monday, they'd decided this might be the last time Mark would get to see the two girls.

They were both waiting for them at Jaclyn's. Since Brad had wanted to drive his car, the girls got into the back seat and the guys stayed in the front. When they got to the theater, though, Brad took Jaclyn's hand and headed inside. Mark smiled at Teri and remarked, "I guess that leaves you and me together again. I hope you don't mind."

"Of course not, Mark. In fact, I wanted to give you my address in Ohio, but I didn't know if I should do it in front of Jaclyn. I'll give it to you now so it doesn't cause a scene later. I'm not asking you to call or e-mail me anytime soon, because I know we'll both be busy trying to get adjusted to college life, but if you should ever like to just talk or e-mail about anything, I'd always be happy to hear from you."

"Thanks, Teri. I *will* have my sister in the same college, so I suppose my parents will ask her to keep tabs on me, but I'd like to talk to you occasionally." He tucked the bit of paper in his pocket. "I've promised sweet little Jaclyn," he chuckled, "that I'll keep in touch with her, too, but I'm wondering if she'll have any time for me when Brad gets here in December to start working at the Law Office. Did she happen to tell you about our first meeting in the grocery store?" he chuckled.

"Yes, she did, and just a little about your first date, too," she smiled. "I think she's a little confused right now about her feelings, but Brad seems to be making the decisions for her tonight. Jaclyn told me that she likes you very much and that you helped her with some kind of problem she was having. But, she also loves to dance with Brad although the rapport is not quite as good. Since she's been able to confide in you, it might help her a lot if you could talk or e-mail back and forth, if it's only to listen and give her assurance that all is well. Being the oldest sibling with no big sister to talk to, it's hard at times to figure things out. As you know, I'm an only child, but I've been so lucky to have a young mother who is like a big sister. I can talk to her about anything, so far at least."

"You certainly don't seem concerned about your future. Do you already have a guy waiting for you at college or somewhere else?"

"No, Mark, I don't. I feel that this is going to be my first year away from home, and I expect to be very busy checking out a lot of people, studies, and other activities, so I'm really not thinking about concentrating on a boyfriend, per se. I really would, however, like to continue our friendship, if possible, because I've enjoyed your company, your attitude toward things, and your thoughts of the future. Right now, I feel that if something were to develop some day between us, I would be very receptive to it, but a lot can happen in four years."

"Thanks, Teri. You are so right, but I think they're waiting for us to go to the movie now," he chuckled. He put his hand to the small of her back and they walked into the theater lobby where they bought some popcorn and a drink. Mark then led the way to find a seat, but then let Teri enter the row first. It wasn't a surprise that Jaclyn was sitting next to him and then Brad. It was, however, a surprise when her hand found his after he'd finished sharing a bag of popcorn with Teri. Glancing to see if she was holding Brad's hand, too, he found her other one was in her lap. *What is she doing? Is this what they sometimes refer to as 'possessiveness'?* Of course, he couldn't stop a grin as he again thought about their first meeting and the mistakes he'd made on their first and only date. He decided if she was going to hold his one hand, he would hold Teri's with his other. He wasn't going to show any favoritism tonight.

Of course, Teri could see what he was doing. She poked him in the ribs with her elbow as he took her hand and squeezed it gently. She glanced at him and smiled as he whispered in her ear. "I feel like the thorn between two roses, but I don't know which one to kiss."

"Neither one," she whispered back. "It'll all work out. I just hope Brad doesn't get hurt by her actions tonight."

Luckily Brad was fully engrossed with the movie and wasn't paying any attention to the things going on around him. *No wonder he hasn't had much luck with girls. Maybe I'll see if I might help my cousin learn a few little tricks on getting attention from the pretty girls. I wish I had brought one or two of my brother's magazines with me, but I can't understand why Brad hasn't been introduced to those during six or more years of college. Has he had his nose in a text book 24/7?*

Jaclyn finally nudged Mark to get his attention. "I have to see you alone before you and your grandpa leave. O.K.?" she whispered.

"I'll see what I can do," he whispered back as he pulled his hand away from hers. It was almost the end of the movie, and Teri had removed her hand, too. Earlier, Brad and Mark had talked about going to the Pub and Grub for something to eat and some dancing after the movie, and when they suggested it to the girls, they were very agreeable.

Brad is a very different person on the dance floor, and he had Jaclyn laughing, smiling, and definitely enjoying all the swings, twirls, and dips he was so good at doing. "He sure has the moves on the dance floor that make me so jealous," Mark remarked to Teri as they sat and watched several couples that were taking advantage of the music, both fast and slow. "Well, what do you think, Teri? Shall we try to burst their bubble with our special brand of dancing?" he chuckled.

"Why not?" she grinned. A fast song was playing and they were soon into the beat of the music and really having fun. Mark always remembers what Liz had told him about moving and swaying to the rhythm and Teri apparently knew that trick, too. The next selection was a beautiful love song, so Mark held her very close as he had the other time they'd been together, and they were soon dancing cheek to cheek.

"This is nice, Teri," Mark whispered as his lips touched her cheek. "I could get used to this dancing, especially with you. Do you suppose they'll have some special dances at college that we could attend together?"

"I'd love that, Mark. We'll have to watch the schedules." They returned to their table after that song ended, and Brad and Jaclyn soon joined them.

"I want to dance with Mark before we leave," Jaclyn exclaimed as she sat down and took a sip of her drink. "It's almost time for him to go back to New York, and I have only danced with him once or maybe twice."

"No one said you couldn't dance with him, Jaclyn," Brad retorted with just a little bit of sarcasm, or was it jealousy, in his voice. "I'd like to dance with Teri, too."

Everyone was rather quiet as they ate their sandwiches and fries. Mark looked at Teri as he sipped from the straw in his glass of lemonade, and what he saw was that understanding smile still on her face. He felt a strong need to get better acquainted and maybe that could be accomplished when they get to college. He then glanced at Jaclyn and the tingles and flutters were there as exciting as ever. *Is every girl I get close to anymore going to cause my hormones to act up in different ways? The next few years are going to be exciting ones, I guess, if there are very many girls around that I love to look at.*

Jaclyn was now on her feet and reaching for Mark's hand. "Are you ready to dance with me, Mark?" she asked a little hesitantly. She'd noticed the look he'd given Teri while he was eating, and she wasn't sure what it all meant. Had Teri so quickly stolen his attention that she was beginning to value so much? Brad had hardly given her a chance to talk to Mark on Saturday or tonight, so she certainly hopes he'll come see her alone before he leaves town.

"I'm certainly willing to give it a try, Jaclyn, although it'll be quite different from Brad's style. Are you going to dance with Teri, then?" Mark looked at Brad with the question.

"Yes, I've been looking forward to the opportunity, if she's willing."

"I'll be happy to give it a try, Brad, although I'm not the dancer Jaclyn is. Did you teach her some of those steps when you took her to the two dances last school year?"

"She's told you all about that, huh? Did she also tell you about Mark sweeping her off her feet when he arrived in town?"

"That wasn't exactly how she described their first meeting or their first date, Brad, but I do think she feels close to Mark now because she found him so easy to talk to. Have you been willing to listen to her problems and show concern about what she's been through?"

"No, I guess I haven't. I've only tried to entertain her with dancing because it was what she seemed to enjoy. Should I come right out and ask her if she's having problems?"

"Oh, Brad, I'm no counselor or advisor to the lovelorn, but most girls like to talk about themselves if given a chance. Ask her what she likes to do, does she have a hobby, does she like her work, does she get along with her brothers and even her parents. Get to know her and also tell her about yourself. Open up as you would to Mark or your own sisters."

"That hasn't happened too often. Mary and Liz were always close and since I was a little older, I felt like I was an outsider most of the time. Liz spent quite a bit of time with me, but we didn't talk about much serious stuff. I told Mark the other day that I was probably the one who needs to change after I told him he seemed like such a casual sonofagun and I sure wondered what kind of an attorney he was going to make. Am I doomed for an uneventful and dull life?"

"I wouldn't think so, Brad. You seem to have many interests, from what I've observed, like the ranch, riding, swimming, and goofing around, movies, reading, eating, and dancing, as well as your studies to become an attorney. That's a good start and you can add to it as you get more acquainted with Jaclyn. Maybe the two of you could drive over to Pueblo, go down to the lake, take a walk around town holding hands, and don't forget to ask her how school is going. She's definitely concerned about this year with Liz gone, so maybe you could give her a call once or twice a week until you come here in December. Of course, you must remember this year's Christmas dance and offer to be her escort.. Is that enough to get you started?" she giggled. "And can you believe we didn't step on each other's toes even once?"

"You are super, Teri. I wish you a lot of luck at college this year and maybe Mark will keep in touch."

The dance was over and it was time to call it a night. Brad and Mark drove the girls to their respective homes and then headed for the ranch. They both had been rather quiet until Brad asked, "Mark, did Jaclyn say anything to you that I should know about?"

"Not really, Brad. She asked if I would come see her by myself before Grandpa and I take off next week. I didn't promise but told her I would try. I do want to stay close friends with her. After all, she was my first heart throb and I still don't know where it's going to end. My heart still jumps every time I look at her."

"That's what scares me. Teri should be a counselor, you know? She gave me a bunch of ideas for getting more acquainted and closer to Jaclyn, and to get out of my shell. I guess when I'm off the dance floor I've been pretty dull, but I'm going to be working on that so you'd better watch out."

"That's great, Brad. I like competition," he chuckled. "My suggestion is to get the girl talking. Ask her to tell you about what it was like in New Orleans and how she has made the transition to Hayes. She really has some very interesting stories about her life and what her dreams are. She can also give you a pretty good history of the people and the town of Hayes after being here for such a short time. I hope you know your way around better than I do, or she may have you way off course if you let her get to talking," he chuckled.

"Thanks, Mark. I'm going to try to become more like the rest of you guys, and maybe it'll be easier when I get down here in December and can be with Brent and Josh. Josh is so much fun to be around and seems to be a natural clown. I'm hoping Jon will also give me some examples about how to be a good lawyer but also a happy-go-lucky guy."

"Well, I guess we made it all in one piece. I hope you enjoyed yourself tonight because I really did have a good time. Thanks for driving and I guess I'll see you early in the morning since those chores will be waiting for another day, at least. I wonder what time Josh and Liz will get home."

"They're flying into Denver so I imagine it will be late afternoon before they get down here. Goodnight, Mark."

"I'm so glad I'll get to see them again before Grandpa and I leave. Goodnight now and I hope you have sweet dreams," he chuckled.

CHAPTER TWENTY-ONE

It was a busy day at the ranch on Wednesday as everyone was helping prepare a big and exciting party for Josh and Liz. The meat was marinated, the grills were cleaned and ready to fire up, the ice cream makers were in position to start the handles turning, the chores were done, and everyone was cleaned up and waiting, including the final three of the Becker family who had arrived from Colorado Springs. Mary had recuperated enough that she was determined to be there to welcome her sister home.

About 6:15 someone on patrol duty yelled that the car was coming down the road, and by the time it was turning into the drive, the whole family was standing in the yard ready for hugs and welcomes. It was quite a reunion. No one had mentioned Mary's surgery when Josh or Liz had called from Hawaii, but it took only one glance for Liz to know something had happened. She was beside her sister immediately and had to hear the entire story. "Why didn't someone tell me?" she wailed.

"You were on your honeymoon, Liz, and we weren't about to disrupt that after all the years you two had waited to get yourselves hitched," her father teased as he took her in his arms to welcome her home. "Mary is fine, but she just needs a few more days before she'll have all of her strength back. We have to thank Josh for inviting Dr. and Mrs. Wilder to the wedding and reception, however, because precious time was saved with him being in Hayes."

The entire evening was a gala affair, Josh and Liz were so tan and so extremely happy, but the jet lag finally took its toll. "This will be continued tomorrow," Joseph laughed as the newlyweds started off to spend their first night in their new home. They will find oodles of flowers and the new 5 and 10" round electric candles to welcome them in the living room and the master bedroom, and the coffee pot is timed for making their morning coffee. A cute hand-made sign "WELCOME HOME" was attached to a kitchen cupboard under which Eleanor had placed one of her yummy homemade coffee cakes on one of their wedding gifts--a pedestal cake plate with a pretty glass-domed cover. All is so well at the Haven of Rest Ranch tonight because all of the family is safely home

Brad and Mark were up bright and early Thursday morning, as usual, to help Brent with the chores. They'd both given Josh orders to sleep off the jet lag before thinking about coming to the barn. It wasn't long after 8 o'clock, though, that he came dashing in with a big smile on his face and a silly remark on his lips. "I've really, really missed this place," he kept repeating as he went to pet a few of the horses and to say thanks again to the guys, which included the hired hands, Jake and Guy. These two workers had grown very fond of Josh and respected him a lot since he'd come to run the ranch for Brent a little over two years ago. That was when Joseph had his heart attack.

One of them approached now with a package in his hand. "Josh, we wanted to get you and Liz something, but we didn't know exactly what you'd want or need. We finally decided this might be appreciated by both of you. It's not one of those fancy wedding gifts, but if you'll open it now, you can decide whether to take it to the house or leave it here in the barn."

"You guys are the greatest, but I didn't expect any gift from you. You really have my curiosity aroused, though, because it's quite heavy. Let's see what you've bought us." When he'd gotten it unwrapped and the box opened, he really had to laugh. "Liz will love this, and I'm sure she'll have it right up by the kitchen door. She'll make sure I use it every time I enter the house whether I need to or not. This really looks like a great one, and it should keep my boots clean from any barnyard residue. Not only does it have a scraper, but also a stiff brush to do the job really well. Thanks so much, you guys." He gave them both a hug. which was just a little embarrassing to the hired hands.

He then turned to Brent. "Well, what can I do to help this morning? I sure hope you haven't done so well while I was gone that you don't need me anymore."

'These two were good substitutes, Josh, but they'll both be leaving us soon, and no one could completely replace you. You've become a valuable asset to the Haven of Rest Ranch, and we're all looking forward to you getting back on the job. Why don't we four go for a ride and check out the grazing cattle? We'll let Jake and Guy make sure the water troughs are full, and also see that the three horses are ready for the students later this morning. We should be back within an hour and a half."

Noah had driven home for lunch Thursday, and everyone gathered on the deck to visit some more since the days were quickly slipping by. David has to return to

Colorado Springs tomorrow morning because of a little boy in critical condition, but Rachel and Mary are going to stay over the weekend to say their last goodbyes to Mark and Lucas.

A little later Josh wanted to go swimming so Mary and Susan agreed to sit on the deck surrounding the pool while the rest of them were in the water. They found a shady spot under the tall trees, and a wonderful breeze was blowing to keep them cool. Josh and Liz had learned some new strokes from the Hawaiian natives so they put on quite a show. Then there was a big water fight, some volley ball and some really competitive races. As Mark watched Brad, Josh, and Liz doing a sidestroke race, he was really amazed at the strength Liz demonstrated in her swimming. He was remembering the stories that Christy had told about Liz when she'd finally joined them in the pool and on the tennis court, and he could certainly believe them after seeing her in action. *Man, would I like to find a girl like her, but, I must say, Jaclyn wasn't bad in the pool either. Is she going to be available, though, for very long?*

Brent and Mark got pulled in to compete in the backstroke with Josh and Brad, and Mark found himself struggling to keep up. *I'm going to find a pool at college this year so I'll be able to do better against these cousins of mine. It isn't fair that they have this beautiful pool available to them almost all spring, summer and fall out here in beautiful Colorado.*

Noah had come to the pool to inform them that he was taking Lucas, Joseph, and David for a ride down to the lake. "Have you boys taken Jaclyn and Teri down there yet?" he asked Brad and Mark as he stood watching a front crawl race between Josh and Liz. He was smiling as he saw Liz pulling ahead of her handsome new husband. *That's not good, though,* he was thinking as he realized what was happening. Then he saw Josh get a second wind and win by several strokes. Of course, Noah wondered if Josh really did win or did Liz let him. *She's a very smart gal, and she'll do well at keeping her husband happy.*

Mark discovered that there was a telephone in the bath house, so he called Jaclyn to see about when they could get together. She would be working in the morning tomorrow so they planned to meet about 2 o'clock. He wanted to keep his evenings open for the family since that was the only time he got to see Christy and Jon.

About 10 o'clock Friday morning Christy told Amy and Beth that she had a few final things to check at the City Hall for the report she was working on, and she should be back in an hour or so. She walked toward that building and it was great that the entrance was on Monroe Street because she felt it would be completely blocked from being seen from the Law Office.

She was soon past there, though, and also past the Library, where she turned onto South Broad Street and in front of the Dr. Noland and Dr. Davis Medical Center. She was so apprehensive when she opened the door, but she had to find out if her suspicions were correct. She hadn't even told Jon that she suspected something wonderful had happened although they had talked about having a baby. She just wanted to be sure before she said anything to him or the family.

She was greeted by Dr. Noland's nurse and immediately taken back to one of the newer examining rooms. Of course, she was instructed to undress and slip on one of those real cute show-all gowns she was handed. "The doctor will be in to see you shortly," she'd promised but Christy had heard a lot of people complain about the waiting time for doctors so she picked up a rather new magazine to pass the time. In less than five minutes, a little knock sounded on the door and Dr. Noland entered with a big grin on his face.

"Christy Holcomb, it's been too long since I've seen you here, you know. If I'm not mistaken, you forgot your annual check-up last year so we've got some catching up to do. Did you come in to get that done, or could it be that you want to be checked for something a little more special?" he chuckled.

"How can you read people's thoughts so well, Dr. Noland? You haven't looked at my chart yet, apparently, because you were able to take a vacation last year and I visited with Dr. Davis while you were gone. I think I'm up to date on all my required tests and shots."

He sat down and studied her file. "I guess you're telling me the truth, Christy, so is this little visit what I think it is?"

"Yes, and let's get to it so I can get back to the office before I'm missed. I want to be able to tell Jon in private before the whole town knows," she giggled.

After lunch, Mark took Grandpa's car and headed for Jaclyn's. He was so excited about getting to see her alone again that his heart was beating out of control. *I thought I'd decided to consider this a summer romance,* he chided himself as he got closer and closer to the girl who had stolen his heart the moment he'd seen her. *I've got to remember the conversation Brad and I had, though, because he has feelings for her, too.*

She was ready and waiting when he got to the door. He'd decided that they would drive down to the lake where he thought they might have a little more privacy, and Grandpa had said they should go there with the girls. Of course, the middle of the day wasn't really a time for any real romance, but if they were lucky and were alone down there, he just might get a few of her kisses before he has to leave for home.

He turned down Wilder Road to drive past Dr. Paul Wilder's magnificent home and there were also some beautiful horses, fabulous scenery, and a couple of nice looking farms to see before reaching Lakewood Drive. The lake wasn't too far from where the two roads meet.

It was a beautiful area and the landscaping was still lush and green even with the warm and dry days they'd been having. They walked down to the beach, slipped off their shoes and waded into the cool water. They'd brought a blanket from the car and were soon lying on it close to the water. "Mark, it's going to be so lonely without you here," Jaclyn was almost in tears as she turned on her side to look at him. "How are we going to stay in touch, especially the way I want to? I suppose you and Teri will get together out there in the East, and I'll be stuck here all alone."

"You'll have Brad to keep you company, Jaclyn. You know he'll be coming down here to stay and work in December. Won't you like that?"

"Not as much as if it were you. He sort of took over the last couple of times we've been together and you seemed happy to be with Teri. Do you really like her, Mark?"

"I like both of you, Cutie. You know how I fell for you the first time I set eyes on you, but I've begun to realize that we are both too young to be getting real serious. Don't you think it's just a summer romance, or the first involvement for both of us? You'll be back in school and forgetting all about me in no time."

"I don't think so, Mark." Before he knew what was happening, she'd moved closer to him and quickly put her lips on his. He loved that she would actually take the initiative, but he was soon taking charge of the kiss by rolling her onto her back and then was practically on top of her. His fingers were getting tangled in her long hair as his thumbs caressed her cheeks, but his one hand then started moving over her shoulder and down her arm. She grabbed his hand and held it tightly. He stopped the kiss because he couldn't control the chuckle that had been caused by her actions. After their first date when she had to slap his face, she, apparently, was not going to take any chances today.

He could feel his body reacting as he had never imagined it could, though. He looked into her eyes, smoothed some strands of hair back away from her face and then was kissing her again as his fingers moved through her hair. He then discovered the bow at the back of her neck that was holding up the halter she was wearing. "Oooh," he whispered as he drew back from the kiss and was trying to find the ends of the ribbon.

"Don't even think about it, Mark," she ordered emphatically as she punched his side.

Suddenly the sound of a car coming down the road surprised them, and they were immediately sitting up, Mark's hands were on the ground behind him propping himself up, and his feet were stretching out into the water. Jaclyn was sitting cross-legged on the blanket and they very innocently watched as a family arrived for an outing. They greeted the parents and even helped the little ones get into the swings while the parents got their other things arranged, but after a few minutes they decided to put their shoes back on, folded the blanket to put it on one of the benches, and then followed one of the trails around the lake.

It was exciting as the animals scurried here and there as they approached, and the song birds were giving them quite a serenade. They soon came to a small narrow marsh, which was below and beyond the bridge they were crossing on the trail, and they got to see a doe and two fawn getting a drink and frolicking together in the shallow water. There was one more area, almost like a meadow or valley between the trees and hills, except it had a few pavilions with picnic tables and also an amphitheater with a stage for performances, etc. There was a great seating area on the ground that gradually sloped down to the stage. Mark and Jaclyn were both quite impressed and would have to ask the family what all was held there. They continued to follow the trail, which led through a dense copse of evergreens, and they found that it circled around behind the theater and back to the lake.

The parents had thrown down a blanket and were relaxing as the kids played in the water or on the swings and slides. A picnic basket was sitting near by. Mark glanced at his watch and decided it was time for them to leave. As they drove toward town, he realized that they'd been saved from some possible trouble by the arrival of that family, but he wasn't quite through talking to Jaclyn. He pulled into a parking space behind the church because there was a nice shady spot under some big trees at the edge of the lot.

"Well, I guess it's about time to say goodbye before we get into any more trouble," he chuckled. "You know you really get to me, Jaclyn, and I may never find anyone else who can do that. Maybe that's why I've heard several people say they'd never forgotten their first love. So, will you still plan to keep in touch with me by e-mail? I'll call you from time to time so we can hear each other's voices, but it's going to be awfully hard to keep a fire going, as my dad would say, if you can't add some kindling to the flame. I so want to hold you, kiss you and touch you, but I know God stopped us this afternoon before I really got carried away."

"Do you really believe that God does that, Mark? I didn't hear much about that sort of thing in my church in Louisiana."

"I do feel that God is very close to me, Jaclyn, and I depend on him for guidance in my life. Maybe you'd like to go to church with Liz and Josh. Christy and Jon both sing in the choir but I don't know if the newlyweds will or not."

"I'd love to sing in a church choir. I've been in the choir at school for two years now and will be this year, too. How do you become a member of a church choir?"

"Just volunteer, attend practices, and show up on Sunday. Christy would help you do that if you're really interested. Maybe you'd rather join the choir in your own church, though."

"Not really. I don't know anyone who goes there, and the service is so formal with a lot I don't understand. I really enjoyed the three or four times I went to Community Church with Liz last year, but I know they were special services during Advent and then Easter Sunday."

"Would your parents be upset if you went to another church? I was wondering if you'd like to go with me this Sunday before Grandpa and I leave."

"I don't think they'd mind. They've remarked several times that we can make our own decisions about careers, churches, and marriage, and they will try to support us as best they can. Why don't you call me tomorrow night? I'll know the schedule by then for my work on Sunday."

"I can do that."

"I really wish we had more time to get to know each other, Mark, but I guess going to New York with you is out of the question," she giggled. "I might be a little worse for the wear if I tried to stow away in the Navigator for several days." "All I can say, Cutie, is that we'll have to take the next few years as they come and see what happens. You understand that I can't promise to get back out here anytime soon, and I do know that Brad likes you a lot. When he gets here full time, you may find him very interesting and that he can fulfill your every need," he smiled mischievously as he ran his fingers down her cheek. He was actually trying to cover up his disappointment of leaving her in the arms of his older cousin.

"We'll see about that, Mark. I'm more concerned about you and Teri than you should be about Brad and me. I've seen the looks she's given you, so I just have to hope my feelings for you will come through loud and clear in the e-mails and letters I send. Since I've spent that time with you at the rehearsal dinner, the fireworks, and the reception, I'm pretty sure I know where my heart belongs and always will. It scares me that I might spend my life with a second choice or possibly even alone."

"That isn't going to happen, Jaclyn. We're both too young to make decisions like that yet. We both just had our first date, so you should at least give Brad a chance to show you how much he cares. I wish I were going to be here to give him a challenge." Pulling her into his arms, he got a few wonderful goodbye kisses before he took her home.

"I'll call you tomorrow night, Jaclyn, about going to church Sunday. The Worship Service we attend is at 10:30 during the summer." He could only whisper because he was so afraid he was going to cry. He definitely felt he was losing his first love as he left her at the door.

CHAPTER TWENTY-TWO

Christy and Jon didn't come and join the family Friday night, and everyone was a little surprised since this was the last weekend Lucas and Mark would be with them. There was one, especially, who was very anxious to know why his granddaughter slipped out of the office this morning but didn't go where she said she was going.

Noah's office has a row of windows on the west side of the building and he had watched as Christy made her way toward the City Hall but didn't go in. He could see her reflection in the windows of the Drug Store across Monroe Street as she'd walked on toward the library. She'd been gone about the length of time for a doctor's appointment, Noah was calculating with a grin on his face, and he thought he'd been noticing a few tell-tale signs the last couple of weeks. *After all these years, not much gets by Grandpa Noah,* he congratulated himself. Of course, he would keep his mouth shut and let the wonderful surprise be hers to tell if that was why she was being so secretive, and of course she'd want to tell Jon first if he wasn't already suspicious.

He glanced over at Marge now, and the smile on her face told him that he wasn't the only one who suspected, or maybe she knew, the reason her daughter and son-in-law weren't joining them tonight.

Saturday brought Dr. Becker back down from Colorado Springs, and the day was filled with viewing more photograph albums, some horseback riding, some tennis, some swimming, and a lot of eating. After the evening meal, they were just relaxing on the deck with Brent and Mark playing the guitars and most of them singing along. Jon and Christy finally stood up together, holding hands, and got everyone's attention.

Jon got to make the happy announcement. "We just received confirmation yesterday that there will be an addition to our family sometime next March or April," he beamed. "We couldn't let that brother of mine beat us at this remarkable event of married life, now that he and Liz are finally married." Of course, that brought shouts of joy with lots of hugs and congratulations by all the family, but especially from Joseph who, not too long ago, had asked Christy and Liz when they were going to help enlarge the family. That was before Liz was even married, but now he's strutting around bragging, "I'll get to be a grandfather twice within just a few months with Brent and Susan becoming parents in December and then another now promised for next spring. Noah just smiled, though, as he'd again predicted a happening before it was announced. *Sharp eyes and insisting on well-placed office windows have given me an advantage over the years.*

Mark had slipped up to his room to call Jaclyn right after they had eaten. "I have to work from 1 to 6 tomorrow afternoon," she said when he'd asked about the possibility of her going to church with him. "Are you sure you still want me to go with you?" she asked a little doubtful. "I suppose Brad and his family will be there, too, since it'll be the last day you'll be here."

"I imagine the entire family will attend church together. Does that make a difference to you?" he asked.

"I was just wondering about Brad and his feelings," she replied.

"Brad and I will put you between us so we can both admire your beauty and see that you hear all the good things about God the Father, Jesus the Son, and also the Holy Spirit. I really wish I were going to be here longer so we could study the Bible together."

"I have a Bible, Mark, and I'm going to start reading it again with a different attitude. Since I've met you, I feel like I've missed a lot of wonderful things that can be found in that book. If you think it'll be all right, I'll plan to go with you tomorrow."

"I'll pick you up about 10 o'clock then. Goodnight, Jaclyn."

Since the choir isn't singing on Sunday mornings yet, special music has been provided by different members of the choir. This Sunday there was a quartet of men, one of them being Jon, singing together, and it was wonderful. Mark could see that Jaclyn was really impressed with the music and also the sermon. She hardly took her eyes off the front of the church.

Brad had been quite surprised when Mark had told him that Jaclyn had agreed to come to church with him. "I hope you'll continue to encourage her to come with you and the family, and maybe she'll come to Sunday School, too, when it resumes again this fall."

"That would be great, Mark. I'll talk to Liz about that. Maybe she can get her to come with her and Josh. She could be really involved by the time I get down here around the middle of December. I don't know how you do it, Mark, but I certainly do envy the ability you have to talk to people. I could've never asked Jaclyn about her faith or about coming to church with me. I hadn't even realized her family was Catholic."

"You just put your faith in His hands, Brad, and the words just seem to come out of your mouth like He is doing the talking. I've been involved with the youth program in my church for several years now, and it really guides my life."

After the service, Brad and Mark took Jaclyn for a quick lunch at the Cafe before they took her to work. Again, Mark told her goodbye and that he'd get in touch with her very soon.

Brad remarked that he'd be calling her before he had to leave to go back to finish the few months of college. "Maybe you and Teri will let me take you to a movie or two before she and I both have to leave."

"I'll look forward to that, Brad. This town is going to be pretty empty without you, Teri, and Mark, but I guess I'd better go now before I'm late for work. I'll pray that you and your grandfather have a safe trip, Mark, and I'll expect to see an e-mail from you real soon."

Mark and Lucas were ready to start their trip home quite early the next morning. A big breakfast had been prepared by Marge, Rachel, and Eleanor, and the whole family was there to send them off with lots of hugs, promises to keep in touch, and hopes for many more reunions in the future. Noah and Eleanor had made a promise to Lucas and Esther, before she'd returned home, that they would travel to New York within the next year, but most likely not during the cold wintertime in New York.

Lucas and Mark had decided to travel on I-70 most of the way back home, so they went over to Pueblo, up to Colorado Springs and then over to I-70. They were hoping to spend their first night in Salina, Kansas, and Mark marveled at his grandpa's ability to read maps and figure mileage because everything went according to plan. The next day they drove to Manhattan to see the 1st Territorial Capitol, the outstanding Kansas State campus, and also get a look at Fort Riley.

They then set their goal on Lawrence, Kansas. A short detour to see the Capitol Building in Topeka was made, but they had to see the KU campus where both the basketball and football teams had become well known by winning a National championship and also a Bowl Game with very good records not long ago. They found a nice motel not far off the Interstate, and as luck would have it, they met one of the coaches who offered to show them around the campus which included Memorial Stadium, the Fieldhouse, and the Sports Museum. It was very impressive. He suggested they could have dinner at the new Oread Hotel and then drive on down to see the business district on Massachusetts Street. Following his directions, they then left Massachusetts and skirted the city by driving west on 23rd Street/Clinton Parkway to Wakarusa, north to 6th, and then east to Iowa Street where they found their room for the night waiting. They were ready to call it a day.

On their way through Kansas City, they visited both the Arrowhead and Kauffman Stadiums and then, of course, the Truman Library as they went through Independence.

St. Louis was their next stop where they went to the top of the Gateway Arch, visited the Art Museum and Zoo, the Anheuser Busch Brewery and Park, and the Busch Stadium. They lucked out because the Cardinals were playing at home, and they were able to get tickets to the game.

In Indianapolis, Indiana, they visited the Motor Speedway and Museum; in Dayton, Ohio, the Wright-Patterson Air Force Base and Museum got their attention;

and then the Ohio River, near Wheeling, Pennsylvania, seemed to be just ahead of them. They turned north there so they could drive along the west side of the river to Youngstown, Ohio, since Mark wanted to see the university where Teri will be attending this year. She'd told Mark that her grandparents lived at one of the lakes, which was fairly close to the university. It was a nice campus and they spent a little time there so it would be a little easier for Mark to imagine about where she was when she'd mention a certain location.

They took Route 80 out of Youngstown over to Route 79 in Pennsylvania and then north to Route 90. It was just a few miles now before they'd turn onto Route 86, and they were both smiling because this meant they weren't very far from home. They did stop to take a look at Lake Chautauqua where they had spent many happy hours over the years. It looked very inviting and Lucas remarked, "That'll be something we can show our relatives when they come to visit."

When they finally drove into Jamestown, they agreed that the trip home had been another exciting and interesting one, although a little faster and more tiring. It had only taken nine days instead of eleven, but they were both ready for a long rest in their own beds. Luckily, they'd gotten home late Tuesday afternoon so they now planned to take the rest of the week to relax and then get reacquainted with the rest of the family.

Of course, they all had to hear about the part of the trip that Esther hadn't been on, and to see all the pictures they'd taken on the trip and also of the current family members at the ranch. There were also quite a few pictures given to them by the Colorado relatives that included ones of Jeremiah, Rebecca, Ruth and Sarah as young girls, and Nathaniel and

Annabelle. To be expected, it got several members of the family very anxious to start planning a trip of their own to this beautiful Colorado ranch and to meet the relatives they'd never known existed.

CHAPTER TWENTY-THREE

The next two and a half weeks were full for Mark as he had to get some new college clothes, register for classes, get his dorm room assigned, and take a tour of the campus to really familiarize himself with the place where he'll be spending the next four years if all goes well. He had been around the campus quite a bit with Stephen and Deborah over the last few years, but he was getting pretty anxious to get started himself and see what he could get involved in besides books.

He did find time to call the ranch several times. He got to talk to Brent, Brad, Liz, and Josh. Brad was planning to leave on Saturday, the 9th, since his classes start on the 14th, and he will finish on the 10th of December. He hopes that will give him time to get to Hayes to take Jaclyn to the Winter Formal. *I really wish I were going to be taking her to that dance, but I just might be busy escorting Teri to a college dance at Youngstown State.* He just vaguely remembers Stephen in a tux once or twice, but doesn't know if it was a dance or a wedding he took part in. *My brother needs to look more closely at those magazines in his room and get his hormones and curiosity stirred up about the opposite sex. I certainly enjoyed my awakening.*

Since he knew Brad would be gone, he decided to call Jaclyn on Sunday, the 10th, late enough in the evening that she wouldn't be working. He had sent both Jaclyn and Teri e-mails just to let them know that he and Grandpa had gotten home safely. Teri had e-mailed back to say that she would be at her grandparents by the 13th. Her parents were riding with her and will stay for a short visit and then fly back home. It wouldn't be long until all of them would be back in school.

Jaclyn sounded a little lonely as she was telling him that Brad and Teri were both gone now, but she got a little more perky when talking about what the three of them had done the last couple of weeks. She said that Brad had been a great friend. He had taken her and Teri to the movies on both the 31st of July and the 8th of August before he left. She and Teri had gone to church together on the 3rd, and when Brad had seen them come in, he'd had them sit with him and his relatives. The three of them had also driven to Pueblo to do some shopping and have lunch on the 5th. She was so excited about all the school clothes she'd been able to find.

"I'll bet you'd make a great model, Jaclyn. Have you ever thought about that as a career where you could wear all those lovely and alluring clothes?"

"What girl hasn't at some time in her life, but I don't think that's for me. I've read too many sad stories about the difficulties of being a model. I'm thinking right now that I'd like to be a nurse, and I could probably find a job almost anywhere in that profession."

"I think you're right about that, so are you taking the subjects you'll need to pursue that career?"

"I talked to the counselor at school last year and she helped me with my curriculum for this year. I'll get some more help before I'm through this year, and maybe I can find out what school would be the best to attend. I don't know if I'll be ready to go too far from home by then, though. I'm afraid I'm more of a home body than I thought."

"Are you going to be all right in school this year? I wish I could be there for you, but life doesn't always make things easy for us. Have you heard if that kid who threatened me is going to be around?"

"I'm going to be O.K., Mark. You helped me so much to realize what I need to say and do around people, and I won't let anyone intimidate me anymore. As for that stupid character, I did hear that his parents enrolled him in a private school some place in Oklahoma."

"I'm glad to hear that. Will you try to keep God in your life, though, so you have His strength and guidance every day?"

"Oh, Mark, I forgot to tell you! Well, I guess I did tell you that I had a Bible and I was going to start reading it. When I went to church this morning, they announced that a Bible Study Class was going to start next Sunday, so I signed up for it. I'm really excited now about learning more about Jesus. I won't be working anymore, now that school is starting, so I won't have to miss any of the meetings."

"I'm really proud of you, Jaclyn, but do you suppose we should call it a night?"

"I think that's a good idea. My eyes are almost closed and I've been trying to keep you from hearing my yawns. I hate to say goodbye but I sure hope you won't forget me."

"That'll be the day. Goodnight, Cutie."

Mark waited until the following Saturday to call Teri because she would need time to get a few things done, too. From the sound of her voice, though, he thought maybe she was sorry she'd given him her number, but then she explained that they were going out to dinner and she was running late. Her parents were flying back home tomorrow, so he promised to call her next week either before he left for school or after he got there.

Stephen and Deborah had both already left for their respective colleges. Stephen's classes in law were starting Tuesday, and Deborah had to arrive early because her sorority had to prepare for Rush.

Monday evening, after they'd eaten dinner, Mark's dad looked over at him with a big grin on his face. "How about you and me going for a ride, Mark? I have something I'd like to show you."

"Sure, we can do that. I was going to start some packing tonight, but I have time to go someplace with you." They climbed into his dad's car and, to his surprise, they soon pulled in at their favorite car dealership.

"Your mother and I have been discussing that old truck of yours, and we decided it wasn't the safest for you to take to college. We're not getting you a new car, but we found a nice looking 2-door, while you were gone, and we had them hold it for us. You can take a look at it, but please be honest if you'd rather have something else."

"Gee, Dad, I wasn't thinking about anything except my old truck the first year, at least, so I'd be extremely happy to have a nicer car, especially after getting to drive that Navigator of Grandpa's. I'll admit my truck is getting pretty old and junky looking."

"You've been very patient with the old Junker for over two years so let's take a look at this one and see what you think. Of course, it's not going to be anywhere near the car of your Grandfather's," he chuckled.

However, Mark was literally flabbergasted when he saw the shiny silver 2-door coupe with a sunroof and rear spoiler. The dashboard was great with a CD changer, which his truck didn't have, a black leather interior, front and side airbags, and an engine that just purred when they took it for a trial drive. "Dad, it looks and runs like it's brand new. Are you sure this isn't too nice a car to take to college?"

"No, Mark, I think you've shown that you're a very responsible young man, especially on the trip to Colorado with your grandpa this summer, and he agreed when I talked to him. It is one thing to have a nice car, but quite another is how you handle yourself while you're in it. Your mom and I told you we wouldn't buy you a new car like so many guys arrive at college with their graduation gift, and this one is actually six years old. It was owned by a young man who was called up to go to Iraq three years ago. One of those horrible roadside bombs took his life about eighteen months ago, and the car has been in his parents' garage until just recently. They couldn't bare the thought of parting with it, the one thing that had meant so much to their son, and they've also asked to meet the person who will be driving it. Would you be willing to do that?"

With tears in his eyes, Mark looked at his dad and said, "I'd be honored to meet the parents of one of our heroes who gave his life so we can be free. I'm just not sure I'm the one who should be driving his car. Maybe it should go to one of the returning veterans."

"I thought that, too, Mark, until Mr. Hemp told me that this boy was planning to go to college, when he came back, and become an attorney. He and I both thought that his parents would like the idea of the car being used by a young man with the same goal in life."

"Thanks, Dad. I'll try to fulfill this young man's dream and make his parents proud, as well as my own."

The months passed quickly. There were e-mails and telephone calls with both Jaclyn and Teri in which they shared lots of news, especially about the Christmas dances. Teri had joined a sorority which held a dance, so Mark had gone to Youngstown to be her escort, and Brad had been Jaclyn's date for the High School Christmas dance again. The trip to see Teri had been fun, but he realized that there were no exciting feelings like the ones he has when he just talks to Jaclyn on the phone. From Christmas to May, more e-mails and telephone calls were exchanged, hearing all about the Spring Prom from Jaclyn, again with Brad as her escort, and of course, about her graduation.

Mark went with Stephen and Deborah to Colorado for a week in late July. Mark had made sure they met Jaclyn and Teri as well as all the members of the Hayes family, and they were really impressed with the family and the ranch.

Stephen and Deborah did try horseback riding, but they decided it would take a while to get used to. However, they certainly enjoyed the swimming, tennis, eating and getting acquainted. Mark, of course, had to catch up on all the latest news. Brad, living above the Law Office, seemed quite content and happy. Jaclyn was excited about a scholarship she'd received from a small college not too far from home, and she and Teri were working again at the grocery store for the summer.

The two babies, Nathan and Clay, were both big enough now for Mark to play with, one seven months old and the other almost four months. Mark actually had spent hours babysitting while the others took Stephen and Deborah to see the area. He held them, talked to them, and played with them, so the week went by much too quickly. Josh and Liz were still the perfect couple, and Mark thought they acted very much like what he felt the one night he got to spend alone with Jaclyn. He couldn't quite understand Brad's actions after all the plans of dating he'd talked about last summer, but from what Jaclyn told him, it was always the three of them being together again now that Teri is home. Apparently, Brad had been quite busy learning his role at the Law Office while the girls were going to school since Jaclyn had received very few calls and no dates except for the two dances. In a rather selfish way, Mark was somewhat pleased about that news. He hadn't found anyone he'd wanted to date and had actually been content to spend time on the phone or computer with Jaclyn.

When school started again, Mark increased his telephone calls to Jaclyn because he wanted to hear her voice and make sure she was doing all right at college and being away from home. He also kept in touch with Teri, but she'd finally admitted she'd found another escort so she wouldn't need him to drive clear over there this year for the dance in December.

He called Jaclyn several times during the Christmas holidays. She'd told him she hadn't seen Brad because he'd said he was taking some time off to be with his family over Christmas. "It was a little strange, though, because Christy casually remarked, when I saw her at the store, that Dr. and Mrs. Becker and Mary were at the ranch on Christmas Eve, as usual, but Brad had not come with them. And, instead of Teri coming home this year, her parents went to Ohio to spend Christmas with her and the grandparents, so it's a little lonely around here. Of course, I love to spend time at the ranch and play with Nathan and Clay. They are so cute and growing so big. Nathan is doing a great job of walking, and Clay's crawling all over the place and is also pulling himself up around tables and chairs.

Oh, Mark, before I forget my manners completely, I want to thank you so much for the gift you sent me. I'm really looking forward to shopping when I get back to school."

Mark had sent her a Gift Certificate from a store he knew would be in the town where she was attending college, and he was glad she liked it. "Well, I didn't expect a gift from you, Cutie, but I'm sure I'll enjoy the magazine when it starts coming. Do you think I can get a few more ideas from it?" he chuckled.

She was really laughing as she tried to explain, "I remembered you mentioning that you'd done a little sneaking around your brother's room looking at his magazines, so I just thought you might like one of your own. I was a little embarrassed while I was giving them the information. I don't know that it will teach you anything, because I don't think you need too many more instructions. I'd rather you remain the Mark I know right now."

"I'll remember that, Jaclyn, and try to remain the way you like me. I certainly don't understand Brad's actions, but I'm rather pleased that he may be looking other places for some romance. It gives me hope that you may still be available for me. Do you suppose he thinks a freshman is a little too young for him now that he's a full-time lawyer with all those big responsibilities?"

"I think it may be more than that, but I'm not going to waste my time worrying a lot about it. I'm concentrating on becoming a nurse, getting good grades, and graduating from college with honors."

"Hey, good for you, Sweetheart. You're my kind of girl."

Mark and Jaclyn continued to stay in touch by e-mail and telephone throughout the Christmas break, but Brad hadn't even contacted her after he'd come back to town. He did finally call the night before she returned to college and wished her well.

"Have I done something, Brad, that has you upset with me?" she'd asked.

"No, why do you ask? It's just that you and Teri are both away at college this year, so I've been concentrating on being a lawyer. I look forward to seeing you both again when you come home next summer. Be sure to drive carefully going back to college, and Good Luck with your studies, Kiddo."

"Thanks, Brad. I guess this is goodbye for awhile then. I do hope everything goes well for you in the coming months. Thanks for calling. Goodbye now."

And I really think it is goodbye, Brad, but that's O.K. Could you have gone to Ohio, too, since you weren't home with your own family? I wasn't so blind that I missed the looks you and Teri exchanged when the three of us were together, and I also noticed that I was always the first to be taken home. I really wish you the best, my friend, and I'll always remember and appreciate your willingness to be my escort to the dances. My heart is still beating for Mark, though. I only wish I knew for sure who his heart is yearning for.

CHAPTER TWENTY-FOUR

December, two years later

It's now Mark's senior year. He had actually tried out and made the baseball team the last two years, and they'd been very lucky during the spring seasons which had caused them to continue into summer vacation. It had caused him to miss going to the ranch when others of the family had gone. Also, when he'd discovered that they actually did have a swimming team, he'd tried out and also made it, and that filled the winter and early spring months. They also had some out of town meets which had interfered with his correspondence with Jaclyn. He loved the sports, but he'd certainly missed talking to the girl who still plays havoc with his hormonal emotions.

Deborah had, after her graduation two years ago, accepted a position at the college as a counselor for freshmen girls, and she had also remained involved in some capacity with her sorority. When a Christmas Formal was scheduled for December 17, she approached Mark to ask a favor. He assumed, of course, that she was going to ask him to be her escort, but why wasn't she asking that guy she's been dating for over a year now? *Why does it always have to be me? Stephen is still single, too.*

Well, it didn't turn out that *she* needed an escort, but rather a new girl who had just transferred at mid-term. She'd explained that this girl was shy and didn't feel she knew any of the boys well enough to ask one for a date to a formal dance where flowers, transportation, and possibly dinner would be required. After several refusals, he'd finally given in since he knew it would only be the one date. He'd been formulating some other plans of his own since Brad had finally let him know in November that he'd decided there was no future for him and Jaclyn. Of course, Jaclyn had been telling him that for the last two years, but he'd never received as much as a hint from Brad that he wasn't still interested.

The night of the dance came, and Mark was supposed to pick the girl up at Deborah's condo. A light snow had been falling for a couple of hours now, which was going to make it a beautiful night for a dance. He was wishing it could be with a girl he knew and cared about, a sweetheart like Jaclyn, and his thoughts were trying to picture her in his arms on the dance floor. He was also wondering if they could still dance together like they used to. He had to chuckle as he was remembering that they didn't move very much on the dance floor way back then. *Maybe she's learned even more steps if she's been dating the last two years, but Deborah has made it her resolution that I would learn a few dance steps, too. Jaclyn hasn't mentioned anything in her e-mails or telephone conversations about dating, but that wouldn't mean that she hasn't. Now, however, I have to get my mind on tonight so I can be a satisfactory date for this girl or I'll really be in trouble with my sister.*

Deborah, of course, was there to answer the door--probably to prolong the agony. He stepped inside, kissed his sister's cheek, and then saw his date standing across the room. The lights were low, but he could see clearly enough to know she was the most beautiful girl he'd ever seen in his life, and he could only stand and stare. She had an almost teasing smile on her face, and she was dressed in an elegant light apricot gown with a deep vee-neck halter top that fastened at the back of her neck. For a second, his mind went back to the day he was going to untie Jaclyn's summer halter when they were down at the lake, but this one was absolutely stunning with a slim floor-length skirt which flared slightly in the back below the hips. Her long, dark hair was pulled back, but a few tendrils were still falling around her face. Those big brown eyes were gorgeous and sparkling with tiny tears as she started toward him, but then her arms were reaching out. He couldn't believe it, but there she was----his dream girl----a most adorable and lovable Jaclyn. Oh, what two years had done to that girl!

"Hi, Mark," she chuckled as she'd almost reached him. "You seem just a little surprised to meet your rather shy and unknown date for this evening. You wouldn't think of turning me down, would you?"

Only being able to shake his head, he opened his arms and embraced her as she clasped her hands around his neck. "Oh, my gosh, Jaclyn, you don't know how much I was dreading this evening with an unknown shy and probably uninteresting female. How were you able to get here?"

He looked from her to his sister who stood there with a very, very satisfied smirk on her face, and he realized then that his sister *had* changed from the self-centered one of a few years ago. The doorbell rang or he might have tried to wipe that smirk off her face, but it most likely would've been with a kiss. While Deborah got the door, he was holding Jaclyn in his arms, just trying to comprehend what was really happening. It was such an unbelievable night.

After introductions had been completed with Deborah's date, Jaclyn finally got to tell him that instead of going home for the holidays, she'd flown out here late last night. She'd also revealed that she and Deborah had been keeping in touch since he and his siblings had made the trip to Colorado 2-1/2 years ago.

It had been no secret to Deborah how Mark felt about Jaclyn, and visa versa, but she'd been so frustrated that Brad would keep Mark in doubt of his intentions for so long. Of course, Mark had been the stalwart cousin who felt that Brad had every right to pursue a relationship with Jaclyn, and he'd always explain that Brad had taken her to the school dances and had also expressed a desire to continue seeing her. Deborah had come to doubt that from her contacts with Jaclyn, so when Mark told her that Brad had finally given his release, so to speak, she'd put this plan together as a surprise Christmas present for her baby brother.

"I rested all day today so I'd be ready for tonight's big event," Jaclyn boasted with a grin on her face and her eyes twinkling. Since she was still being held in his arms, she leaned back to look up into his face. "I'll be staying for almost a week here with Deborah before flying on home to be with my family for Christmas."

"Wanted to check out the New York winters, huh? Well, if you haven't looked out the window in the last few minutes, you'll be surprised to see that you're getting your wish with a nice supply of falling snow. I suppose that means I'll have to carry you since you only have on those dancing slippers."

"Isn't that what you big strong handsome men are here for?" she giggled.

"It's certainly good to know that your sense of humor hasn't changed over the last two plus years. I hope your dancing hasn't changed a lot either. Although my big sister had made it her objective to see that I learn a few steps, I'm still not a very good dancer, and I remember how you and Brad used to whirl and twirl."

"There hasn't been a lot of time for dancing the last two years, Mark, so we'll still try to learn a few steps together. O.K.?"

"As long as you're in my arms, I'm game for almost anything, Sweetheart," and he felt his future had just opened up beautifully. "Is it time to get the show on the road, Sis?"

"Let me give you your tickets and you can be on your way. Douglas and I will be right behind you in case they don't want to let you in," she chuckled. "The chaperones are sometimes a little persnickety when a girl they don't know tries to invade their premises. I informed them but you know how it is. There may have been one or two who didn't hear or care to listen."

"We'll find someplace to dance if we have to dance in the snow," Mark laughed as he held her coat for her and they walked to the door. The snow was still falling steadily so Mark got to sweep her into his arms and carry her to the car. He also swiped a little kiss on the way and a few more on the dance floor and afterwards. It was a night he'd never forget.

Sunday morning they attended the Campus Chapel, but unknown to Jaclyn a trip down to Jamestown was also on the schedule. She got to see the grandparents and Stephen again, meet Mark's parents, James and Ann Louise, as well as the other relatives who were at a dinner held the night before she headed home.

They'd done some ice skating, just a little cross-country skiing, and taken a toboggan ride. The best, she thought, was sitting in front of the huge fireplace roasting marshmallows and then feeding each other the sticky gooey treats. She wasn't used to this winter weather in New York, and although she wouldn't dream of complaining, she'd almost frozen while they'd been outdoors. It was so terribly hard to say goodbye now, but Mark had invited her to come back for his graduation in the spring, and she definitely planned on being here.

The months from January to June seemed to move swiftly for Mark with more e-mails and telephone calls crossing the wires from New York to Colorado as well as the last of his college studies and exams to get finished. Mark's graduation was then a memorable day with all his family attending. Of course, Jaclyn was there for him to admire and introduce to all his friends.

Jaclyn had only planned to stay three or four days this time before flying home, but she was totally surprised when Mark announced that he was going with her to Colorado. It was on a Saturday when they rented a car in Denver and drove out to the ranch unannounced. It was a wonderful day, everyone was thrilled, but neither Mark nor Jaclyn was prepared for the news they received when the family had gathered on the deck and were catching up on the latest happenings. After Mark had given them the news of his family, his graduation and Jaclyn being there for him, the shock came when Joseph announced, "Brad and Teri are going to get married in late July in Youngstown, Ohio. He gave her a diamond last Christmas, Teri's been offered a teaching job right there in Youngstown, and her grandparents have helped secure a job for Brad in a law office there, also. Brad is no longer with the Hayes Law Firm and has left the little town and ranch he'd always said he loved."

"I can't believe it, but I certainly wish him the best," Mark softly spoke as his mind was racing back to November when Brad had finally told him he'd decided there was no future for him with Jaclyn. *Why had he waited so long to tell me if he knew he was giving Teri a ring for Christmas? He has certainly been one difficult guy to understand.*

He then looked at Jaclyn and smiled. "I'm so glad it worked out this way because I can now proceed with my own plans for the future. Miss Jaclyn Lambre, would you give me your full attention for a few minutes?"

"Of course, Mark, but what in the world is so important right now?"

He took her hand and almost fell down as he went on his knees in front of her. The whole family had gathered to welcome them since it was Saturday afternoon and they are now anticipating what this means. With the biggest smile on his face, Mark said, "Jaclyn, I can just barely remember that day and how long it has been since I first saw you in that grocery store and fell so hopelessly in love at the first sight of your darling face. My love has continued to grow while I had to wait for Brad, that unpredictable cousin of mine, to inform me that he'd let you go so he could ask Teri to be his wife.

But now, I'm asking you, Jaclyn, if you'll consider being *my* wife. I know I have some schooling yet, and you have another year of training to be a qualified Registered Nurse, but would you let me put this ring on your finger today with a promise that we'll become man and wife when the time is right?" He took the small ring box from his pocket and opened it for her to see the sparkling diamond in a dainty white gold setting that he had bought shortly after she left New York last December. This seemed like the perfect time to present it to her.

"Oh, Mark, it has been so-o-o long that I've been wishing this moment could happen, but I would've never dreamed it would be here in front of this marvelous family that has been so kind to me and my family. Yes, Mark, I'll be very happy to accept and to wear the ring you have there for me." He quickly slipped it on her finger.

There was an immediate round of applause, along with hugs and kisses, from all of those who had been waiting patiently for the same outcome. They hadn't, however, known that Brad had been keeping Mark uncertain of his future all these years. They were visibly upset, especially Rachel and

David, because it had never occurred to them that their son could be so thoughtless and deceitful.

Happiness soon overcame the disappointment, however. It was a wonderful month that Mark spent at the ranch and also visiting with Jaclyn's family. Almost every evening there was music on the deck when Brent handed a guitar to Mark and the two of them began to play.

Jaclyn's family joined them some nights for the music and also for swimming in the pool, but it always ended with Mark and Jaclyn getting away alone to discuss their love and their future.

Mark had so much fun getting reacquainted with the growing boys during the day after he'd helped with the chores and spent time with Brent and Josh. Nathan is almost 3-1/2 now, Clay was 3 in March, and now there's also a two-month old little boy, Cody, who belongs to Josh and Liz. Brent and Susan are expecting again soon, and Jon and Christy just learned that they will add a set of twins in November. The family is steadily growing.

Mark also went to see Noah and Jon at the law office. When he informed them that he was registered to start at Michigan Law School this Fall, their eyes lit up and more future plans were discussed. Brad was gone, so if and when Noah wanted to retire, it would be leaving Jon in the office alone. Would Mark even consider joining them here in Hayes, or had Jaclyn been intrigued by New York?

It left Mark with a lot to think about. He hadn't been sure how Jaclyn would like living in New York. She'd mentioned many times how she loved the small town of Hayes, and she is as attached, emotionally, to the Hayes family as he is. Would it be possible to consider coming here and working with Noah and Jon? His dad and Stephen could easily handle the office in New York when Grandfather retires.

"But what if Brad would want to return here someday?" he asked.

Noah and Jon were both thrilled with the possibility that Mark would even think about coming to join the firm in a few years, and there was no hesitation in Noah's answer about Brad coming back. "Brad did not prove himself to be a compassionate counselor like we want in this office and town. He had not taken the responsibility of being a part of this law firm as seriously and as dedicated as he should have as a family member. He had acted like, since he *was* a family member, he could do his own thing without concern for anyone else, just like we realize now he did with you and Jaclyn. Hopefully, he will grow up and take his new job and his marriage with a resolve that will be successful. I understand that he and Teri both like the Youngstown area and are definitely planning their future there."

"I'm sorry he didn't see the wonderful opportunity he had here, but Teri seemed to be a good influence on him, so maybe she can change his attitude toward life's important decisions. He remarked once that she would make a very good counselor," Mark replied.

Jon then spoke, "There is one more thing, Mark. Would you consider working with us during the summers while you're in law school? It would give you some experience in the actual workings of a law office, and you'd be helping us out since we're shorthanded with Brad gone and Christy only working part time since Clay was born and now expecting again. I did that for my uncle and I feel it really helped. Think about it and let us know. We realize this is a lot being thrown at you all at once, and it *is* a long way from the rest of your family."

Jaclyn was ecstatic, when he discussed it with her, because she had already talked to Dr. Noland, Dr. Davis, and Dr. Becker about working at the Clinic when she'd finished her training. Dr. Becker had finally fulfilled his dream of becoming the pediatrician for his grand-children and great nephews and nieces by joining the two doctors at the enlarged Noland Clinic here in Hayes, and he is happier than he'd been in years. He didn't realize there were so many little ones in the small town until he'd been introduced by Dr. Noland at church and at the Fall Festival. Of course, Dr. Noland is forever threatening to retire, but he just continues to be in the office to take care of his faithful patients, and everyone expects him to be there for quite a few more years.

Everything seems to be in place except for the years ahead of Mark to finish Law School, and one more year for Jaclyn to become a Registered Nurse. Their love has surely survived the previous four years, and Mark is sure it will be even stronger and sustaining in the years ahead. He now has his first and only love with a ring on her finger and a solemn promise in their hearts. God has guided them to unity with Him and with each other.

From college the following year, Mark wrote this song, and with his own guitar as his accompaniment, he sang it to her many times as they continued their telephone calls and e-mails:

When each new day begins and when it's through,

My thoughts and prayers are always there with you. We'll be together soon, I know it's true,

God loves us both, and I pledge my troth. You make it very, very easy to be true, My love will never falter or be untrue.

The life I've chosen proves that it is true, God loves us both, and I pledge my troth.

They were married the following June in the Community Church where Jaclyn had, because of Mark's influence, been confirmed, attended Bible study, and sang in the choir until going to college. It was a beautiful wedding with Deborah as maid of honor and Liz and Christy as attendants. Of course, Stephen was best man for his brother, and Brent and Josh were groomsmen. Jaclyn's two brothers served as ushers, and Jon--well, Jon had elected to be an official babysitter along with Susan.

Jaclyn then worked at a hospital in Ann Arbor for the two years while Mark was still finishing his law school studies and at the Noland Clinic during the summers while Mark was working with Noah and Jon. They are now in Hayes to stay; Mark established with the Hayes Law Firm and Jaclyn working full time for the three doctors who are so glad to have her.

Brent and Susan built a home just past the beautiful yard that had been the setting for the weddings of Christy and Jon and then Liz and Josh. Between theirs and the home Josh and Liz had built before they were married, is another big yard also beautifully landscaped, but it contains a large assortment of playground equipment for the growing number of children. Four more babies had come to join the family since Mark had given Jaclyn the engagement ring on the deck three years ago. Brent and Susan's second had been a girl, Jon and Christy had added twin boys, and Josh and Liz just recently welcomed a little girl to join her 3 year old brother.

David and Rachel Becker now live in the vacated wing of the Main House where Brent and Susan had lived. It was like coming back home to Rachel since she had been raised in that house, and she and Marge had always been very close. Mark and Jaclyn are living in the apartment above the law office that they had redecorated to their liking, but they hope to build a home at the ranch in a year or two. That leaves Mary, who is about to finish her final requirements of becoming a doctor. She and Damon Roberts, who had been dating since their senior year in high school, were married

A Summer's Adventure

last year and have been busy checking out different places to start practicing in their special fields of Gynecology and Oncology. Could it possibly be in Hayes, Colorado?

Of course, Brad and Teri usually make a short visit during the summer if they come back to see her folks. His parents are still upset with him, and Brad still acts a little embarrassed or self conscience around Mark and Jaclyn, but he has never apologized for the way he handled the situation that year when he didn't tell Mark until November that he was no longer interested in a future with Jaclyn, and then gave Teri a diamond for Christmas. They do seem to be enjoying their work and life in Youngstown, and Mark and Jaclyn are happy for them.

The visits from the family in New York are a little more frequent with Mark living here now, and all the members of the family in Hayes have made the trip to New York. What a wonderful discovery was made when Lucas had been determined to find out about his mother's heritage and had taken Mark along for the ride.

ABOUT THE AUTHOR

Sally's grandfather, C. Z. Nelson, had come to America from Sweden with his parents when he was only 2 years old. His father had then died when Grandpa was 10 years old, and as years passed, no one seemed to be interested in the history of the family or if there were any relatives still in Sweden. Sally's two older sisters, Julia Rude and Mary Thompson, decided to trace the ancestry and they were eventually able to find that an equivalent to the American side was still residing in Smaland. The trip they took to discover their Swedish relatives proved to be a wonderful and very informative experience.

It takes a lot of research and a lot of time to discover your ancestors, and this story tells how one man persisted in finding out if the few stories he had heard from his mother were true. It is, of course, a fictitious story, but an adventure for a grandfather and a grandson that fills an otherwise dull summer with a lot of excitement.

This is the last of the Haven of Rest Ranch series and Sally hopes you have enjoyed reading it. Learn more about Sally and her books by visiting her Web site @ www.sallymrussell.com.

www.ingramcontent.com/pod-product-compliance
Lightning Source LLC
LaVergne TN
LVHW091536060526
838200LV00036B/625